The
Sentimentalists

ROBERT HUGH BENSON

Once•and•Future Books

www.Benson-Unabridged.com

Foreword to Robert Hugh Benson's

The Sentimentalists

In one of his early short plays for the German-Reeds (an acting family that took as its self-appointed mission the moral improvement of the theater), W. S. Gilbert lampooned in his inimitable fashion the late Victorian taste for "sensational" literature — *i.e.*, that which attempts to arouse an intense and usually superficial interest or emotional reaction.

The sketch, *A Sensation Novel (In Three Volumes)*, probably suggested by Captain Marryat's hilarious "How to Write a Romance" in *Olla Podrida*, is clever, witty and, unfortunately, dated. No one today would fully understand the Gilbertian satire of spirits of the departed sentenced to expiate their sins (such as frequenting music halls and singing comic songs) by playing characters in a hack writer's "sensational three-volume novel."

The modern "media mogul" looks at the issue of quality entertainment from a perspective different than that of Marryat or Gilbert who viewed popular tastes with amused contempt. Measuring the ratings for American "reality television" (and noting, the more pointless and sensational, the higher the ratings), the TV executive would determine that this is what sells. His conclusion: there is no mass market for moral or mentally challenging entertainment.

Yet, Mel Gibson's *The Passion of the Christ,* defying the predictions of the media pundits, was an outstanding popular success. Nearly a generation ago, in a similar vein, Alan Bloom's *The Closing of the American Mind,* a somewhat dry academic study, became an overnight best seller, stunning the author and the publisher. A century ago, Robert Hugh Benson took the bull of popular culture by the horns by publishing *The Sentimentalists.*

Much to the surprise of just about everyone (himself included), Benson achieved a popular triumph with a "sensational novel" that went against the current by having a definite point to it. This was even more surprising in that the novel was written by one of the most unlikely authors the public at the time could imagine — a Catholic priest!

Despite its grounding in sound philosophy and morality, *The Sentimentalists* verges on the lurid in parts, at least by Victorian standards. However, Benson never portrays anything so obvious as to "bring the blush of shame to the cheek of modesty" — to quote that quintessential Victorian Gilbert again. [The quote is from *Patience, or, Bunthorne's Bride (An Aesthetic Opera),* a production about a couple of *poseurs* using the æsthetic movement to get girls. The "Bunthorne" character is traditionally believed to have been modeled on Oscar Wilde.]

Still, the raw emotionalism of some of the scenes in *The Sentimentalists* — absolutely necessary to drive home Benson's point — made some readers decidedly nervous. The theme, while similar to *Patience,* is much more serious and intense in its treatment. Even Benson was a little embarrassed by the scenes he created in which a human being's pretensions are stripped away and the consequences of his affectations and selfish egotism come home to roost. All that happens to Gilbert's Bunthorne when he is revealed as a phony is that all the women — even the ugly ones — lose interest in him. Benson's Chris Dell attempts suicide.

The public didn't stop reading *The Sentimentalists,* for all the uneasiness it may have caused. The very "sensationalism" (tame by today's standards) that Benson built into the story, is the quality that underpins one of the most thought-provoking novels of the early 20th century.

As Benson relates in a letter:

> Did I tell you about my yet more new one? to be called, probably, *The Sentimentalists* — modern times — relating the reformation of a *poseur* by brutality. Sometimes I think it Extremely Good, and sometimes Extremely Bad. It's certainly one of the two, and I don't know which.

Odd words from any author! Still, Benson was very worried about the book:

> I have begun *The Waster* [Benson changed the title when he began writing, and then back again when it was published], but I am seriously concerned as to whether it will be possible to publish it. It is the grossest caricature of X. I can say honestly that it is not him, but a violent parody of him .... HONESTLY, it has already ceased to be him. It is his dramatic element, caricatured to absurdity, and practically none of his virtues, which are many.

Finally, though, Benson was able to complete the work:

> Half an hour ago I finished my book. It will probably not be called *The Waster.* Perhaps *The Conventionalists.* I am not sure. I really am all right. It is perfectly true; though I dare say reviews will say that I make a deal of fuss about nothing, but I don't think that they will deny its truth. I have employed a device of Henry Kingsley's at the end — suddenly telling the story from my point of view, and relating what I saw happen at a garden party, with which

the thing ends. It makes it startlingly real — as if a statue suddenly moved.

The critics, apparently confused by the appearance of a sensational novel with a point, reacted ambiguously. The public reacted with enthusiasm — even those who claimed to hate the book. Discussion was endless over the real identity of the model for "Chris Dell," who was never explicitly revealed except to a select few individuals. (Everyone, of course, "knew" who it was ... or at least thought they knew.)

Far from being insulted, the real "Chris Dell" was, by his own account, absolutely delighted with the novel and the effect it had. He even undertook to write his own novel (apparently never published) in which he caricatured Benson, a sort of friendly "tit for tat."

When it became known that the real Chris Dell approved of the book, the critics had to take other tacks. First, the critics sniffed, "Chris Dell" wasn't "true to life." He wasn't supposed to be — as Benson had pointed out even before publication. "Chris" was a composite of several individuals, although inspired chiefly by one.

Second, the critics declared that the author, being completely sane, couldn't really understand or depict the insanity of egomania. That, however, wasn't the point. Benson was concerned with the redemption of a *poseur* drowning in self-pity, not the details or causes of his disease. (There's very little offered as to *why* "Chris" is the way he is — Benson's priority was to get the character to stop being that way.)

None of these criticisms detracts from the value of *The Sentimentalists*, which, along with its sequel, *The Conventionalists,* has had something of a small cult following since its first publication — handicapped, as we might expect, by the scarcity of copies. This lack Once and Future Books is pleased to rectify with the publication of this edition. Perhaps more people will be able to appreciate what Benson hoped to accomplish with his "sensation novel":

I did not ask myself if it would make converts, but rather whether it would make things any more hopeful for the thousands of souls who are going straight to hell because no one understands them or makes the best of them . . . . I don't know what the good of being in union with our Lord is, unless we try to do what He did — *i.e.*, make *the best of sinners, and not the worst* — and, above all, never expect gratitude, and never allow the faintest self-love or bitterness or resentment to remain in one's heart.

— Michael D. Greaney, editor

SATIUS ESSE PRODESSE ETIAM MALIS PROPTER
BONOS, QUAM BONIS DEESSE PROPTER MALOS.

Seneca, *de benef.*

Dedication

My dear Max, —

In dedicating this book to you who allowed me to write it, I must express my gratitude for your extraordinary generosity in giving me that permission. I think I know no other man in the world who would have consented not only to be depicted with the colors which I have used, but to supply details without which the book could not have been written. But then I do not know any other man exactly like you. "Dick Yolland," with whom I am staying at this moment, of course told me a great deal which your modesty would have forbidden, but I have to thank you for your leave to me to use it as well as the information that I had from others. "Mr. Rolls," as you know, was obdurate to the end; I have been obliged to guess at the processes of his mind as well as at the details of a few conversations, since "Lady Brasted," of course, has not been consulted. "Jack Hamilton," however, who, I am glad to know has made friends with you again at last, has told me enough about her ladyship to justify what I have written of her — (I saw her, by the way, on Waterloo platform last week) — and has given me his "imprimatur" for these pages.

The other principal personages of the story are, as you know, beyond the reach of my application; and, in any case, considering the time that has passed, my adroit disguisings of "Lord Brasted" as a motoring peer, "Mr. Rolls" as a lean, clean-shaven man, my description of the clergymen concerned as respectively stout, fair-haired, long-nosed, and so on, my subtle mention of Norfolk as the scene of your experiences, and all my other devices — I think you will confess that I do no wrong to the dead or the living in revealing the history of those two or three years. (You know I always did rather sympathize with "Mrs. Hamilton.")

I wonder very much whether the world will be in the least interested in that history; I am afraid, at any rate, that it will be sadly disappointed. People would infinitely have preferred that you should have hanged yourself comfortably, for I fear that pessimism is regnant, if not supreme, amongst us. But for you and me, my dear Max, who believe in God and the Catholic Church and one or two other things, a convinced optimism is the only reasonable philosophy, and, after all, in this case it happens to be justified by events.

May I add an expression of my own gratification that you did not succeed in your design? Had you been a little more, or "Mr. Rolls" a little less, cautious, I could never have enjoyed a friendship which I value exceedingly — a friendship which dates, to my mind, at any rate, from the evening when we met on the lawn here, and "Dick" introduced us amid the garden chairs.

> Believe me,
> My dear Max,
> Yours very sincerely,
> Robert Hugh Benson
> "Amplefield,"
> "Norfolk."

P.S. — "Dick" sends you his love, and bids me tell you he is looking forward to Christmas. I, too, shall be here again, I hope, at that time. — By the way, I must congratulate you on your new book. I'll tell you what I think when we meet.

CHAPTER I

An Old Sufferer

(I)

R ichard Arthur Molyneux Yolland, priest of the Catholic Church, sat over his fire on an October evening saying his office.

He was not at all true in his appearance to the type of Roman cleric conceived by his fellow countrymen; he was neither blue chinned and gross, nor spare and furtive eyed. On the contrary he had a clean looking freckled face, blue eyes, stiff sandy hair, a snub nose, and an appearance of honesty. He was about thirty years old, and resembled, said his friends, an intelligent Irish terrier.

His room, in these lodgings that he occupied in Soho, was, to the discerning eye, a palimpsest; — there were two records to be read there. Plaster statues of Saints Joseph and Mary, one on either end of the painted mantelpiece; a row of theological books — Lehmkuhl's "Moral Theology," Liguori's "Glories of Mary," Bishop Hedley's "Retreat," Tanqueray's "Dogmatic Theology" in three volumes, breviaries, a tattered missal with gay crumpled markers, and a number more of their kind, — a Breton china stoup near the door, a tall wood-and-metal crucifix hung about with a rosary on his kneehold table by the window — all these revealed his calling as of a seminary-bred priest. On the other hand a Louis Quinze table, two pairs of antlers over the fire, a Khelim hearthrug, a grave leather-fringed bookshelf, filled with miscellaneous books — Stevenson, Henry Kingsley, some suspiciously clean editions of the Fathers of the Church, works on travel and sport — a pair of silver candlesticks on a carved coffin stool at his right hand — all these told another tale.

There was therefore no unity in the room, and an observant psychologist, knowing that the room reveals the occupant, would have pronounced that here was one more example of that numerous class of persons who have combined but have not yet fused dissimilar elements of character.

I am sorry to be obliged to state that Dick Yolland was not attending to his prayers.

Saint Callistus, Pope and Martyr, who, as the second nocturn related, established the Ember Seasons, built the basilica of Sta. Maria Trastevere, enlarged the old cemetery in the Appian Way, reigned five years, one month and twelve days, made sixteen presbyters, four deacons and eight bishops, and migrated to the Lord through the gate of martyrdom under Alexander, Emperor — this great confessor did not now prevail to win his son in Christ from the venial distraction of his thoughts. Dick was trying his best to attend; but, as a matter of fact, was chiefly thinking, with pleasurable anticipation, of the following Monday, when he was to go home to Amplefield, Norfolk, for four days' shooting. The pheasants were doing phenomenally, his father had told him in a letter received that morning; and the mustard fields were full of birds. There would be only three guns — himself, his father and Jack Hamilton. Jack was no good; that would mean that he himself, with the boy's full concurrence, would have the warm corners. . . . Jack was a poor shot.

Then he frowned a little.

"*Jubedomnebenedicereevangelicalectiositnobissalusetprotectioamen,*" he said all in one breath.

He had hardly began "*Nihil est opertum quod non revelabitur,*" when a tap came at his door, and he lifted moving lips and distraught eyes to his old housekeeper who stood there in cap and apron.

"Please, Master Dick —"

He leaned back with his finger on the page.

"There is a gentleman, Master Dick. Shall I ask him to wait?"

"A gentleman? What is his name?"

"He won't give his name; he says you know him."

Dick hesitated.

"Well, ten minutes; tell him I am just finishing my office."

He bent himself to his book again as the door closed and the footsteps went down the passage.

Here then was another distraction. The birds, Jack Hamilton, and the warm corners retired to the middle distance; beyond them could be faintly discerned the mitered figure of the Martyr-Pope moving about fields of pain and glory; and across the foreground flitted questionable shadows. . . A gentleman whom he knew and Betty did not — not a priest; then it could not be this or that or the other man. Who in the world was it? . . . Why had he not given his name? . . . What could he want at nine-forty-five p.m.? . . . It was not a sick call.

Once more he frowned, pursed his lips, and began Lauds — *Deus in adjutorium* . . . .

It was exactly seven minutes later that he stood up slowly, still with moving lips, and ten seconds after that that he said *Divinumauxiliummaneatsempernobiscumamen* at the top of the steep stairs. Then he no longer attempted not to wonder who his visitor was, and went swiftly downstairs two at a time, his zimmara flapping behind him, and opened the dining room door on the first floor.

There was something dramatic in the very pose of the figure that awaited him there.

Beyond the single candle on the white and crumby tablecloth, stood a man a year or two older than himself and a couple of inches taller; one hand was hidden in a buttoned-up Chesterfield coat, the other, with a silver ring upon it, rested with fingertips on the cloth; a bowler hat with a caved in top lay beside a knotted blackthorn near his hand. The man's face, as Dick saw it in the candlelight, was smooth shaven and long; he had a long nose that appeared slightly pressed into his thin cheeks; his black hair was neatly parted in the middle; his full lipped mouth and projecting chin seemed tilted in a kind of tragic appeal, and his sharp black eyes looked at him under half-lowered lids.

Dick had an instantaneous recollection of a visit to the Adelphi of ten years before, as he stared at the stranger; then he stopped.

"Why, is it Chris?" he said.

The man laughed shortly in such a manner that Dick suddenly realized the meaning of the word "sardonic."

"It is," he said; "all that is left of him."

Dick came round the table holding out his hand. "My dear man," he said, "it must be five years —"

"An eternity," said Christopher Dell. "God — the gods help me!"

He paused again dramatically, drawing back a little as the priest came near.

"Do you know, Father Yolland — my dear Dick," he exclaimed; "do you know all?"

Dick had a sensation as of being obliged to act a part at short notice in private theatricals; he had not an idea what to say, and yet his cue waited.

"I don't know what you mean, Chris?" he said feebly.

"Do you know what I am?" spouted the other again with fierce-shining eyes. "A tramp — a publican."

"Oh! My dear man, don't talk like that. What does it matter?"

Chris looked at him with working lips.

"I believe you, Dick," he said; "you are not like the others. God bless you!"

He brought his hand down in a splendid sweep, and gripped the priest's.

"That is why I came," he said; "it was you or the river for me tonight."

He loosed his hand, and drove his own into his trouser pocket.

"Not a sixpenny piece," he said.

A faint jingle sounded from his pocket. His face fell ever so slightly.

"Two half-pence," he said; "enough for a crust. Shall I go then?"

Dick took his arm.

"Come upstairs, Chris. I am delighted to see you. Have you dined?"

He saw the other "curl" his lip (there was no other word).

"I dined, Dick! Yes, I dined on the Embankment — God's restaurant — a banana and a crust of bread."

Dick jerked the bell handle, and waited, strangely uneasy, until the door opened.

"This gentleman wants some supper, Betty," he said. "Bring

something up to my room. Come upstairs, Chris."

His friend took up his hat and stick, and remained in a carefully deferential attitude for the priest to pass out first. Dick had a spasm of impatience.

"Oh! Don't be a — Come on."

He observed him very carefully as he climbed the stairs behind him. His trousers were not at all frayed, as they ought to have been; on the contrary they were neatly turned up, displaying a very tolerable pair of patent leather boots, a little old but sufficiently smart; his hair was beautifully smooth behind; his coat was well-brushed, although not glaringly new. On the whole he seemed very prosperous for a gentleman who had dined off a banana and a crust. Dick wondered to himself about the caved-in hat.

Chris set down the hat on entering the sitting room, and Dick instantly took it up.

"It's got a dent," he said, and pressed it from within. It sprang out, and immediately looked perfectly respectable. The other laughed bitterly once more.

"One does not attend to such things," he said "when one looks death in the face."

Dick blinked his blue eyes a moment. He could not help wondering whether it was from lack of attention that the hat had suffered.

"Where are you staying tonight?" he asked.

"I suppose in the Salvation Army shelter, or in the river. My bones —"

"Do you mean you have no rooms?" asked Dick, blinking again. Chris laughed again.

"Don't ask too much," he said; "it will only give you pain."

"My dear man — where did you sleep last night?"

"Do you really want to know? Well, then, on a bench in the Green Park."

"Good Lord! And — and for how long?"

The other's face fell again ever so slightly.

"I had rooms till yesterday," he said, "then I was turned out."

Dick drew a breath of relief.

"I am very glad you came," he said. "You must stay here tonight at any rate."

Chris, who at that moment was drawing up his trousers at the knees, preparatorily to sitting down, looked up with such an emotional face that the priest hastened to go on.

"Was that your parcel downstairs? We'll have it brought up."

"It contains everything I have in the world."

"Pajamas?"

"I believe so."

"And Boccaccio?" asked Dick grinning nervously.

Chris grinned back, and then looked stern.

"Well, yes. I will never be parted from that."

"Where did you sleep last night?"

The door was pushed open, and Betty came in with a tray.

"Just get the spare bedroom ready, will you?" said the priest. "Mr. Dell will be staying here a day or two. And just bring up the parcel down below."

"Yes, Master Dick," said the old lady.

It was pleasant to see the hungry man sit down to the cold grouse and stewed fruit. He poured himself out half a tumbler of claret first, and drained it.

"Ah!" he said. "I suppose it is three months since I tasted wine."

His impatience, however, seemed slightly overdone; he ate, Dick thought, as a suburban actor would eat, who impersonated a starving gentleman; his hands trembled a little, his black eyes shot to and fro from plate to dish, and the food vanished with dramatic swiftness.

Dick said nothing, but watched him uneasily, wondering how far the genuineness went, and whether he himself was being brutal. Chris had always been an odd creature from Oxford onwards, strangely vivid and impulsive and theatrical all at once — subjectively sincere but not always objectively genuine.

Chris sprang up suddenly, made a large sign of the cross, darted his hand to an open box of Egyptian cigarettes, and then paused.

"May I?" he said. "I am your pensioner, not your guest."

"Oh! For God's sake —" said Dick, twisting in his seat.

"I may then?"

He seized a cigarette, put it to a candle, filled his lungs with smoke, and sank down into the easy chair.

"My dear Dick, this is heaven! And to think that I shall have a bed to sleep in!"

Dick turned briskly to the parcel that Betty had laid silently on the table three or four minutes before.

"Tell me what you have got," he said. "Razors? Sponge? Toothbrush?"

"Open it," said Chris superbly.

Dick cut the string, pulled out the paper, and the contents lay displayed.

There was a neat pile of pajamas — silk, for he felt them incredulously — a spotless collar, an Indian silk tie, a pair of pumps, a neat little dressing case with "C. D." in silver on the back, a pair of clocked socks, a volume of Boccaccio in chiseled vellum, a china snuffbox, an amber cigarette holder, a revolver, and a missal.

"My dear man," he said, "I see you have saved something from the wreck."

Chris was looking with rapturous eyes at the ceiling through a cloud of smoke.

"Dress suit went on Monday," he said, "and my last white shirt yesterday."

"But these pajamas?" asked the priest smiling.

"One can at least preserve one's self respect by night. It is cheaper too," said the other.

Dick leaned back and took a cigarette himself.

"Just tell me the whole thing," he said.

Chris waved his hand.

"The old story," he said. "Chatterton, George Gissing and the rest. You know it all: melting money; articles unpaid for; things going one by one; a brutal landlady; and behold me!"

"Was it your own fault?" began Dick.

"Oh! I suppose so; it is always the fault of the unsuccessful," cried Chris with emphatic bitterness; "it is always the fault of the damned; each makes his own hell. You can make a good sermon out of me, reverend Father."

"Tell me," persisted the priest steadily.

Chris flung out his hands, dropping his cigarette. He stooped to pick it up, which spoiled his gesture; so he repeated it.

"I do not ask much from the gods," he said. "A little plain food, a shelter over my head, a little red wine to drink and cigarettes to smoke, decent clothes to wear — I am content with that, but — well, I have not got it."

"What have you been doing for the last five years?"

"Oh! This and that. I went to Italy for eighteen months and lived in the Abruzzi; then I wrote some articles on it and got them published. Then I was in Paris afterwards for six weeks —"

"At a hotel?" put in Dick swiftly.

The other eyed him a moment.

"No," he said, "staying with a friend. I went to the devil then, who is a gentleman, for he paid me what he promised. Then I chucked it, and thought I would try Almighty God; and I cannot say that He — I beg your pardon, I forgot you were a priest."

Dick began to tap his foot impatiently.

"My dear man, continue to forget it if you like. I am not a fool."

"I believe you are not," said Chris earnestly. "I believe you are a good man. Well, I have kept tolerably straight for a year; trying to do my best — I swear that I have; and then yesterday the end came. I went and stood a long time looking at the river last night till a Bobby moved me on. I looked at it again this morning. Then to-night I saw your name on the church door — and here I am — happy for one night. Tomorrow —" he shrugged his shoulders like a Frenchman.

"Tomorrow you will be here still," said the priest, "and the day after and the day after — till Monday at any rate. Then we will see."

"God bless you! cried Chris passionately.

He leaned back once more and drew on his cigarette.

Dick's mind worked like a mill. He was not very clever, but he was clever enough to know his own limitations; and he frankly told himself that he did not in the least understand Christopher Dell, that he never had understood him, and that he probably never would.

On the one side there had always been this glaring theatricality; he had thought it beautiful at Oxford, then he had got a little tired of it. On the other side there had been a great deal of worth in Chris; he was generous beyond all bounds, running himself into debt in order to give expensive presents, injuring himself again and again by unrestrained talking as often as not in defense of his indefensible friends for he was extravagantly loyal; he was kind beyond all others. Dick still remembered with gratitude his patient nursing when the two had been in lodgings together. Once more, against all this had to be placed a certain sinister reputation that simply horrified this wholesome-minded young man; but Chris had never spoken of it, and Dick had never attempted to question him. He loathed it all far too much.

All this produced bewilderment now in the priest's mind. Christopher was a man of black-and-white, which had never merged in gray. Dick had never known such an ardent convert as his friend when he had been received into the Church ten years before; he had bought a discipline, a breviary in four volumes, and a spiked belt which he sedulously left about his rooms; but his new-found faith had not hindered his getting drunk three weeks later; and, less than a year after, a white bust of Hermes with a red lamp before it looked across his room at a blue lamp before the image of the Mother of God. Chris had burst into an eloquent defense then of the truth of all religions; and Dick had fallen into a fit of helpless laughter that offended the other far more than the reproof and horror that he had evidently expected.

He was certainly a *poseur,* the priest reflected now; but he was a good deal more as well.

He stood up.

"It is half-past ten," he said. "I must go to bed. I have to say Mass at the convent at seven. Will you look after yourself? Your room is the first door on the right."

Chris sprang up, and looked at him with ardent eyes. Then he stooped, caught up the priest's hand and kissed it.

"The gods reward you!" he said.

"Cigarettes there," said Dick passionlessly; "soda in the cupboard. There is no whisky. Goodnight, Chris. Breakfast at eight."

"Goodnight, my dear Dick. God bless you! Remember me at Mass."

(2)

Mr. Dell was dressing, Betty reported, in answer to the priest's slightly irritated question at twenty-five minutes past eight on the following morning. She had met him just now coming from the bathroom.

"Just ask how long he will be," said Dick, looking hungrily at the buttered eggs before the fire.

A voice presently cried over the banisters.

"Dick, Dick! I am horrified. I thought you had begun. I will explain when I come down."

Dick smiled, called up reassuringly, and took him at his word.

"I never eat much breakfast," remarked Chris, coming in ten minutes later, speckless as usual, with a white shirt of his host's shining at throat and wrists, "and I have had a miserable night —"

"I am sorry," said the priest stolidly. "Help yourself, will you?"

"Neuralgia again," went on the other, putting all that was left of the eggs upon his own plate. "I am a martyr to it."

"Do you mind smoke? . . . . Then I will just sit here and tell you my views."

"Er — may I ask for some fresh coffee? This is a trifle cold," remarked the layman.

Dick pulled the bell.

"Now, listen, Chris. This is what I think. I am going home on Monday. You had better come with me. (Some more coffee, Betty.)"

"My dear fellow," exclaimed the other, "it is impossible. No clothes, no shirts."

"We'll arrange that. Give me your pawn tickets after breakfast."

"Dick!"

"Please don't be absurd. Or you can go round yourself. Whichever you prefer. We'll see to that presently. Well, will you come?"

"Come! Why, I would come to the world's end —"

"All right. Well, you will have time to think things over there, and make an arrangement or two before the end of next week. Have you any prospects?"

"There is the *Saturday Express*," explained Chris, helping himself to a quantity of black coffee. "They have promised me a job, but I don't know —"

"Can I be of any use? I know the man."

"My dear man, it would be the greatest use. You see, I have not many references."

"Very well, I will write presently. Now look here, I am more or less free today and tomorrow morning. Tomorrow afternoon and all Sunday I am useless. Please tell me quite plainly by lunchtime everything you want. We must get everything by tomorrow at midday. We start first thing on Monday."

"Oh! My dear man —" murmured the other brokenly.

"For God's sake let us be reasonable. You would do as much for me, would you not? Very well then; let's have no jawing. I tell you plainly that I have plenty of money: you needn't be shy; and if ever I am in trouble I will come to you. Now then, make a decent list after breakfast and let me have it by lunch; afterwards we will go out together. Give me a paper; no, the *Daily Mail*."

Then Dick was gone, trembling a little at his own speech, and Chris sat a moment, genuinely moved. He clenched his fists, murmuring a benediction like a man in second rate literature; for he posed as much when alone as when with others; then he sighed, finished his coffee, wiped his lips delicately, and lit a cigarette.

He was really very grateful indeed as he sat by the fire, gazing at his cuffs, his slender fingers among which his silver ring looked very well, and stooping to pull up his creased silk sock.

Dick was a dear man, he told himself; a little stupid, of course, as he had always been; even just a little uncouth in the fine affairs of life; but his heart was undoubtedly in the right place. He was whole regions above his coarse brethren in the priesthood, who had bade their interesting suppliant pawn his velvet-collared coat and his silver ring before he applied for charity again. Dick had not even hinted at that; he had understood that some things were more necessary

even than food and red wine and cigarettes — such things as a respectable appearance, a well-groomed hand, and self-regard. But Dick
Yolland was a gentleman, and his brethren were not.

Amplefield would be delightful for a week or two. He had once
been down there, nine years before, alone with Dick. That was in
the years of fatness; they had risen at ten o'clock, played a little
piquet till lunch, shot afterwards, talked incessantly, played piquet
again till dinner and once more until about two a.m. — Probably
that would be impossible now; there would be old Mr. Yolland to
be entertained and deferred to. Chris, as his manner was, almost
unconsciously to himself began to consider the pose that he would
present to that Catholic country gentleman. He had best be an earnest young journalist; some hints as to the power of the Press and
his own sufferings as a conscientious Catholic would probably be
his best policy, with a touch or two of the man-of-the-world thrown
in. There was nobody else to be conciliated, except the butler and
the man who waited on him. He must raise thirty shillings somehow for these officials.

Then he sat up, produced an exquisite little morocco pocket book
and began to make his list.

It seemed a little formidable as he ran his pencil down it an hour
later, and he regretfully struck off an item here and there. He must
be content with only one more suit of pajamas; and he must obviously do without a dressing gown; in fact, he could borrow one of
Dick's. He reduced eighteen collars to fourteen, deleted the Beeston
strop altogether; but he left the twelve white shirts as they stood,
with other things. Then he went through a swift calculation, and
added an item of three pounds in cash for general expenses — say
five pounds.

Then he sighed, eyed the whole list with dismay, crumpled it up
and threw it into the fender. Then he sighed yet more deeply, rolled
his eyes passionately to the ceiling, picked up the list, smoothed it
out, put it back in his pocket book, and took up the *Daily Chronicle*.

He was in an attitude of deep depression, with his elbows on his
knees, and his head in his hands, as Dick came in half-an-hour
before lunch.

"It's no good, my dear fellow," he said, "no good. I can't face you. Let me go! Let me go!

Dick's honest face became clouded.

"Don't talk rot, my dear man. What's the matter?"

"I can't," cried Chris again, looking at him despairingly. "I can't sponge on you like this. It isn't as if I could ever repay you."

The priest sat down.

"I repeat," he said, "wouldn't you do as much for me?"

"Why, of course —" exclaimed Chris radiantly.

"Very well then. Let's have the list."

Chris dropped his face once more into his hands.

"I can't, I can't," he moaned. "I tell you I have nothing. I cannot come with you as a pauper. I must be decent. Let me have a few shillings instead, and go and get a lodging somewhere."

"Oh! Do be reasonable. Of course I understand; but don't talk rot. Where is the list?"

Chris eyed him miserably a moment; then, as with a great effort, he drew out his pocket book, and looked at the list for a few seconds. Then once more he dashed it into the fender.

"I threw it away once before," he cried. "Let me burn it! I daren't show it you."

Dick picked up the list that had fortunately fallen quite clear of the fire; smoothed it out and looked at it a minute or two.

"This seems all right," he said deliberately. "What's this you've crossed out?"

Chris leaned towards him, and the priest was aware of the faintest imaginable aroma of violet scent.

"A dressing gown and a Beeston strop," groaned the pauper.

"Oh! But you had better have a dressing gown," observed the priest; "it is sure to be useful."

"No! No!" cried the other, "it is not necessary; it is not necessary. I ask no more than the simplest necessaries."

Dick folded the list and put it away in his pocket.

"We must go out after lunch," he said. "Where do you generally go for your things?"

"I used to go to the Haymarket," murmured his friend.

"Very well, then. You are sure there is nothing else?"

"You are too good to me! No, nothing else, upon my word."

Dick had a very queer afternoon. Mr. English's assistant in the Haymarket directed all his deference towards the vivid gentleman in the blue coat who demanded shirts with such an air, fingering the linen delicately and surely; and begged pardon more than once when the priest was privileged to step forward and give his address as the place to which the goods were to be sent immediately.

"Just have them marked," said Chris brusquely.

"Yes, sir — er — what name?"

"'C. Dell,'" said the priest.

"And now pajamas," put in Chris over his shoulder, posing a moment before a tall glass, and passing his hand smoothly over his chin. "Silk — not that half-and-half business —" He turned abruptly. "That is —" he said, and eyed his friend a moment.

"Yes, silk," nodded Dick.

He felt a hand touch his arm affectionately a moment.

"You are too good," murmured Chris, as they passed further into the shop.

Dick had just a minute of silence as they drove homeward through the lighted streets in the hansom that Chris had hailed; and almost before he was aware of it himself he perceived that the man beside him knew it.

"You are displeased with me? What have I done?"

"My dear man, what do you mean?"

"I know it; I feel it. Have I been too free? I thought you meant—"

"Good Lord! Of course I meant it. All; everything. Didn't I say so?"

"You are sure?"

"Sure."

When he looked at him again half-timidly, Chris was eying himself in the corner-glass with that peculiarly solemn and mask-like expression of the male sex before a mirror.

They had a delightful evening together between tea and dinner; and Dick was at once amused and annoyed at the pleasure he found in the other's company. Chris was so absurd, he assured himself now and again; he had all the faults of an overdrawn portrait; there was not a movement of his that was not an exaggeration. When the priest dropped his cigarette, Chris was on the floor instantly, and handed it back with a scrupulous exactness not to finger the wet end. When they spoke of Oxford there came into his friend's face such a passion of sentimental retrospect that Dick laughed nervously. All that Chris said of himself too and of his life during the past five years was uttered with a wealth of melancholy penitence that was plainly a great enjoyment to him; he hinted at incidents, at escapades, at misfortunes; he accused himself in general terms of infamous affairs; and yet he told the priest nothing at all. It was like the confession of a fashionable woman unable to condescend to details, but desirous of making an impression; and when Dick once ventured to particularize, he was met with such indignant repudiation that there was nothing to be done but to apologize and explain.

Chris still smoldered a moment.

"No, thank God! I have fallen very low, but not that. I may say that I am scrupulous in money matters. I have gambled — yes — far beyond what I should have done, but I have paid."

"My dear fellow, I am very sorry. I thought you meant — I thought you said that you had some debts."

"Not debts of honor," protested Chris. "Tradesmen — yes. Surely there is a difference; and they shall be paid some day, too — the blood-suckers."

Dick indulged in a humorous reflection, and again, by that swift intuition that Chris had always possessed, he was detected.

"You think they have not sucked much from me! But they have! Tears and anguish at the thought that I could not pay them! And they will have the money, too. Well they know that!"

As regarded the actual objective side there could be nothing but disapprobation or laughter, but on the subjective side this man was undoubtedly as attractive as he had always been. Dick remembered the extraordinary power that the other had always had over women. They began by being amused by him, they laughed while they liked his fine attentions, his gifts of flowers, his alertness at the door;

then they generally pitied him for the mysterious misfortunes which he allowed to make a swift appearance in his conversation and his apparent self-repression; they always quarreled with him presently, and were piqued by the icy and aloof dignity that he assumed in place of the cordial flattery which he usually displayed; and they generally ended by falling in love with him more or less. Dick had often wondered why, and on the whole the best explanation seemed to be that there was a kind of essential virility underlying his soft and ardent theatricality; he was elaborately made up, there was a glimmer as of footlights about his personality, and yet under the paint and the posing there was a very real male creature.

Children also loved him. He was so dainty and vivid, and took them so seriously; it was among men of his own age that his enemies lay. Dick had heard him abused as a strutting fool, an effeminate ass, an affected *poseur;* and he was aware that there was truth in such remarks, yet, in his defense, delivered with some stiffness, he had always maintained that such accusations were extremely shallow and one-sided, and that there was a great deal more in Christopher Dell than these blockheads had wit to recognize.

It was this inner side that Chris presented to him this evening; he was unfeignedly affectionate, full of self-reproach, alert in his attentions, and extravagantly grateful; and by the time that Dick took up his bed-candle, he had forgotten altogether the slightly unpleasant impression of the afternoon, the freeness with a friend's money, the all but imperceptible touch of patronage; he only remembered the warm nature, the sincerity beneath the unreality, the loudly expressed gratitude and self-depreciation.

He went up to bed, pleased with the thought that he had been of service to his friend, pleased with the consciousness that they were beneath the same roof, and yet more pleased to think that the situation would continue for another ten days. But he wondered what on earth his father would make of the guest.

(3)

Christopher Dell was conscious of a very pleasurable atmosphere as he stepped out of the train at Marlesdon Junction three days later, and caught sight of the grave, saluting footman on the platform, and, beyond the paling, the heads of two black horses erect and aristocratic.

It was an atmosphere which he had not known for some years, although, he told himself, it was the one proper to a man of his parts and tastes. He stood, a stiff important figure for a moment, in a long fawn-colored coat and a gray hat which had been among the items on his list, waiting for Dick who appeared to have seen some acquaintances on the platform. He noticed two ladies, one middle-aged and the other young and with them a stoutish man in a mackintosh.

"The luggage, sir?" observed a deferential voice at his side.

"Two portmanteaux," said Chris brusquely. "Father Yolland's you know. Mine is a new one, with a red star."

Dick came up presently.

"Beastly bore, my dear man — I couldn't help it; and they want us to dine on Thursday. I couldn't get out of it."

"They?"

"The Hamiltons — you won't mind, will you? I played you, but it was no good. They want you to come too."

Chris murmured something in the nature of delighted assent, and the two men went off together.

The luggage was in the phaeton already, it seemed, and Chris climbed up beside Dick, who took the reins. It was extremely pleasant to draw the fur-lined rug over his knees, sitting back in the deep, springy seat, and to look out at the tossing, jingling heads and the sleek backs before him; it all symbolized so much that was so foreign to him now, and yet full of reminiscences of the days of plenty. A slight drawl made itself perceptible in his talk as they drove homewards through the mellow October air.

They turned in after a mile or so through a lodge gate where a child in a white pinafore bobbed decorously at the carriage, and Chris felt his heart overflow with satisfaction.

"My dear man!" he said suddenly, "how good you are to me!"

Dick growled softly, and the carriage sped on.

On either side of the drive lay the deep autumn grass, slope be-

yond slope, melting from a heavy green at hand to an indescribably sweet blue in the distance. Tawny clothed trees trooped down
as on promontories among the tawnier bracken about their roots;
the clear, hard blue sky lay over all; the very sounds were opulent; a
cock-pheasant crowed among the copses; there was a melodious
jangle of a cowbell from beneath the trees; once through the brisk
air came the quick double-pulse of a gun fired far away.

Dick turned suddenly.

"Will you shoot after lunch?" he said. "There are plenty of guns."

Chris reflected for an imperceptible instant.

"I think not, thanks. Let me walk with you instead."

In that fraction of time a couple of alternative poses had whisked
before his mental vision — in one he appeared as an apologetic
sportsman, the contempt of keepers, an object for compassionate
excuse from Dick; in the other as a distinguished gentleman in a
fawn-colored coat with a cane in his hand, holding his tongue at
critical moments, dropping shrewd compliments and comments
at the proper time.

There was no doubt that the latter was the more impressive; he
remembered the terms well enough, and he had been but a poor
shot even five years ago. He could certainly do the talking; it was
wiser not to risk the shooting.

The Georgian house presently appeared before them, a squared
white building, with a pillared porch and a balustraded roof, startlingly ugly, and yet satisfactorily suggestive of comfort. The very
exterior told of high, dignified rooms, chintz covered armchairs
and classical cornices. It stood in a lake of gravel, flanked by shrub-
beries; the gardens, Chris remembered, were upon the other side.

As they drew up, the inner glass doors opened, and a tall old
man, gray-bearded and sanguine, came out, in loose gray clothes
and a knotted black tie, and simultaneously the opulent sound of a
gong boomed from the hall behind.

"Well, then," said the old man, smiling.

Chris had an opportunity to observe his host, as father and son
greeted one another, and came to the swift conclusion that he was
what he had expected. He would be a good Christian man, aware

of his dignity, reasonably generous, staunch, wholesome, and a little stupid; the pose of an earnest young journalist who had suffered for the Faith, pathetically anxious for sympathy, would do very well.

He found his hand taken presently with an air of slight reserve, and hastened to put as much deference as he could into his bent back.

"Dick will show you your room, Mr. Dell."

It was a large hall, stone-floored and classically adorned, with a tiger skin or two, some mahogany furniture, and an array of buffalo horns; a broad solid staircase rose out of the inner hall towards the glass dome that lighted it, and disappeared in galleries to right and left.

The bedroom too was entirely in keeping, carpeted and furnished with a dull splendor; a green-curtained bed stood out from the wall in the very middle of the room, as if to assure the visitor that he was in nothing but a bedroom; a deep chintz sofa stood at its foot; a heavy knee hold table with a stamped blotting book, new quill pens, a painted china ink stand and a morocco paper-case, assured the observer that letters could be written there; a tall rosewood wardrobe with a beveled glass in one of its doors afforded an opportunity for self-contemplation; and a highly polished fireplace with square black shining coals within a white paper screen awaited but a match to burst into comfortable flame. It was dignified, chilly, rather expensive, rather funereal, and cried, "spare bedroom" from every shining surface; there was nothing familiar or domestic in it; the inhabitant was a guest, not an intimate.

"Find your way down, will you? The dining room is at the foot of the stairs."

Dick glanced round, nodded and was gone.

Chris took off his coat with the precision that was so characteristic of him, rolled up his stiff cuffs, slipped off his silver ring on to the white marble, and stood soaking his chilled fingers in stinging hot water. He felt a little unhappy, and, for a wonder, a little shy.

He was not sure how he would get on with Mr. Yolland, nor what was expected of him. Perhaps it would be better to postpone committing himself; to observe, to be deferential and complimentary. It world be a sad pity if nothing came of this visit; it was his first return into the respectable world after a five years' absence, and he yearned for respectability and an assured position. What a pity there were no women; he could not go wrong there.

He found his way down presently, walking with a slow dignity down the heavily carpeted stairs, shooting his cuffs, looking at his nails, and intensely conscious of wealthy ease about him. He passed his ascending portmanteau with an admirable *hauteur*.

Dick and his father meanwhile were exchanging a word or two before the dining room fire.

"He is a good fellow," said Dick softly. "I found him almost starving. He has no idea of money."

"A little — er — theatrical, eh?" remarked his father, warming his tails.

Dick grinned.

"Just so," he said, "but it is only superficial. He is all right, really."

Dick was pleased with his friend's bearing at lunch. Chris was amusing, unostentatious of poverty, extremely polite, and not at all shy. Only once did he overdo his pleasantness in hastening to ring the bell before the son of the house.

"I think I shall go out with a gun," said Dick; at last, emptying his coffee cup. "Will it bore you to come?"

"Won't Mr. Dell shoot too?" put in Mr. Yolland. "If he hasn't a gun here —"

Chris hastened to decline.

"The fact is I haven't shot for a long while; perhaps before I leave —. I should like to walk with Dick if I may. Will you not come, sir?"

An expression fleeted over the old man's face.

"I think not, Mr. Dell. I have my bailiff coming up."

Dick compressed his lips as he noticed a look of extreme disappointment in his friend's features; he wished he would not be so eager to please.

They had a long, placid afternoon in some outlying parts of the park, walking over the dry leaves beneath the dying trees; the whole radiant air was full of fragrant death; the tawny pheasants that clucked and whirred like defective clockwork seemed a part of the English landscape; even their deaths harmonized with the dying year.

They took it easily, more for the air than the sport content when a hardly-escaped bird, crying with nervous exultation, buzzed across the rising mists to the home coverts; and once Dick missed a cat on purpose by two yards.

"Thank the gods!" said Chris earnestly

Dick's face twitched with amusement. He refrained from even one look at the keeper.

There was not much opportunity for talk, and Chris was too tactful to insist upon it; he tramped alongside with a severe and reminiscent face; once or twice he dropped a word or two in the keeper's hearing that suggested rather than stated his own desperate prowess in past years; and, still in his fawn-colored coat and gray hat, he presented exactly the figure he supposed and desired.

He had another burst of good-feeling as he walked homewards under the luminous sky, and saw the pleasant lights of the house beginning to glimmer beyond the trees.

"How happy you must be, Dick! And you deserve it all!"

Dick murmured incoherently. He wished the other would not talk like this; and yet he recognized that it was inevitable.

"Tell me about the Hamiltons," said Chris suddenly. Dick had given up his gun, and the two were walking over the dew soaked grass towards the glimmering gray line of the garden terrace.

"Oh! I don't know. They're not Catholics. They're mother and daughter and Jack. That was Brasted with them."

"Who?"

"Lord Brasted, the motoring-man. I think he knew Mrs. Hamilton's husband. He often comes down here."

"Oh! Where do they live?"

"Hinton Hall. It's a fine house, quite new. The old man built it."

"And Jack?"

"Jack's a cousin who lives there."

"No sons then?"

"No."

Chris had an overwhelming desire to make inquiries then about the daughter; but he restrained it, and approached the matter from ambush.

"Tell me more about them, Dick."

"Well, they're very pious, I believe. I heard the parson say that they were sound Churchpeople, whatever that means."

"I know exactly. You see you hadn't the advantage of being a convert. Well, what do they do?"

"Oh, nothing much; they live pretty quietly. The girl is not out till next year —"

"Go on, I like to hear — if you don't mind, old man."

"There's nothing to tell; they're all right. They're very nice to me."

Chris deplored in his heart his friend's lack of discernment. It was just like Dick. Well, he must observe for himself on Thursday night.

They passed in together through the garden door, and stood blinking at the lights in the warm, redolent smoking room where they had played piquet years ago. A tea tray winked pleasantly near the fire.

Chris went to bed early that night; he said he had a headache, and the father and son sat up a few minutes more.

"I'm rather unhappy about Chris," observed Dick suddenly.

"Why?"

"What is he to do? He's got nowhere to go when he leaves this. You don't know of anything, I suppose, Father?"

Mr. Yolland knocked out his pipe before answering. He was aware of having been slightly touched during the evening by the young man, who had been so eager to please, so alert in his manners, so carefully deferential; an enemy might have called him servile, but it would not have been true. Even the almost imperceptible tinge of over-emphasis had faded with his absence, and his pathos remained. Besides he was scrupulously well dressed, and knew how to wear his clothes, and that pleased Mr. Yolland, who himself wore a V-shaped front to his shirt and a straggling tie under his beard. He was also his son's friend.

"What about that journalism he was talking about?" he said at last.

"Oh! It won't come to much. And, anyhow, what is he to do in the meantime?"

"What sort of a thing does he want?"

Dick smiled, and glanced at his father.

"He would make an excellent — er — well, I don't know. He is wonderful with women; servants always like him; he tips them magnificently with his last penny. He has got lots of tact, of a kind."

"I know of no openings," said Mr. Yolland gravely.

"Well, a sort of secretaryship — so long as someone else did the accounts. He writes very well."

Mr. Yolland blew long and meditatively through his mellow briar.

"He seems to me rather like a man in a book," he said at last. "Where did he get his clothes, if he is as poor as all that?"

Dick evaded.

"Oh! That sort of man always keeps his clothes to the last. If he killed himself he would do it in evening dress, you know."

Mr. Yolland was silent.

"Does he know anything about books?" he asked at last.

"I believe so," said Dick eagerly — "at least about some sorts. Do you know of anything?"

"I don't know," said his father slowly, rising. "I will think. Soda water, Dick?"

CHAPTER II

An Attack of Feverishness

(I)

Miss Annie Hamilton had just finished dressing for dinner, and stood a moment before her glass, listening to the sound of wheels and looking at herself.

She saw, framed in walnut wood, a pretty figure and a pretty face; but she did not quite know how pretty was that slender, long-limbed self, the thin round arms emerging from deep sleeves at the elbow, the pleasant pallor of the face heightened by a pair of very dark eyes and eyebrows, and a crown of black hair. She crossed her hands, let them drop again, advanced a foot and withdrew it. Then she became aware of the sin of vanity, and turned resolutely away, a little annoyed with herself. It would have to be mentioned to the Vicar on Saturday, too. But before she had reached the head of the staircase she was wondering how she would look in a low-cut frock next year.

A charming-looking fair-haired rosy boy of seventeen came out of his room as she passed his door, his smooth chin held rather high by reason of a collar, his hands deep in his pockets, and a stiff breastplate of shirt-front bulging from his waistcoat.

"I say! They've come," he said.

She nodded.

"I like that chap Dell," proceeded Jack, going down beside her. "He wouldn't shoot, though."

"How much did you get?"

Jack mocked her for her phrase, and proceeded to give her the statistics of the day's bag; he had only got back an hour before from pheasant-driving at Amplefield.

"I don't think you'll like him, though," he interrupted himself suddenly.

She put her finger on her lips and pointed below to where two figures, one in black clerical dress and the other in ordinary evening dress were crossing the hall. Each was making strange movements with his arms; that would be their cuffs, she supposed. What odd creatures men were!

She dropped her eyes, composed her features, and went forward into the room.

She was always a little excited by Father Yolland's presence. He ought to have had all the mystery of the Erring Sister behind him, but he seemed so extremely natural. She had wondered more than once whether his frank ease were not a triumph of training after all at the hands of those clerical masters of deportment, the Society of Jesus. A priest, she thought, ought to have somewhat of a pontifical air at all times, such as the Vicar had, who always spoke on a monotone, and pronounced all his vowels the same.

She shook hands with the priest, and then glanced up momentarily as her mother made Mr. Dell known to her. No, she decided; Jack was right; she would not like this long-faced man with the smoldering eyes; his face was too much like a mask, and he bowed too low. She was sure he was cold and calculating, with a spice of mockery.

Before she could begin to speak, the door opened again and Lord Brasted came in, and introductions began once more.

This nobleman was of the Pink Type, stoutish, with tufts of light-red frizzed hair above and below his ears. His dominant color pervaded all the rest of him that could be seen, and presumably what could not; his hands had a slight growth of the same hair on their backs. Annie disliked his hands very much; they were too well padded, too soft, and too square.

Yet he had an undoubtedly agreeable manner. He stood now on the hearthrug in the exact position and with the precise manner that indicated his standing in the house. He was a guest, but so old a friend that he was very nearly the host. Yet he always deferred charmingly to Jack, and over herself assumed the protection without the severity of a parent.

"You had a good day, I hear, Mr. Dell," he was saying.

"Ah! I was not shooting, but it was excellent. I had great pleasure in watching Mr. — er — Mr. Jack Hamilton."

The boy flushed with pleasure, and came a step nearer.

"I am sure you can shoot, Mr. Dell," he said. "You know all about it, I expect."

Chris smiled brilliantly — he had very white, even teeth, the girl noticed — too white; it was part of the mask.

"My dear boy, I couldn't hit a haystack. I haven't shot for years."

The boy came even nearer

"Come out tomorrow," he said, "if you would care to pot rabbits, at least,"

Mrs. Hamilton rose as the door was opened, and a soundless-voiced butler presented the top of his head.

"Mr. Dell, will you take my daughter in? Father Yolland, do you mind coming with Jack?"

It was all muddled, thought Chris, as he moved out with Annie's hand on his arm. Then he turned to her, and said an enthusiastic word or two about the oak pendants of the ceiling.

Mrs. Hamilton did not get a word with him, till the fish had disappeared; but she listened, during Lord Brasted's remarks on her right, with considerable complacency to her daughter's conversation. She seemed to be talking really well, and she was usually shy.

It was good for her to meet men of the world, even if they did look like melodramatic actors; it would break the shock of next year.

"My dear lady," protested her other neighbor at last, "you are not listening to a word I am saying."

Her shrewd gray eyes twinkled pleasantly at him as she slowly turned her head.

"I was not," she said. "I was thinking how cheerful Annie was."

Lord Brasted lifted his head like an amiable ram to glance across.

"Who is he?" he asked in a soundless voice.

"I don't know. A friend of Dick Yolland's."

When Chris had helped himself delicately to a sweetbread on toast she laid a slender jeweled left hand on the table.

"You are here long, Mr. Dell?" she said.

"I beg your pardon," said Chris impulsively. "How rude I am! But really Miss Hamilton —" he broke off with an admirable air of confusion.

She was pleased with this; it was so natural. No; the man was not really so very like an actor after all; it was only that he was very well groomed.

"I am so glad you had a good day," she said. "Jack has taken a great fancy to you. I suppose you know that."

He smiled cordially.

"Well, yes." he said. "And what a charming boy he is — an Etonian, I suppose?"

"I had to take him away last half to cram for the Army. They are no good, there, you know."

"No, but what a color it gives to life! I think I envy Etonians more than anyone in the world. I would give anything —"

"You were not there?" she said, knowing that he was not.

He smiled full at her.

"Thank you! No, I was not."

He seemed very melancholy for a moment or two after that, and crumbled his bread in silence with a delicate hand.

"Dick Yolland and I were up at Oxford together," he went on presently. "What a good fellow he is!"

She had noted two facts by now, and hastened to add to them.

"Do you see much of him in town?" she asked.

"I have not seen him for a good while," explained Chris. "I have been abroad such a lot, you see, and now my work —"

"Your work?"

"Well, I am a sort of journalist," he said, "when I can get anything to do — articles and that sort of thing. When I can't —"

He stopped abruptly.

"Yes, Mr. Dell?"

"I starve," he said, with the utmost frankness and seriousness.

Mrs. Hamilton almost gasped. This was very startling; at least the man was not designing as she had been inclined to suspect. It was almost inconceivable that this trim gentleman could mean what he said.

"That is relative, I suppose," she observed presently.

He shook his head, looking at her intently for a moment, and then dropping his eyes humbly.

"No, absolute. I meant it, Mrs. Hamilton. Forgive me —" he broke off again with every appearance of distress.

Before she could summon up any answer to this she heard her daughter break in.

"Mr. Dell, do attend a moment. Father Yolland says —"

Then Lord Brasted's suave voice made a remark about cylinders, and she forced herself to listen and answer.

There was a good deal of laughter during the rest of dinner between the other four; they were at an oval table that made such communication possible, especially when Jack leaned his head between the ferns to contribute his share; and Mrs. Hamilton was able to exchange a good many remarks with her old friend.

"He is a very odd man," she said presently, with scarcely moving lips. "I think I like him."

The other put his head politely on one side; he was not interested in odd young men; he liked them conventional.

"He has been saying such curious things," she went on. "I wonder if they are true."

"To Miss Annie, too?" he asked.

She looked at him an instant.

"Of course not," she said. "They were exchanging reminiscences of childhood when I last listened. He appears to have worn diamond socks."

Lord Brasted murmured something appreciative.

"Why don't you like him?" she demanded.

"Dear lady, I have no views at all. He is extremely well-dressed; that is all that I have observed at present."

"Observe some more," she said. "Make him talk when we go. I should like to know what you think."

She was astonished at her own interest. She had a hundred criticisms — of his talk, his bearing, his sleek head, his thin suggestive hands; and yet she forebore to formulate them even to herself. They hung for the present suspended. She would see after Lord Brasted had given his opinion, and she would also like to hear Annie's.

She gathered her fan at the earliest occasion, and swept out with her daughter, bowing her gray-piled head towards Chris, who was of course at the door, alert and trim, with his napkin in his left hand.

She said nothing at all for a moment, but sat warming her pretty blue-veined hands at the fire, and watching Annie bring up a stool.

"No, my dear; don't sit there, or move before they come in. What do you think of Mr. Dell?"

"He is delightful, Mamma. He told us such funny stories."

Mrs. Hamilton's face had a shadow of amusement on it for an instant, then she reminded herself that the contrast might be the result of pluck.

"What sort of stories?"

"Oh! About the Italians, and the way they behave in church — all sorts of things, Mamma."

"Is he a Roman Catholic?"

"Yes: I asked him."

Mrs. Hamilton fell to warming her hands again.

"There are plenty of men like that, my dear," she observed presently.

"Like what?"

"Like Mr. Dell."

Annie was puzzled. She had completely reversed her opinion of Chris long before the end of dinner. She was still afraid that possibly he was not a very good man, which, of course, would be very sad, if true; but he was a very nice one. He was not stout and red like Lord Brasted; he did not patronize her at all; on the contrary he had asked her for her opinion on several matters; he had given enthusiastic praise to that dear boy Jack, and he had somehow conveyed the impression that he thought her very charming and good. Perhaps that was vanity, she reflected; but he had certainly said some very true and touching things about the influence of good women in general — even of girls. Why, then, did her mother not like him?

She was apt to be a little afraid of her mother, but she determined to be brave just now.

"Don't you like Mr. Dell?" she asked, innocent-eyed.

Her mother laughed.

"My dearest, how can I tell? I have hardly spoken to him. You monopolized him altogether."

Annie smiled with pleasure.

"He would talk to me, Mamma," she said.

"Well, you must let me talk to him when he comes in. Don't forget, I want to."

There was no question as to who was to talk to Mr. Dell that evening. Mrs. Hamilton, sitting now on a high-backed sofa apart from the rest, swept aside her silken skirts and called him by name.

"Come and talk to me, Mr. Dell."

There was no help for it. Annie drifted off to a table with Father Yolland and talked countryside, intensely conscious of the two on the sofa. Lord Brasted came and chimed in presently with an air of one who makes concessions, and Jack, after revolving round the sofa for ten minutes disappeared, presumably to the smoking room, closing the door unnecessarily sharply behind him. There was no question, thought Dick Yolland, as he observed these phenomena, that his friend was a success. But then he always was on such occasions.

The butler presented the top of his head again before either of the groups was re-sorted, and this time his news was audible. Father Yolland's brougham was at the door.

Annie shut the book they were looking at — the countryside had proved rather sterile — and stood up with a slight air of resentment, looking towards her mother. They seemed very busy in conversation; then Father Yolland stepped forward.

"I am afraid we must go, Mrs. Hamilton. It's rather a cold night."

The two rose, still talking, and then, to Annie's amazement, Mr. Dell, taking her mother's hand, raised it to his lips. She did not seem in the least disconcerted.

"Then on Saturday," she said, "about five."

Chris murmured something.

Annie shook hands with the two men, secretly terrified at the thought that Mr. Dell might kiss her hand too, but he only looked at her with a kind of melancholy admiration, and then followed his friend out. She could see Jack, with a very sulky air standing outside to see them to the carriage.

When she turned again, her mother was talking to Lord Brasted.

"I don't want to hear," the girl heard her say. "I have my own opinion now. I may tell you he is coming to stay here on Saturday."

Annie was so much pleased at the news that she hardly noticed Lord Brasted's shrug of his broad shoulders.

"I will not dispute your intuition," he said. "But —"

"No ' buts,'" she said. "Goodnight, Annie."

"Mamma, why did he, why did he —?"

"Well, my dear?"

"Why did he kiss your hand?"

She laughed naturally, but her eyes were bright and interested.

"It is a pretty Italian custom," she said. "Go to bed, child."

(2)

Dick Yolland was silent for sheer amusement for a full hundred yards from the house door. Chris had been so entirely characteristic of himself — so superb, so adaptable. What in the world had he talked to Mrs. Hamilton about, that had elicited that invitation? Jack, too, had accompanied Chris to the carriage door, pressing entreaties to pot rabbits up to the last moment; Annie had been a new creature; she had talked with sparkling eyes; her reserve had been melted.

At last he broke silence.

"You are a wonderful chap, Chris."

By the glow of the cigarette that the other had lighted in the porch from one of Jack's matches Dick could see a pair of eyes look at him sideways.

"What do you mean, Dick?"

By the tone the priest thought he was slightly offended.

"Why, — wonderful," he said. "You have made three conquests. How do you do it?"

"Not four then?" came the voice.

Dick had forgotten the fourth.

"Oh! I daresay four. I don't know about Brasted. He is a tough chap. How do you do it? What did you talk to Mrs. Hamilton about?"

Chris was silent a moment.

"My dear man!" he said; and there was a ring of expostulation in his voice.

For a moment the priest was astounded; yet he had known Chris before now take offense at what he considered ill manners.

"Oh! don't be a fool," he said. "How was I to dream it was private? Do you want me to apologize?"

A hand was laid on his arm.

"My dear chap, of course it isn't private to you. I — I talked about myself."

For one instant a thunder cloud of *fou rire* enveloped the priest; but he fortunately restrained himself. Why, of course! What else should Chris talk about with such earnestness? He thanked Divine Providence that the brougham was dark.

"It interested her, at any rate," he said, trying to keep the quaver out of his voice.

Chris drew sententiously upon his cigarette and expelled the smoke with pursed lips. Dick could feel the aromatic sting in his eyes.

"I showed her my heart," said the egoist. "Dick! There is no limit to the power of a good woman."

The epithet "good" was perhaps one of the last, though not the least, true, of all those applicable to Mrs. Hamilton, but the priest knew what Chris meant by it it signified what he would have called sympathy.

"And to her daughter?" he inquired.

"My dear man, of course I shouldn't talk like that to a girl. But what a dear creature she is — pure and good and virginal. Oh! My God!"

This was nearer the mark; but Dick had heard those epithets applied to not less than five other maidens before.

They were both silent for perhaps a hundred yards. Then the

voice went on out of the darkness.

"Oh! my God! If I had known such people ten years ago, what a different man I should have been!"

There was again undoubted sincerity in the man's voice, but how far was there genuineness?

"Well — I'm delighted you've made friends," said Dick serenely. "How long have they asked you for?"

"She said till Monday."

"And what about Lord Brasted?"

There was a swift movement beside him.

"You noticed it too?" cried Chris. "That man was trying to pump me. I saw it at once. He's my enemy, Dick."

"My dear man, he's perfectly harmless. He spuds dandelions."

"I don't care, he's my enemy; I knew it at once. I hate those red-haired, white-skinned, fat men. They smell, too."

"You're talking complete rubbish. I know him well. He's nothing of the sort."

"You don't understand," said Chris; "it's a question of magnetism. He hates me as much as I hate him."

"Bosh!" said the priest.

Chris threw himself back without a word, and Dick did not care to break the silence. This man was really too absurd. Neither moved till the carriage stopped in creaking motionlessness at the lodge-gate. Then Dick felt himself seized once more by the arm.

"My dear Dick, forgive me — I'm a wild fool. But I must trust my instincts. They're all I've got."

"You're quite wrong about Brasted," repeated the priest steadily

Chris said no more, and they drove in silence down the long drive, till the open hall door shone out pleasantly and the carriage stopped.

Dick slipped out and stood waiting on the steps. Chris came out looking rather constrained, passed him in the hall and took up his bed-candle.

"You're not going to bed?" cried the priest.

The other nodded.

"I'm tired out; this kind of evening exhausts me. Goodnight, dear man."

When Dick got to the smoking room he found his father with a book and pipe.

"Well?"

Dick shut the door and sat down, helping himself from a siphon.

"Chris has been a great success. Mrs. Hamilton asked him to stay there when he leaves here."

Mr. Yolland's eyes grew amused.

"As you told me," he said. "Well, I have been thinking too. I am very sorry for that young man. How about the library here?"

"How?"

"Well, it's in shocking bad order. Do you think he would think it beneath him to arrange and catalog? It would give him breathing-time."

"I'm awfully grateful," said Dick, "but how about you? Wouldn't you hate to have him here?"

"Oh! We should only meet at meals. That would have to be understood. What do you think of it?"

"I think it excellent."

He mused a minute or two.

"Why didn't he come in?" said his father.

Dick roused himself.

"Oh! I think he was rather annoyed with me. It's his way, you know; he takes offense rather easily."

"What's the matter?"

"Oh, there was some rot about Brasted. He didn't like him. I told him he was a fool."

"Is he likely to lose his temper with me?" asked Mr. Yolland gravely.

Dick laughed.

"I must talk to him. I've been meaning to ever since last week. He'd be such a good chap if he'd only take himself in hand. He's got no will, you know, except when he's excited. He was always like that."

Mr. Yolland put his book down with an air of finality.

"Dick," he said, "I don't want you to answer if you can't, but I wish you'd tell me more about him. I want to know what he's really like."

Dick's snub-nosed face grew serious.

"About morals, you mean? Well, I'm afraid they aren't very good. I expect he's done most things. I've never actually inquired, you know. But I should think he's gone pretty deep. But you can trust him here."

"You're sure there'll be no trouble? I shouldn't like a scandal, you know."

"Oh! That'll be all right. He's got too much sense of honor. He's perfectly honorable. And I've no doubt he'll tell you everything you want to know, in a week or two, at any rate. He's often wanted to tell me, but I put him off. I can't bear that sort of thing. Besides, it isn't really a part of him — Oh! I can't explain."

Mr. Yolland filled his pipe before answering.

"Well, then, what about his religion? He hasn't been to Mass at all."

"Oh! He talks a lot of nonsense about all religions, but he's a Catholic all right. He's rather like a Renaissance man; I think that's his ideal."

"But he goes to Mass and all that?"

"Oh! Yes, when he gets up in time; and he's very fervent indeed now and then. It's all rather feverish; but I haven't a doubt as to his faith, though he would probably deny that he had any. That's the worst of these converts; they never can distinguish between faith and emotion."

Mr. Yolland's mouth twitched under his gray moustaches.

"Your father, for example?"

Dick laughed.

"Oh! You don't count. You're practically an old Catholic."

"Except as regards sending you to Winchester?"

"Yes, except that," answered Dick smiling.

"Well, then," went on Mr. Yolland presently. "Then that is settled so far as I am concerned. You will sound him, please, tomorrow. I suppose the cataloging will take not less than six weeks. He will have everything supplied here; and money —? How much shall I say?"

"Fifty pounds," answered Dick promptly. "If that's not too much."

"It shall be fifty pounds."

Mr. Yolland rose.

"Then I shall go to bed. By the way, Dick, Rolls is coming out to lunch tomorrow. I shall shoot too, I think."

Dick nodded.

"Goodnight, Father. It's most awfully good of you. I don't know what to say."

"Oh! I hope it'll turn out well. Goodnight, Dick."

The priest sat on, letting his cigarette burn itself into a long unheeded curl of gray ash.

At times like this his affection for his father waxed into a sort of passion. He was always so sensible and youthful; there was no jawing — there never had been. Dick had been flogged as a boy more than once by his father, and it had been always done with the same promptness and humanity; and his first pony had been given to him with the same decisive air. A certain time was devoted to consideration first, and then the announcement of blame or praise came out clear and precise. When Dick was in need of funds for charity in Soho he met with the same treatment. His father either said no, or sent exactly the amount asked for without question or comment. Lately it had been the latter more than the former; Dick felt that his father had begun to trust his judgment, and it was very delightful to him.

Now here was this new thing, and this crowned all; his father had accepted his recommendation practically without inquiry, and, on the strength of it had laid himself open to the risk of severe inconvenience. Dick sincerely trusted that his confidence was secure. Surely Chris would behave himself!

He must have a long talk to him tomorrow. There was a number of small points on which advice was necessary; Chris must understand the situation; he was not in any sense to be a servant, but neither was he to be a guest with a right to entertainment; also he must do what he was told; he was to be a professional in the matter of the library, not an irresponsible amateur. Then he must really be down to breakfast in time, and must go to Mass on Sundays;

and he must keep himself tolerably employed for, say, seven hours a day. That was not too much to ask.

As regarded graver matters of behavior Dick did not propose to speak; Chris knew perfectly well what he thought. He would do no more than indicate the general course of life.

The priest stretched his legs to the blaze, threw away the ash of his cigarette and took another.

There were other things he would say to his friend tomorrow. He would tell him not to sulk, not to make a childish exhibition of himself if he thought that his pride was injured. That little affair in the carriage coming home was really absurd. It was only a small thing — even Chris could not make it a great one — but it should not have happened at all, and the going to bed in a huff was the pinnacle of folly.

He would tell him that he needed ballast, a wholesome tranquility, a grip on himself, greater faith in other people. It was all very well to be emotional but emotions should be servants, not masters, or at least not tyrants.

The secret lay in the will, as it always did the priest reflected, secure in his ramparts of casuistic reading. The personality should reside there as in a castle, and issue orders to the passions and intellectual apprehensions, who, in their turn should inform their master of external happenings and await his decision. Now Chris's personality did not reside in his will; it ran about the battlements, mixed in the fray, ordered and counter-ordered at random, was swept off its feet in panics and sallies, and all the while stormed or paced or attitudinized according to mood in a hundred varying postures.

This was an excellent analysis, Dick told himself; it was Chris to the life; he wondered he had not thought of it before. Well, his friend should have the benefit of it tomorrow, tactfully given, and without any assumption of superiority. Had not Chris told him a hundred times how wise he was? Very well, Chris should hear wisdom.

And all the while the priest did not recognize how really fond he must be of his friend to give him all this inspired thought. He honestly believed that he was impartial and just.

He threw away his cigarette end and stood up looking with steady, honest eyes at the dying fire. A good fellow, Chris, but a child in some things!

Then old Mr. Rolls was coming to join them at lunch tomorrow — that queer lean man who lived all alone in his fortified house. What would Chris make of him — and, as an afterthought, what would he make of Chris?

Then Dick Yolland blew out the lamp, and went up to bed, well pleased.

(3)

Chris was rather silent at breakfast, and disappeared soon after, saying that he would have to be extremely busy that morning with correspondence as respected his desired position on the *Saturday Express,* and would join them, if he might, at lunch.

Dick saw very well that he was in one of his moods, of which the small affair last night had been a symptom, so he left him alone, indicated the cottage where lunch would be served, and went off to the gun room without saying a word about the library scheme. If Chris was still sulky, he reflected, the offer would fall on him with greater reproachful force; if he were not sulky, it would do no harm to wait till evening when the matter could be talked out.

They had an excellent morning; both father and son shot well, and a little before one o'clock found themselves close to the cottage. Chris emerged from the door as they arrived.

Again Dick noticed that air of extreme trimness in his friend. As he stood there with his hands in his deep pockets, the cap of a proper tint upon his head, well-shaved, slender and virile, with a due amount of spat appearing beneath a neat trouser, it was almost impossible to believe that this man was practically penniless and homeless.

He hailed them with an inquiry as to the bag, was informed, and turned with Dick into the gamekeeper's cottage.

It was a charming room, low-ceilinged and raftered; a few fallowbucks' horns sprouted from the walls; an ancient gun or two hung from a beam; a neat glazed gunrack glimmered in the corner; the floor was cheerful red-brick with a couple of skins upon it; an oak table was set out with steaming food — maigre, for it was a Friday — diamond-paned windows looked out on to the deep autumn woods, and a wood fire blazed pleasantly on the hearth.

Chris sat down by it, pulling up his trousers first, and spreading his thin hands to the fire.

"Rolls hasn't come then," observed Dick.

"Who?"

"Rolls — he was going to meet us here."

"Oh! Who is he?"

Dick finished taking out his cartridges, snapped the breech, set down his gun, and came across to the fire.

It was evident that Chris had not recovered; there was still a little vibration of nerves in the air. It was too absurd, Dick told himself; it was like a schoolgirl — not a man.

So he answered rather coolly.

"Oh! Rolls is Rolls. He lives near here; I don't know that there's much to say about him. He's — he's rather odd. You can't help attending to him, you know."

"Oh!"

"He's got a fine house — fearfully old. It's got a moat, and so on. He lives there alone."

"Oh!"

This was discouraging; it was more than discouraging — it was irritating. After all, the man might try to behave civilly! Dick made a mental addition to his list of subjects to be laid before his friend that evening.

There was a sound of voices; the door was darkened, and a tall old man came through, followed by Mr. Yolland. Chris sprang up and stood at a sort of attention.

"Here he is," said Mr. Yolland. "Mr. Dell, let me introduce you to Mr. Rolls."

Dick watched the little scene with interest. There was Chris, with a deferential curve of the back, looking, as most men did, about three sizes too small by the side of this tall old man, gray-haired, with a brown, clean-shaven face like a hatchet, covered with wrinkles. Dick saw his eyebrows twitch, and his melancholy eyes going through the stranger like swords, but he said nothing.

Chris recovered his upright attitude, and stood, as he always did after an introduction, with a sudden air of fierce independence. Once more Dick remembered the melodramatic stage.

Chris's air of slight resentment vanished wholly as lunch proceeded; he talked briskly about sport, about the deceptive flight of certain kinds of birds, and was at first at least as conventional as it is possible to be. He handed things about smartly, was punctilious in helping his neighbor before himself, and, on the whole cut a decent, if an overdrawn, figure.

Mr. Rolls sat silent most of the time, but his silence was oddly significant, as it always was. It revealed rather than obscured his personality. Dick could see that Chris was affected by it; his mental face was turned continually towards the newcomer; he twice broke off in a sentence to hear what the other was saying in his melancholy voice; he upset the salt, and was extravagantly apologetic in his eagerness to serve him. Yet the priest was not sure whether it was a favorable impression or not.

Chris, in fact, did most of the talking. Three times it was he who broke a silence; for Mr. Yolland talked little too, and the young man exerted himself considerably. It was one of his ideas, Dick remembered, that sociability depended on conversation; yet he was not wholly successful towards the end of lunch.

He was talking about Russia, and happened to mention that he had once learned to speak the language of that country.

Mr. Rolls looked up.

"Indeed, Mr. Dell? Do you speak it well?"

"Yes, I speak it all right," said the young man airily.

The other instantly uttered what sounded to Dick's ears like a string of hauks and spits, and looked gravely at Chris, who glanced back uneasily.

"Er — I don't see the point of that," he said.

Dick felt uncomfortable and also amused. What on earth had that sentence meant? He determined to ask. But he had no chance then; Chris deftly swept to another subject.

"The woods are charming now," he observed, finishing his last glass of red wine. "They are like the best Persian rugs. Who was it who said that nature imitates art?"

A profound silence fell. Dick's heart sank; he remembered that sort of conversation at Oxford. Chris would do it sometimes. He hastened to break in.

"Yes, very clever," he said. "That sort of paradox won't do though."

Chris eyed him sharply.

"Won't do, Dick?"

"It is too easy. One can make any number like that?"

"Make one then," said the other sharply.

Dick was conscious of a moment of profound irritation. It was too much; he had tried to show his friend that this kind of thing would not do at all with Mr. Rolls who sat with his glass in his hand saying nothing, and he had received rather a rude rebuke. He was also conscious of having spoken tactlessly, which made it worse.

He drove down his annoyance with an effort.

"You have me there! I can't. One to you."

But Chris did not smile. He turned to Mr. Rolls again.

"Were you ever in Monte Carlo, sir?"

Again the priest's heart sank. He knew this mood too well. Chris was astonishingly obtuse sometimes; he summed up situations too quickly, trusting to what Dick now called privately his infernal intuitions. He had apparently taken Mr. Rolls for what he would have named a "man of the world," but he had chosen a singularly unfortunate subject.

Mr. Rolls turned a courteous face.

"Yes, Mr. Dell."

"Ah!" went on Chris airily, "it is a wonderful place — a place of passionate beauty and passionate sins. It is like wine. It flames like these autumn woods."

Dick could not bear it. He pushed his seat abruptly back, and got up. Mr. Yolland rose opposite with a look of extreme gratitude, and Chris snarled soundlessly. But Dick was too much annoyed to mind. Here was his friend, whom he had recommended so earnestly, making quite the wrong kind of exhibition of himself. It was trying, because no one would understand how superficial it was, who did not know him intimately. Besides, Monte Carlo was really too much.

He took up his gun.

"Shall you come, with us, Chris?"

Chris was dead silent for a moment, standing before the fire. Dick repeated his question. Chris looked sharply round, and then answered in a head-voice.

"I beg your pardon. I was thinking. No, I think not; it is rather cold."

There was no more to be said and Dick went out ashamed and miserable.

Outside he made an opportunity to draw near to the older guest.

"What did that sentence, you said, mean?" he asked. "Was it Russian?"

The other looked at him without a smile in his melancholy.

"Yes, Father Yolland. It was nothing remarkable. It meant 'Do you speak Russian?'"

"Oh!" said Dick.

He had a reflective afternoon and shot abominably. It was hateful that Chris should behave like this, and try to show off so unwarrantably, especially when such schemes were in hand on his behalf; no doubt it was his idea of independence, to receive favors boorishly with the intention of depriving them of the sting of charity.

Mr. Yolland apparently was following the same course of thought. Once at a corner father and son were together for a moment, and the elder man spoke without any preface.

"What was the matter at lunch?"

Dick tried to be airy.

"Oh! He was upset. He's a good chap really."

"But that kind of remark —"

"It's a trick," said Dick decisively. "It isn't him. He thinks it smart and epigrammatic."

"Oh."

Dick was yet more upset by this incident. He had tried to hope that his father had not noticed — and what about the library-scheme now? He was almost appalled by the reflection that his father and Chris would breakfast, lunch and dine together in solitude for six weeks; if Chris engaged in that kind of talk what in the world would happen?

He was not therefore in the most tranquil of moods when, after leaving his father at the farm, he came up in the dusk to the garden-gate and saw Chris standing there with that eternal cigarette at just the wrong angle protruding from his mouth.

Chris said nothing, but turned with him towards the house.

In front lay the row of square Georgina windows, glimmering oblongs of light; overhead was the ruddy evening sky promising another clear, bracing day for the morrow; the sting of frost was already in the air, and the gravel of the broad walk was crisp to the tread.

But Dick was sore and irritated; he had the slight headache that sometimes follows shooting; he was rather wet and dirty, his shoulder ached a little. So his gambit was not soothing.

"Look here, Chris; I wish to goodness you hadn't said all that at lunch. You mustn't mind my saying so, but Rolls isn't a bit that kind of man. I only say this because —"

"I don't know what you are talking about."

This was said with such a venomous kind of breathlessness and was so entirely unexpected that Dick felt every nerve in his tired body thrill with excitement. He felt like one who had leaped into what he thought water, and found it a gulf instead.

Before he could answer Chris had gone on.

"Do you really mean that you are telling me to mend my manners?"

"Look here, Chris, don't let's have a row —"

The two men were standing perfectly still, facing one another, though Dick was scarcely aware at what point they had stopped walking. Chris instantly snapped back — "Row! Why — why — my dear man — good God! You tell me to mend my manners and then jaw at me for making a row!"

"I didn't," said Dick, seriously roused. "It wasn't a question of manners at all. It was the choice of subjects —"

"Isn't that manners? Do you think I am a cad? Or a fool, and don't know what you mean —?"

"Look here! Chris. For God's sake let's both keep our tempers —"

"There again! You insult me at every word. I know I'm your guest. You seem to forget it —"

"Chris!"

"And I'm your pensioner —"

"Hold your tongue, Chris; you don't know —"

Chris recoiled with such a savage agility that for one instant the priest really believed it would be a question of blows. The affair had developed with such astonishing speed, and Chris's temper was obviously so evil, that he would have been surprised at nothing. Then he heard a swift indrawn breath hiss between the other's teeth.

"Dick!" began his friend, and his voice sank to a horrid kind of calmness. "Dick! There are some things that no man can stand. If I owed you my life — instead of — how much? Thirty pounds? Thirty pounds! If I owed you my life I wouldn't stand it. I never dreamed of such a thing! It was bad enough at lunch. You snubbed and interrupted me enough then; I could hardly believe my ears — and now — Do you know why I was waiting for you here?"

The priest shook his head; he could not speak. His heart was laboring, sick and hot, at the root of his throat; he felt twinges of emotion thrill along to his fingertips.

"Well, then," said the other, looking at him with cruel, hating eyes — "I was waiting because I thought you would wish to apologize. I was waiting —" The two were moving on now mechanically; they stopped again at a sundial in the center of the path. "I was waiting because I thought you would long to tell me how sorry you were. Oh! My God!" he wailed, suddenly breaking off.

He took a quick, faltering step forward, threw his arms across the dial and buried his face in them, sobbing heart-brokenly.

It was so swift and unexpected that the priest stood absolutely motionless a moment. It was surely unreal; a dream, or a mad melodrama!

A bird was chirping goodnight from the laurel shrubbery twenty yards away; the light was inexpressibly tender and peaceful round him, and the tawny autumn flowers burned ember-like in the box lined beds on either side. And there in the middle, not a yard away lay that body of his friend, grotesque and ludicrous in the contrast of the fashionable coat and spats and of the piteous, passionate attitude of a hysterical woman.

Dick felt the heart in his throat stop beating for an interminable instant; then again it began to beat sharp and quiet like the engine of a racing-boat. His nerves thrilled and quieted into tenseness.

"Chris!" he said. "Chris!"

Then the wailing voice began.

"I thought you were my friend — that you really cared — you were generous and good — I know I'm a brute — I can't help it — and you insult me — and despise me!"

"Oh! Chris — for God's sake —"

He came a step nearer, hesitating to touch that fawn-colored coat. He was conscious, with a knowledge that he hated, of an intense desire that this miserable sight should not be seen from the windows; it was such horribly bad form, he thought. How could he explain? And was it his fault?

The moaning was going on, but he was mentally framing sentences of appeal, of rebuke, of anything that would end this shocking business; but he rejected each in turn.

"Chris," he said again. "Chris."

Still the other did not move, but the moaning died into dry sobs, and the sobs to silence, till the heaving shoulders lay still. Dick began to think bitter things — trying to steel himself; he told himself that Chris lay there to be admired for his *abandon,* his passion — that the whole affair was the other's fault. Then he told himself that he was a brutal bully — that he ought to have remembered that hot, hysterical nature, and the hardships the poor chap had gone through, and his sore soul.

An inspiration rose from despair. He went past the sundial, treading sharply, and spoke over his shoulder as he went, in a perfectly controlled voice.

"I am going in. Come."

For a moment yet there was silence, then he heard a sigh, and steps following him.

He paused an instant till the other almost came up, and then went on, taking care not to look at him; he passed straight up the steps into the smoking room, lit a cigarette elaborately over the lamp to give his friend time to dispose himself; then he sat down in a deep chair and glanced up.

Chris was standing by the mantelpiece with one arm resting on it, and his head on that, in an attitude of deep dejection. One neat boot was placed on the brass fender.

"Chris," said the priest, "let us have this out quietly. Help yourself to tea. And first, I wish to apologize sincerely and humbly for my tactlessness and — and rudeness."

The other turned his face slightly, and let a spasm of emotion be seen upon it; but his tears had been objective enough, for the rims of his eyes were a little red.

"Say no more, dear fellow," came a low, trembling voice from the mantelpiece. "It was I who was wrong — I was hasty and — and —"

The head went down again on the sleeve.

"You don't know how I have suffered — my nerves are in tatters. I know I'm a fool," came a broken moan once more.

"Tea," said Dick cheerfully, but with a heavy heart. He was beginning to think again about his wild library-scheme. He helped himself, trying to make a normal jingle with the cups. But he had poured out and drunk two cups before the posed figure by the fender moved again.

This time it turned completely round and extended a hand, after the manner of Sir Henry Irving. Dick took it, half-ashamed and half-satisfied, and let it drop quickly. He felt indignant that he was smiling so tremulously.

Then Chris sat down languidly, took off his cap, unbuttoned his coat, and helped himself to bread and butter.

"Look here," said the priest after a pause. "Let me explain, it's the only satisfactory —"

"No, no, my dear man. You have apologized; I ask no more."

Dick gulped rather at this. Still, it was true.

"All right, old chap. We won't say any more. There was something else too I wanted to say, which will show you that —"

He checked himself abruptly. Was it as well to make the announcement without further consideration? But Chris looked up so sharply that he thought it as well to go on.

"Look here, it was this. It was my father's suggestion. He asked me last night whether I thought it possible you would do him a great service —"

"Delighted, my dear man; anything —"

His tone was decidedly convalescent, and Dick went on reassured.

"Well, you know the library here is in an awful state, and I know you know about books, and all that. Well, do you think you would have time to arrange it for us? It would be most awfully good of you —"

"Why, my dear chap —"

"Yes, I know," went on the priest hastily. "I know it's a lot to ask, but of course you must not do it for love; though I know you would."

"Oh! My dear Dick, you must indeed allow me. It's nothing at all — I couldn't dream —"

"Stuff and nonsense," said the priest, and corrected himself hastily. "I mean — I mean, of course we couldn't ask you to do such a thing unless you had some — some sort of remuneration. My father thought that — that you might stay here — it'll take at least six weeks — and — and, say fifty pounds. Do you think that —"

"My dear chap, I couldn't possibly —"

"Oh! Yes; yes. Then that's all right. Have a cigarette?"

He pushed the box rather nervously across the tray. Then he hastened to add — "It's most awfully good of you, really, Chris. It's an awful job. I don't know how ever you'll get through it —"

He glanced at the other, astonished at the silence. He had expected protest, gratitude, even tears. But he was yet more astonished by the complete and businesslike self-command that he saw. Chris was rolling his cigarette delicately, pushing a slender finger into the end to drive back the protruding tobacco.

"Well, of course, Dick, I'm delighted," he said quietly. "It's very good of you to think of me. That puts it all on a more satisfactory basis."

"Yes, just so," said Dick blankly.

"I'm really grateful," went on Chris briskly. "You have done it so delicately too. You have given me back my self-respect. I hated taking your money for nothing. And now —" he extended a hand once more. "Thanks, old boy."

The priest took it, and sat back in dumb bewilderment.

Chapter III

Infection

(I)

The Vicar of Hinton, the Reverend James Stirling, was a very good man indeed, but he was not a very clever one. His attitude towards those whom he would have called his brethren of the Roman Communion was one of polite suspicion; he was accustomed to say that their training was of such a character in the seminary that it was impossible to be quite certain of the behavior of even their most English-minded men; and in this manner he was able to preserve a certain reputation among his small and devoted flock for the generally incompatible virtues of charity and shrewdness.

Another of his views was to the effect that the more detached and the more scrupulously uncontroversial the conversation of a Romish priest, the more certain was his skill and subtlety in the art of proselytism; and he was accustomed therefore, with a kind of secret pride in his own vigilance, to make a point of paying a little visit to Hinton Hall as soon as possible after Father Yolland, or Father Maples the rector of the little church in Amplefield village, had set foot there.

On the Saturday evening, therefore, towards five o'clock, his buttoned-up figure appeared at the door of the drawing room.

Annie was the first to see him, as she sat next to Chris who had arrived half-an-hour before. She signaled with her eyes to her mother who was not feeling in a clerical mood just then, and who showed a slight air of patience as she turned round.

"Good evening, Mr. Stirling. May I introduce Mr. Dell — Mr. Stirling."

Annie watched the two shake hands, with a touch of new interest. The two men represented very tolerably the two sides of her nature, though she could not have so formulated it. The Vicar stood for the clerical, the supernatural, the restrained, the orderly, the established; the other for the new and strange, the daring, the chivalrous. Chris had been talking vividly of Italy since his arrival, bringing in sonorous Southern words into his conversation; she had learned the meaning of *polenta, loggia* and *simpalicissimo,* and, to her, the very atmosphere of the pretty English room was instinct with Southern passion.

"How do you do, Mr. Dell?" murmured the Vicar in his pained monotone.

For the first time in her life, his figure seemed to her less than morally gigantic. His clothes were almost too neat, his little gold Latin cross hanging from a gold-clasped hair-chain — which in itself had a pleasing suggestion of a hairshirt — almost irritating; his voice almost conventional.

Chris said nothing, but his attitude was less deferential than usual.

Then the two sat down and the Vicar was presently balancing a Derby teacup on the point of a lean clerical knee.

"I was talking to Mrs. Wendy about the harvest decorations," began the clergyman, with a comprehensive glance round the company. (Lord Brasted had gone away that afternoon, and Jack was not yet come in.)

"The loaves were really too large this year — they were almost — almost grotesque. It is very helpful I think, to have loaves — they are — are symbolical of — of so much. Yes, and grapes too; but they must not overshadow the real nature of the Festival."

Mrs. Hamilton murmured politely, and the Vicar was presently launched on a discourse respecting the high spirituality of daily bread.

Annie had a sense that she was being disloyal in her thoughts, for her meditations for the last twenty-six hours had made a certain change in her; and she was conscious of a very slight feeling of impatience as her pastor proceeded. Harvest decorations and their symbolisms were of course very beautiful and helpful — it was hardly possible to imagine anything more so, but just at that moment she wished to hear about Italy. Maize was not at all the same thing as *polenta*.

She looked at Chris; he was stirring his tea meditatively with compressed lips, and it seemed to her that he was behaving very exquisitely. Roman Catholics did not have harvest festivals, and yet this one was listening with decorous attention.

"It is *Corpus Christi*," ended the clergyman at last, "without — without the materialistic ideas embodied in that Feast; not but that I —"

Chris looked up.

"I beg your pardon, sir; but do you think that? I should have thought it was almost the other way."

Mr. Stirling twitched slightly all over, and his spoon rattled. He was as much astonished as if a member of his congregation had disputed a statement from the pulpit.

"I beg your pardon?" he said kindly.

Chris glanced almost apologetically at Mrs. Hamilton, who smiled ever so slightly back. He was encouraged and went on.

"The bread that perisheth," he said, "is surely more material than the bread which does not —"

The Vicar lifted the teacup, changed legs, and went on.

"Certainly, Mr. — Mr. Dell. I quite take your point. It is very — very shrewd. Yes, yes; I quite agree, but I am afraid that you do not —"

Mrs. Hamilton broke in.

"Mr. Dell is a Roman Catholic, you know, Vicar."

Again the clergyman twitched.

"Oh, indeed. Yes. No; I was not aware."

He looked so unhappy that she hastened to soothe him.

"But pray go on, Mr. Stirling. It is most interesting; we are all on your side, you know. Mr. Dell, you must fight alone."

"As a priest," began the Vicar sonorously (on G sharp); but Annie was not attending to him. She was thinking how cleverly the guest had answered; it was very shrewd, and rather startling.

How easy and competent he looked now, again with lowered eyes and a slight air of embarrassment. No doubt he had not meant to provoke a discussion. Of course he was bound to protest; the other had made an attack; but how bold to enter the lists with a learned and holy priest, and how courteous to be so silent again now!

Once more the Vicar ended (on E sharp) "as a priest," and waited for a reply which he proposed to interrupt; but no reply came.

"Well, Mr. Dell?"

"I am silenced," said Chris smiling. "I could not presume —"

Annie drew a breath of admiration; it was beautifully done. Then her mother began, and the conversation shifted off into quiet waters.

The Vicar's bearing as he took his leave at last was that of an awakened sentry, alarmed but alert and prepared to go to any lengths in the defense of his post. He said a priestly word or two about the importance of being in time for evensong, and Bishop Dupanloup's remarks on the subject, and took his leave, with a confidential hand-pressure to the two ladies, and a bow, like the salute of a dissatisfied duelist, to Chris.

Then he was gone, and Chris sat down again.

"He is such a conscientious clergyman," observed Mrs. Hamilton, setting down her cup. "A model to his neighbors. Yes, Mr. Dell?"

"I am sure of it," said Chris heartily.

"Of course he thinks you very dangerous."

"I am very much gratified."

He was feeling very much gratified with himself too; he had turned that corner well, and he was perfectly aware that he had made a good impression. For himself, he had the greatest dislike of clergy of all denominations with the exception of a few of his own communion. He liked priests who were human and unprofessional, like Dick; and he liked those who were no more than picturesque offerers of sacrifice, such as the strange, stiff-vestmented mask-like persons who made gestures in Roman basilicas, and resembled priests of Cybele, Venus and Isis. In other words he loved sacerdotal images and human creatures, but hated clerical personages.

Yet he had behaved, he thought, with extreme tact just now. He had drawn an inch or two of the blade of his sword for an instant from its sheath, in defense of his professed Faith, and had snicked it home again and bowed dramatically at the menace of an assault. It could not have been better done. He had shown courage, tact and courtesy. Besides, the irony of his defending dogma pleased him considerably.

The girl made a little movement beside him.

"What is it, Annie?" asked her mother.

"Italy, please," said the girl shyly.

Chris smiled indulgently and began all over again.

His discourse was really effective, for he knew his subject. It was like an article in the third column of the *Daily Mail.* It bristled with rather elementary allusions; it was gemmed with Italian words; it was richly enameled with odorous languorous pictures; *cicadas* sang in it; the scent of cigarettes and flowers floated through it; it was lighted with volcanic sunsets. Veiled women peeped through its meshes; brown-limbed Italian boys lounged in the foreground; scarlet cardinals rustled in the middle-distance; and now and again, like a peep into a pagan heaven, a Pontiff showed himself, as on Renaissance clouds, surrounded by Greek gods, stiff, sacerdotal, ivory-faced, in vestments of a heathen priest, uttering Latin epigrams and Horatian odes and Apostolic benedictions.

It came to the girl almost as a revelation, adding, bright points of color in the misty picture that stood to her for Italy. Things, histories, pictures, blue seas, the Renaissance, the Popish religion — all alike fell into their proper tones and became significant; while on the other hand, during his actual words delivered in the manner of a second Othello with a spice of Don Juan, English matters appeared cramped and provincial; her home a colorless place, herself and her mother limited barbarians, and even the Vicar more of a clergyman and less of a priest.

Jack burst in presently, bringing a whiff of heather and gunpowder, and was made to sit down and hold his tongue; and, as Chris went on, even this wholesome cousin of hers seemed a little raw and imperceptive; and it was with a real sigh that she heard the bell for evensong actually ringing half-a-mile away, and rose to go for worship and spiritual direction.

Chris too sighed, for he was enjoying himself immensely, and rose with her, spruce and alert.

"Please go on afterwards," said the girl. "I love to hear it."

Chris smiled indulgently once more.

"You must go and see it all for yourself, some day Miss Hamilton. My poor words —"

Jack laughed abruptly.

"By Gad!" he said, for he felt a little awed by this verbose and profound traveler.

"It is all very nice," said Mrs. Hamilton sedately. "But you must go and put on your things, Annie. Thank you so much, Mr. Dell."

Jack too went with her, to change his things, and Chris sat down once more.

"Yes, do smoke, Mr. Dell. How very well you talk!"

Chris looked up deprecatingly from the silver cigarette case that Dick had pressed upon him on leaving.

"Talk, Mrs. Hamilton, but what is that? It is feeling that matters — inspiration not expression."

She looked at him gravely, and he saw that he had touched a wrong note.

"Oh! Yes. Of course you think me artificial and unhealthy, and all the rest. I only hope I did not say anything I ought not, to Miss Hamilton. But it's in my blood; I can't help it, and I do so long for simplicity. Cannot you help me, my dear lady?"

He spoke with a kind of dejected helplessness which touched her; while he reached for the matches.

"My dear Mr. Dell, I don't think you are unhealthy, really."

"But indeed I am," he sighed.

Really this young man was rather an appealing person. He plainly had great powers; he must have had a stormy youth, and now regretted it. He was so simple at heart, she felt sure; there was a great deal of good in him. She began to feel more motherly than ever. Besides he obviously had not done anything very bad; he had been very frank with her two days before, and nothing of that kind had appeared. He seemed to her a tarnished sort of Sir Galahad — tarnished, not corrupt.

So she folded her hands, bowed her gray head a little, and began to talk.

Chris went to bed that night in a bright, dimity-furnished room with a brass fender, blue carpet, and a *prie dieu* — well content with himself, and with a kind of melancholy delight in simplicity.

He had had a charming conversation too with Jack in the smoking room, during which he had exalted the cleanness of English youth and simple, gentlemanly ideals, much to the embarrassment of that shining example of them. He had been beautifully reminiscent too of wasted years and a passionate adolescence, painting them in alluring colors at the same time that he warned Jack against their deceptiveness.

But he had cleared the air finally by a brisk story or two of Renaissance love and war, and the rest had slipped from the boy's innocent back like oily water, leaving him still pleased and admiring, though with an added whiff of wonder.

He had lighted bed candles for the ladies with deft grace, and had looked once into the virginal eyes of Annie who was a little pale this evening.

And now here he was in his lavender-scented bed, clothed in exquisite pajamas, with the prospect of a sheltered Sunday before him. He thought perhaps he would wander in the churchyard on the following evening and listen to the simple English hymns. His eyes would fill with beautiful tears; there would be a shake in his voice as he met his friends afterwards. It would be as well if there was a little rain, but not too much; it would give him an air of the homeless wanderer.

But again he was not exactly conscious of posing; he wished no more than that the innate picturesqueness of his character should be apparent, for he sincerely thought now that a cultivated simplicity was the subtlest grace of all.

He would be very simple tomorrow. He would not eat too much breakfast; (besides they would probably bring him an early cup of tea;) he could add a word or two about Italian meals.

His mind recurred to earlier events, and he lay a minute or two, with the eiderdown drawn to his chin, reflecting on Dick Yolland, the breeze that had blown between them, and the future prospects of the Amplefield library.

Indeed it had not been his fault; Dick did not understand that there was pride left even in a pensioner. It was a privilege to bestow charity, scarcely to receive it, and patronage must be out of the question. Of course Dick was not a man of the world in the full sense, but he had had a lesson now. And he was really an excellent chap, and the library was a good thought of his. He could accept it without misgivings; it was an honest piece of work that wanted doing, and fifty pounds was not excessive for six weeks' skilled labor at a dirty job.

He did not even regret the tears; they were not wholly without grace, and the moral effect had been tremendous; they had drawn an apology. Besides, he had felt deeply wounded, and they were natural to a man of his temperament.

Once more his thoughts sprang back.

Really, that virginal English girl was a dear creature; so simple and wholesome, like a draft of spring water, and he could see her often now for the next six weeks. He glanced out, as he leaned to press the switch of the electric light, at his *Boccaccio* laid like a totem beside his bed. . . No, he would not read that tonight; he would think about Annie instead.

(2)

Annie scarcely understood her own symptoms.

She was extraordinarily ignorant of herself, of men, and of the world she lived in — of everything except the small graces of life and moderate High Church theology. She knew that there were such things as good and evil, the first practically, the second theoretically, but of the bewildering combination of the two — of the fiery gas called romance or passion or glamour, she knew nothing at all.

All she perceived now was that this man excited her.

The little ecclesiastically-smelling church in which she sat this Sunday morning had an unreal air to her, as it had once or twice before, after a late children's party or a servants' ball. Her spirit

ebbed and flowed as she stood, sat and knelt, bringing now a flush
of pleasure, now a spasm of discontent. Her hands seemed a little
hot and dry, and she drew off her gloves in the middle of the psalms,
to clasp the sleek, cool pitch pine rail before her. She wanted to sit
down, to stretch her knees, to drink a glass of cold water. She sang
vigorously at one moment, and the next wondered why the chants
were set so high. And all the while her thoughts fled here and there
like circling pigeons; sometimes dwelling above Mr. Stirling in his
short surplice and elaborately embroidered stole, sometimes on
the solemn ruffed Elizabethan who lay in cool gray stone where
the guild-altar had once stood, sometimes on Mrs. Wendy's purple
bonnet in the front pew, and the Markham girls to the left; sometimes soaring away over all that she had heard last night; but again
and again they returned, as to their cote, to the figure of the
melancholy-faced young man whom she would see again when
church was over.

He would be walking back now over the park. He had gone off
at ten o'clock to Mass; and she imagined him far away, coming
with that deliberate ease that was so characteristic of him. He was
in his yellow coat — the very sight of it on Sunday morning had
struck her as attractively profane, for God surely wanted black on
His day — he had his gloves in his hand, — white wool, a malacca
cane, brown aromatic boots, and a pleasantly sacrilegious gray hat
with a furrow down the middle.

How curious it was that such a costume and religion should
really go together; such clothes, she had hitherto believed, were the
marks of unbelief; Jack, who now yawned, now boomed like a
hoarse bee in the hymn beside her with closed lips, wore, of course,
his black tailcoat, a gray silk tie with a pearl pin, and black boots;
and his shining hat reposed in the aisle. Yet religion seemed more
essential to the guest than it did to her cousin. Jack was obviously
bored with the supernatural, though he performed its duties with
decorum; Mr. Dell managed to find it romantic; at least he had
succeeded in so representing it last night. That of course must be,
as Mr. Stirling had so often pointed out, from the worldly spirit
imported into Romanism. "My kingdom is not of this world," he

had said, implying that it was not for the vulgar but the select.

She thought about this with such absorption that the recitative sermon passed like a dream, and she was presently on her knees again to ask her Maker's pardon for her distractions and to receive Mr. Stirling's benediction.

As she followed her mother through the private door from the churchyard to the Hall garden, her heart quickened a little, for there he was, a slender autumnal-colored figure, hands behind back, pacing slowly down the long path before them between the tawny ribbon-beds. It was as she had hoped; he had come back across the fields, and was waiting to walk with them to the house.

There was about him to her eyes a faint air of mystery, for it could not have been long since he had knelt in the Popish church, but this was soon lost in his vivid present personality.

"I had a word with Father Maples," he said to her mother. "He told me he knew you."

Mrs. Hamilton assented. She was in her purple silk, carrying her skirt carefully over the loose wet gravel, and did not seem greatly interested.

"And I saw Mr. Rolls too, in the distance."

"Ah!" she said. "Do you know him?"

"I met him at lunch on Friday," said Chris briefly.

"And what did you think?"

"A fine old fellow," said Chris, with an air of appreciative patronage.

"And was that all?"

"He hardly spoke," explained the other, anxious for his intuitions. "I — I should think he has suffered," he added, as he always did when in doubt about anyone.

She walked in silence through the gate that he held open, and dropped her skirt on the broad dry walk.

"I think he is the most remarkable man I know," she said presently.

Chris uttered an interested murmur.

"He is a solitary since his wife died — thirty-five years ago, I suppose; he does not entertain; he sees no one but Mr. Yolland and the extraordinary creatures that stay with him."

"What sort of creatures?"

"All sorts."

Chris walked with his head on one side like an interested terrier, waiting for her to go on.

"Annie, I have left my prayer book. No, don't go, Mr. Dell, you won't know where to find it. And where is Jack?"

"Jack stopped to talk to the Markhams," explained Annie.

"Well, go and get it for me, will you, and come on with Jack."

The girl was astonished at her own annoyance as she walked down the path; she told herself that she wanted to hear more about Mr. Rolls, who was always something of a terrifying mystery to her mind; there were, as her mother said, odd rumors about him and his guests that she did not understand. Yet she knew at the back of her mind that curiosity was not her chief motive in resenting the message.

Jack was not to be found; she looked about fretfully for him and then gave it up. By the time that she had reached the house, Mr. Dell and her mother were gone indoors.

She was rather silent at lunch, and sat with her eyes on her plate, but she was vividly conscious of every word that he spoke, and of every movement of his deft hands. There was no more talk of Mr. Rolls, and she pretended to herself that her sense of resentment arose from that fact.

It was not until coffee was brought in that the conversation had for her the smallest intrinsic interest.

Her mother asked Chris whether he was going to town next day.

"No," he said, "back to Amplefield. I told you about Mr. Yolland? It begins tomorrow."

She looked up quickly and met his eyes with her own. Was that true?

"I am to arrange the library," he explained. "Mr. Yolland is kind enough to take pity on a pauper; besides his books are in terrible disorder."

"But that's ripping," broke in Jack. "You must come over here a lot before I go."

His face showed a rather wan smile.

"My dear boy," he said, "I simply can't. I shall be hard at work. You will have to come and see me."

There was an indescribable melancholy in his voice that set the girl's heart stirring. Of course he had not meant that about being a pauper; it was only a picturesque way of saying that he was not rich. But was it really true that he would be in the neighborhood yet for a while — that she would be able to hear more about Italy? She dropped her eyes and sat absorbed in the assimilation of this new fact.

Outside one window of the schoolroom on the ground floor projected the end of a long glazed verandah that ran along to the smoking room door. It was a pleasant place on a sunny winter day, set with rugs and cane chairs; the windows of the two rooms that looked into it opened to the ground, and were often left ajar, allowing the smell of the musk pots and geraniums to flow into the house.

Annie came into the schoolroom after lunch, and sat listlessly down by the fire. Her mother and the guest were gone off somewhere to talk, and it had been hinted to the girl that her presence was not required.

She sat now with her arms behind her head, wondering what in the world they were talking about. She had never seen her mother so much interested in anybody before. It would be untrue to say that she was jealous; but it was a fact that she was slightly displeased. She had hoped to hear him talk again, and now half Sunday was gone and he had delivered no more discourses. She crossed her slender feet and sighed a little.

Then she heard a door open and voices in the verandah.

"Well then," said her mother's voice, "to continue. Yes, take that chair, Mr. Dell — don't you think perhaps that you have been a little wanting in — I won't say courage — but —"

"Yes, yes," cried a pathetic voice. "You are perfectly right; it is courage that I need — courage against the hardness of the world, treacherous friends — may I move a little? There is something of a draft just here — courage against Fate. I know it; I feel it; it is perfectly true."

Annie was so much astonished that she sincerely forgot that she was not meant to hear this conversation.

"Well, then — Mr. Dell —"

"Dear lady, you have helped me enormously. I shall always look back on this day; I feel I can face anything — poverty, starvation — you have awakened me."

Annie stood up trembling. It was horrible to her to hear such things.

"Even the clothes that I wear are Dick's gift," went on the male voice, shaking with passion; "they scorch me as I sit here. To think that I —"

Then the girl remembered, and her hands went instinctively to her ears. She must get out of the room. She understood nothing of the dramatic instinct with which Chris spoke; she only knew that she had been listening, and had heard a secret. What he had said carelessly at lunch was literally true; this man of delicate tastes, of a fastidious and sensitive spirit, was living on the charity of others, was on the verge of penury. It was a terrible and an admirable secret.

Then she went out on tiptoe, trembling a little.

(3)

Mrs. Hamilton was rather ashamed of herself as she stood at the door next morning and saw Chris drive away in the dogcart.

She was ashamed, as her prayer book instructed her to be, of what she had done and of what she had left undone. On the one hand she had shown this curious young man a great deal of sympathy; the motherly feeling had become even stronger on the previous afternoon as she and he had sat together in the sunny verandah, while she held her hands in her lap and listened, and he smoked a cigarette or two and confessed his failures and shortcomings. He had done both in a theatrical manner, but that, she told herself, was his way, and he certainly had been frank enough; he had confessed in scarcely veiled terms that he had been led seriously astray in his youth by a seductive middle-aged woman, and he had cried out with passion that the rest of his life must be de-

voted to expiating his guilt. But she was a little ashamed now of
her sudden interest; it was not her custom to melt so quickly and
with so little excuse. It was almost as if she had been entrapped.

She was also slightly ashamed at what she had left undone. She
had said goodbye cordially enough; she had even, in general terms,
expressed a wish to see him again; but there had been no actual
specification of date. He would be busy, she told herself; she must
not tempt him away from his work. Yet she knew that was not her
sole reason for her silence; there was just in the back of her mind a
suspicion that she had been somewhat remotely resembling a fool.
Yet, she was ashamed of her silence for all that; it would have been
but natural to ask him to dine, for example, next Sunday, before
Jack went back to his crammer's. Jack had looked sulky enough at
the omission.

There was one more reason, so shadowy that it scarcely deserved
the name, connected with Annie. That maiden had been very silent indeed last night; she had not spoken one word between supper and bedtime except what was absolutely necessary; she had
not even referred to an Italian lecture; and her eyes had been rather
bright. It was ludicrous of course to materialize this thought into
form, but its spirit had been there when she had compressed her
lips to hold back a specific invitation. Annie was too much excited,
she said to herself; she did not wonder, but it would be time for her
to meet men-of-the-world this time next year.

She stood now, with Annie behind her and Jack on the gravel in
front, and the three waved together as the dogcart, with a raised
hat protruding from it, whisked round the corner by the laurels.
Then she turned and went without a word into the house.

It was just a little flat at Hinton Hall that day. Jack disappeared
half-an-hour later, gunned and gaitered, taking lunch with him;
Annie went upstairs to her own room, and Mrs. Hamilton proceeded to household matters. It was what they did on most other
days at this time, but the disruption appeared significant now; it
was as if a certain bond had been withdrawn, and they had fallen
apart in consequence. the elder lady at least, as she jingled off to
the housekeeper's room, thought the hall a little chilly and empty.

Then she once more compressed her lips and set about her tasks.

Annie was listless at lunch too; she lifted her upper lip ever so slightly at the chicken *salmi* and said that she was going to ride if she might.

"Why not?" said her mother. "Miss Annie's mare then at — what time? — at half-past two, with the groom; and the pony-carriage for me at three. I will drive myself. Where are you going, Annie?"

"To the woods, I think," said the girl.

Mrs. Hamilton was sitting in her room after tea, looking vaguely through Mr. Walter Pater's *Renaissance*. She scarcely knew why she had taken it from the shelf; it had been almost an unconscious choice, and she was turning the leaves when Jack came in, in dress clothes and a homespun jacket.

"I thought Annie was here," he said.

"So you've come back. Have you had tea? No, I haven't seen Annie for the last half-hour."

"She's not in the schoolroom," said the boy.

"Well, I don't know then. Tell me, Jack — sit down first; I can't bear to talk while you're standing up. How did you get on with Mr. Dell?"

"Oh, he's ripping!" said Jack, yawning a little.

"Is he coming over here again to shoot?"

"I don't know; he wouldn't say."

"Would you like him to dine one day?"

"Rather."

"Well —" she put down the book — "How about next Sunday?"

"Oh! Yes; that'll do."

"What did you talk about last night?"

"Oh! I don't know. Lots of things. He told me some stories —"

He was obviously rather impatient, so she let him go, and went to her desk to write a little note to Mr. Dell. It would go by the first post in the morning. She had just signed herself his very sincerely when the door was opened again rather hastily, and Jack came through, shutting it behind him.

"I say, Aunt Mary, Annie's in her bedroom."

"Well, why not?"

"I think she's crying, or something."

She stood up abruptly.

"Nonsense."

"She is; she told me to go away, and I could hear."

Mrs. Hamilton stood quite still for a moment; then she went straight past him and out. Annie had been listless all day, she remembered.

She had plenty of time to form theories as she went along the corridor and up the stairs from the hall, but she accepted none of them as final. Then she tapped on the door of the girl's bedroom. There was no answer, and she tapped again.

There came a rather startled voice from within, asking who was there.

"Let me in at once," she said sharply.

There was a murmur of dissent, and she tapped again.

"Do you hear me, Annie?"

Then the door was unlocked, and she went in.

The girl was in her dressing gown, with her hair down her back, and her face was still tremulous with tears. There was one candle only burning on the dressing table, and the bed was all tumbled as if it had been lain upon.

"Now what is it?" asked Mrs. Hamilton rather sternly.

Annie's face broke up into lines, and she brushed her hand quickly across her eyes.

"Are you ill?"

"Yes," whispered the girl hesitatingly, still staring pale-faced at her mother.

"Annie — that's not true. Tell me!"

Her voice showed a sort of relenting, and the next instant she had caught her daughter by the shoulders and kissed her.

"Sit down, my pet, and tell me."

She drew her across to the fire, and sat down; and the girl sank beside her on to the white hearthrug, leaning against her knee with her face turned away and half-hidden in her hands.

"Now tell me," said the elder woman softly, passing her arm gently round the girl's throat.

There was a long silence. She could feel a little pulse beating in her daughter's throat, and the silky texture of the skin, and over her hand fell the long black hair. Outside all was very still in the hush of an October frost, and within the little flames leaped and laughed between the coals. The theories poured through her brain, but they were fewer than before; and still she accepted none as final; it might be any one of half-a-dozen things, or two or three together. She had known her cry like this before for the death of a cat.

Then she heard two words.

"I can't."

She tightened her hand a little on the smooth throat that heaved and jerked with sobs.

"No, not yet," she said. "When you are quiet."

Again the silence fell. She waited until the heaving throat grew still, watching the fire intently as if for inspiration.

"Now, my darling. Have you done anything wrong?"

"No — at least —"

(That swept away one group of theories.)

"Has anything happened when you were out this afternoon?"

"No."

(Another group was gone. There were only two left now.)

"Is it anything to do with Jack?"

"N — no."

She tightened her grasp yet more firmly, drawing the soft head back against her knee, and put her other hand on to it.

"Well, then, is it anything to do with anyone you have seen lately?"

There was dead silence once more. Then the girl wrenched her head free and buried her face in her hands.

Her mother resolutely drew it back again.

"Now, my darling, I think I know all about it. It's about Mr. Dell, isn't it? Now I'm not going to scold you. You can wait until you are quite quiet, and then you can tell me all about it."

She had contradicted herself, but it was a comfortable sort of contradiction, and she did not trouble to correct it. She remained perfectly still, scarcely knowing whether love or anger ruled her, and stroking, always stroking, the smooth, shapely throat and shoulder beneath her hand.

At last she spoke again,

"Now, my dear; tell me exactly what you are crying about. Is it because he has gone?"

"N — not exactly."

"Well, then, what is it? What do you know about him?"

There was no answer.

"Did he tell you anything?"

"N — no; but — but I heard."

"Heard? What? Don't be afraid, my dear."

"I heard him — talking to you — in the verandah. I — I — didn't mean to listen."

For one moment her heart stood sick with fear. But she fought it down.

"Tell me what you heard."

Her voice rang a little hard, and she knew it by the shrinking under her hand.

"No, my pet; I am not in the least angry. I know you didn't mean to listen. But tell me what you heard."

"He — he is so poor."

There followed a storm of sobs, and the girl tore herself loose and leaned forward, crying as if her heart would break.

Jack, waiting below in bewildered perplexity at the vagaries of women, stood up as his aunt came back to her room twenty minutes after the dressing bell had rung.

She seemed a little disturbed, and went straight across to her writing desk without speaking to him. There was an open letter lying there, and she took it up rather sharply.

"Annie's got a headache," she said, tearing the paper across and across. "She won't come to dinner; I have sent her to bed. Tell them to put off dinner five minutes."

Jack rang the bell as his aunt left the room. It was a comfort that there was nothing wrong. But what queer people women were! Why couldn't Annie have said that she was ill?

CHAPTER IV

An Interlude of Letters

(I)

D ick Yolland had gone up to town on the Saturday morning completely bewildered. He sat with the morning-papers unopened on his knee from Marlesdon to London, staring at the flying landscape, and doing his utmost to bring the threads to a center. Chris did not appear to be one person at all, but half-a-dozen, and the perplexity of elements had reached its climax of tangle in the interview on the previous evening.

His friend had stormed and wept at a criticism so delicate that it ought scarcely to have scratched the skin; and had immediately after received, unshrinking, an offer of charity so miserably disguised that Dick had hardly dared to make it. Was there ever, he asked himself, such a distorted vision, that magnified this and minimized that?

The next question was: would Chris do the work assigned to him? And if he did do it at all competently, would he not make his own presence in the house unbearable by indiscreet conversation? The picture of Chris and his own father facing one another three times a day across a table was a ludicrous thought. Yet Chris had tact of a kind; he had come back, as it were, flower- and laurel-crowned, reeking of delicate incense, from the dinner at Hinton Hall.

Once more; Dick was aware that he was fond of Chris, that he liked to have him in the room, even to know that he was in the house; yet he was equally aware of a sense of relief at having said goodbye to him for the present; the atmosphere was too electric for comfort; and finally two more points clashed and fought in his brain just as he thought he was coming to a conclusion. Chris was a profound egoist, he began to tell himself, and on the moment remembered that he was lavish of money and generous to a fault.

He sighed, gathered up his papers, and stepped out of the carriage at King's Cross, feeling both flat and baffled. He would at any rate say Mass for him tomorrow.

It was not until the following Thursday morning that he saw two notes lying on his table, one addressed in his father's handwriting, and the other in Chris's fifteenth century script. He tore the first open rather eagerly, and turned quickly in spite of filial piety to the last paragraph.

"Mr. Dell is doing very well. He worked for nine hours on Monday, four on Tuesday, and seven today. He went out for a ride this afternoon to cure his neuralgia. He is very kind indeed to me, and talks down to my level, about farming in Italy and the superior quality of the beans grown there; he has a quantity of information. We have had no more rubbish, and I think you are right about him. I am very willing for him to stop his six weeks. The servants are devoted to him.

"Your affectionate father,

"Richard M. Yolland."

Dick wrinkled his snub-nose with amusement, and then opened the other letter.

Amplefield, Norfolk, R.S.O.

"My dearest man, —

"Your father is too kind to me in offering me such work, and I am happier than I have been for months past, and it is all your doing! I hope to earn my money well — for the books are in terrible confusion though there are some treasures amongst them — I found a Wynkyn de Worde yesterday on a top shelf; and I am working steadily. I did nearly ten hours on Monday, and should have done as much today if it had not been for my neuralgia. Your father kindly offered me a horse, and I rode quietly for an hour or two, when I met Miss Hamilton, and went back with her to the lodge gates, though I was hardly able to speak for pain.

"My dear Dick, what a charming girl she is! So quiet and innocent. What a power women have, if they only knew it! Thank God they do not! I told the poor child some of my troubles, though I knew it was wrong; but I could not help it, and twice I saw her eyes fill with tears. I asked her if she often rode, and she told me that she did. Happy the man who wins her! If the gods had only given me the good fortune to know such an one ten years ago, what might not have happened? She *understands*, Dick, I know she understands, though she is but a child!

"I had a very pleasant Sunday at Hinton, and a good talk with Mrs. Hamilton. She too! Now what a good woman is that! She gave me some excellent advice, and God knows how much I need it! Oh! What a mess I have made of my life; I sometimes hope that it is not too late, but these things are on the knees of the gods.

"I have also made Father Maples' acquaintance. He seems to be a man of the world, but he is *antipatico*. Mr. Rolls I have not seen again.

"Dear man, I must stop. Have you heard anything from the *Saturday Express?* God bless you for what you have done for me! Write me a long letter, and give me your advice, you best of priests!"

Yours,

Christopher Dell.

Dick propped this letter, smiling to himself, against his coffee urn, and read it again two or three times before he had finished breakfast. The flattery was so disguised by its own extravagance that he scarcely recognized it at all.

It was all better news than he had hoped; Chris really seemed to have some notion of duty left, and the slight difference between the reports as to the hours spent in the library was exactly what he would have expected.

The paragraph about Annie Hamilton was also characteristic; there was no gray with Chris; women and men were either whiter than snow, or blacker than hell. On the whole the tidings were most encouraging, and he began to consider the next step.

Dick Yolland was, in his way, a very devout priest. He had no more doubts as to the truth of the Catholic Religion than he had regarding the Constitution of the British Empire. They were equally obvious, and he conformed to both with equal contentment. It was entirely natural to him to pray for Christopher Dell, and he did this duty with punctuality and fervor; he had mentioned his name

at Mass every day, and devoted a decade of the rosary to him on
Mondays and Thursdays, ever since their meeting; the Joyful Mysteries appeared to him the proper antidote to his friend's gloom.
He had also sent in his name to the Poor Clares, asking them to
present it in the proper Quarter, and to see that it was suitably
considered. But all this did not appear to him sufficient; it would
have been foolish to pray without making a corresponding effort
towards the object of those prayers; so this morning, when he went
up to his room, he selected a sheet of paper and a smooth pen, and
set himself down to answer his friend's letter.

He had intended to say some plain words last week, but the dis-
turbance on Friday had made it impossible. However, Chris was
not to escape, and for a full hour the priest wrote, weighing every
word, rejecting, as he thought, every expression that could be in
the least open to misunderstanding. He farced his counsel with
remarks appreciative of Chris's good qualities, and expressive of
his own esteem, and by the time he had ended was tolerably content with himself. He read it over carefully, folded, directed and
stamped it; and then stood, weighing it in his hand, smiling and
wondering what Chris would say. At least it was impossible for him
to take offense. Had he not asked for advice?

The little plaster statue of God's Mother stood on the mantelpiece beside him, and with a sudden movement he laid it at Her feet.

"Do what You will with it," he said. "I leave it to You."

Then he took it up again, pleased at the thought, for was not
Chris devout to Her? — more devout than to any Olympian? —
and put it on his table for the post.

He went about his business for a couple of days with restored
serenity. Chris still formed the background of his thoughts, but it
was lighted by hope. Surely the poor man wanted nothing but peace
for his recovery — peace, and a little judicious counsel.

He had given in his letter the benefit of his meditations a week
ago. He had told him, with many pleasant periphrases, that will power
was what was wanted; or, rather a concentration of it. He advised
him to form small habits, and to make them laws to himself; he in-
stanced physical exercises as a parallel — dumb-bells, deep breath-

ing and afternoon rides. He had poured out his own optimism, and had even ventured to refer to the Providence of God. In fact he had given him exactly the advice that he would have followed himself under similar circumstances — exactly the sensible normal advice by which sensible normal persons direct their lives.

On the Friday evening he came in tired out from his visiting, and found the answer lying in the hall. It was too dark to read it there, but he took it upstairs, pleased at the thought that his friend had written so soon; he sat down in his easy chair and opened it. It was one long lament at being misunderstood.

"My dearest man, you have said some cruel things to me, just when I thought you were beginning to understand me at last. I am most bitterly disappointed.

"You tell me I am without will power! Was it lack of will power then that kept me going all those years, when I received no help from any man, not even from you? True, I gave in once, and went to Paris, as I told you; but is it fair to reproach me with what I told you in confidence? Was it lack of willpower that held me struggling on, denying myself the very necessaries of life, that kept up my self respect? Again it is true that I came to you at last, as to my last hope, but is it generous to refer to that?

"I am afraid I have made a great mistake in coming here. It is true that it is honest work, but I hate to think that I depend even for that upon one who distrusts me, as you do. Is there only one way out of it? Are you sure you wish me to remain? It seems to me that there is no hope anywhere. I had better make an end of it once and for all. If there is a God I think He will be more just than you. Dear man, I know you do not mean to be hard; but you have wounded me cruelly. You do not understand me. No one," (there followed a complicated erasure) "does understand me.

"Yours regretfully,

"C. D."

Dick Yolland went through a series of movements when he reached the end.

He first threw the letter violently upon the floor and jumped up; he then went up and down his hearthrug several times with his hands clenched and his nose twitching. He hit the wall three times violently with his fist. He gave two vicious kicks in the air with a muddy boot.

Then he sat down again, picked up the letter, and read it once more.

It was hatefully plausible, shockingly unjust and ungenerous, maddeningly sentimental; and it was exactly the kind of letter that he ought to have expected Chris to write. He could see him doing it, bent over his desk in a cloud of smoke, his lower lip thrust out, and his pen held sideways tracing the words carefully on the page. How pleased he must have been with it! In what a charming pose he must have seen himself — the blighted, homeless, friendless wanderer, lifting pathetic eyes and hands to an unfeeling world!

What a blazing fool he had been, he told himself, to have thought that Chris meant what he said when he asked for advice! He did not want advice; he wanted sentimental flattery. He wanted another motive for melancholy purring.

Then Dick jumped up, holding the carefully written sheet between finger and thumb, and sat down to his table. He wished to tell him on a post card not to be a blighted fool, and leave it at that. It would be too absurd to give the *tu quoque* at length and tell his friend that he himself too was misunderstood.

It was terribly difficult to decide; and he remained long, with a pen poised over a sheet of paper, asking himself whether he should write at all, and why in the world it was that he took so much trouble over a worthless ass, vowing that he would never again take him at his word.

At last he wrote. It was short, but not so short as he intended when he began.

"My dear Chris, —

"I am so sorry for my mistake. I really thought you wanted me to say what I thought. I won't do it again. But you ought to put a footnote saying 'This is rhetorical.'

"But I dare say I am perfectly wrong, and that you are quite right in attributing all your misfortunes to Fate, and all your successes to yourself.

"Please do not suggest giving up your work at Amplefield; if for no other reason, because it would be extremely inconvenient to get another man now; he might not understand your methods —

"Oh! — I can't go on like this. But you know perfectly what I mean. Is it not just conceivable that you may be wrong in your estimate of yourself? You can take or leave my contribution to the discussion as you like. I expect it will be 'leave.' But don't talk nonsense about cruelty. Let us drop this; you won't ask me again for advice, and I promise not to volunteer it. Let us both be reasonable and charitable.

"Ever yours,

"R. Y."

He folded it quickly lest he should change his mind and become either harder or softer; put it in an envelope, stamped and directed it, and stood it up once more before the little tawdry image.

"Please do better with it this time," he said. "But I know it was all my own fault. I am a fool. Make me wise — and him," he added.

(2)

The answer came on the Monday morning, and it consisted of two words on a post card.

"Dear Man."

Dick grinned, spun it across the room to the corner where he supposed the wastepaper basket to stand, and looked up at the image.

"Thank You," he said. "I thought so."

That was really all that could be done for the present, so, in the back of his mind, and in the front of it when he was at leisure, he began to mature further schemes.

He had a month before him, and only that, because he held himself completely responsible for his friend. It was simply inconceivable that Chris should pack up his things at the end of the six weeks and drift back to town with fifty pounds in his pocket. It would not even be fifty pounds. Five at least would go to servants, five more, probably, on small graceful gifts, and, if Chris was in a pious mood, probably a statue or a silver heart or something of the kind, to the church. If he retained thirty-five pounds it would be as much as could he expected, and he would probably retain that for about a fortnight, for he would certainly give a small dinner at the Savoy to celebrate his prosperity, and be offended and wounded and all the rest, if Dick demurred or declined to come. And what at the end of the fortnight?

He could not have said why it was that he held himself responsible, beyond the fact that he did so. There was no reason really. Chris had neglected him wholly during the last five years; he had only sent the priest a line or two from France. And yet any other prospect was impossible. Chris had a marvelous knack for taking up acquaintances where they had dropped. After the first half-hour of the first dolorous interview on the Thursday night, Dick had felt exactly as if they had met after a fortnight's absence; he had found himself remembering his friend's ways, weaknesses, virtues, crimes, as vividly as he had known them at Oxford.

No. Chris must be set on his feet somehow. The priest wrote another letter to the Editor of the *Saturday Express.*

It was a week before he had an answer, but when it came it was worth waiting for.

The editor regretted he had not answered sooner, but press of business had made it impossible, and he had not understood the urgency. He was acquainted with Mr. Dell's writings, and thought they might be really popular. He would be happy to offer Mr. Dell a small post on the staff, and his duties would be to write a descriptive article once a week, of two thousand words, and his salary would be one hundred and twenty pounds — that is if Mr. Dell cared to accept it. The engagement would begin at Christmas.

Dick beamed with happiness and something of astonishment, enclosed the letter with a line of congratulation, and sat down to consider.

There would be rather under a month during which Chris would have to be financed. That would not be a very difficult matter; he would ask him to come and stay in town, and there would be about thirty five pounds for minor expenses. By the end of that time he would know better whether it would be possible to ask Chris to stay with him altogether but he determined there should be no more question of charity. If he decided to ask him he would do so on strictly business terms. Twenty-five shillings a week, exclusive of red wine and cigarettes, should be the sum mentioned between them. If he decided to make this offer, and Chris decided to accept it — well, it would be very pleasant. But the priest, bent on his friend's reformation, was clear that the other must depend on himself. There would be no hope without that. Besides he gave Chris the credit of thinking that any other offer would be an insult.

Dick went into church this time to say "Thank You"; and he said it for a long time, kneeling under the low smoky roof, staring up and smiling towards the gilt tabernacle that shone tawdrily splendid in the gloom. How pleased Chris would be, he told himself.

Then he marched back to his house swinging his umbrella and walking on air.

No answer whatever came from Amplefield. At the end of three days Dick sent an impatient post card —

"Are you dead?" and twenty-four hours later received one in return.

"Yes, and buried. Am writing from heaven."

The priest was more annoyed than amused, and his annoyance waxed even greater when twenty-four more hours passed without a word.

But Chris was obviously in a good humor, or, as Dick reflected, he would have named the Other Place, as his manner was; so he contented himself with a wire.

"Then — presume — no — need — for — post — on — *Express.*"

Still there was silence, and then on the following morning as the priest came in from his Mass he saw a fat letter lying in the hall.

He did not quite know why he was excited by the look of it, but he took it up, again without opening it, and in his zimmara and biretta passed straight upstairs to his room. He laid down his *Horae*, sat down in his easy chair, pushed back his cap, and with his heart hammering in his throat, tore open the envelope.

The first sentences drove the blood from his face, and he read on unconscious of all else till the very end.

"My dearest man,

"How can I tell you what has happened to me? I am in bliss, in BLISS. God has had mercy at last; I thank Him with all my heart. I ask His pardon for all my mistrust and rebellion.

"Mary has heard my prayers. Set up a great candle to Her, if you please. How little I have understood!

"Well, this is it, in a word. The dearest girl in God's creation, the sweetest, the purest, the simplest, belongs to me! What have I done to deserve this joy? You know who she is, and I need say no more.

"This is how it happened.

"I told you that I had met her out riding. Well I met her again. Her mother did not know, but I did not know that. I sent her messages again and again, but the dear child, it seems, did not dare to give them; she knew our riding together would be forbidden — and — can I say it? — She could not bear that.

"Well, the inevitable thing happened, as indeed it had happened, though I did not understand it, at the first moment that I saw her; and at last I told her one day, in the dear woods of Amplefield. And then I found — oh! Dick — how can I tell you without shame? — but she had thought of me ever since we had first met. You remember the Monday that I went away from Hinton? Well, the poor child had a fit of crying that night, and her mother found her, and of course, as was perfectly right, though I did not understand it at the time, did not ask me to the house again.

"But my dear Love could not bear this. — Dick, how can I say this to you? — and she rode out alone every day, and we met; the blessed saints must have been with us.

"And now all is arranged.

"You know of course that she will be very wealthy by and bye; I told her mother that that was the one thought that restrained me, and that I could not bear to live on my wife. I offered to take her to Italy as she was, but her mother would not hear of it. I had a hard struggle; she said some things to me that I am trying to forget. No — they are forgotten! — and these are the conditions — I am to be in receipt for two years, of an income of £200. She is only seventeen now. Of course the waiting will be hard for both of us, and I am no Jacob. Yet I could wait a thousand, if I did not die of love.

"Oh! Dick. What a blind devil I have been! Eating husks with swine, complaining against God!

"All that you said of me was true, TRUE. I have been a weak, drifting creature; there is hardly a sin of which I have not been guilty; and now I see, I SEE. Yet I cannot repent as you would wish; I do not believe in that kind of repentance. All I know is that the whole world is changed for me; that it is full of sweetness and purity and love. All my faith has come back, and yet I can respect my wife's faith too. Is there any difference of creed between those whose creed is Love? There is nothing but love anywhere for her and me.

"Dick — I owe all this to you! You saved me from despair and death; you treated me generously, and I behaved to you like a devil. I do not deserve that you should forgive me, and yet I know you will, so I do not even ask for pardon. And now it is through you that this has come about. It was you who took me to her house. Dick! If ever I show you ingratitude or coldness again, I give you leave to strike me on the face.

"I am mad with joy and love. *Domine non sum dignus! Domine non sum dignus!* What can I say but that over and over again? Pray for me! Pray for me that it may not be a dream, that I may not die too soon! Come down quickly; I cannot come to you. I am held here by the cords of a man.

"Your affectionate loving friend,
"Chris. Dell."

"P.S. — Mr. Stirling is very angry and will not speak to me. But Father Maples is pleased. Your father is more than kind, though he says very little. Oh! God bless you, Dick! I cannot say one hundredth part of what is in my heart."

CHAPTER V

Convalescence

(I)

It was a heavy November afternoon turning to dusk as Dick
stepped out once more on to the Marlesdon platform. The
sun had gone down in an angry, clear glory, and a pale gash of
primrose still shone in the west, and in the sheets of water that lay
by the side of the line. The fine rain that had fallen all day had
ceased, but the lampposts, roofs and platform of the station were
still gilded and outlined with the reflected splendor.

The dogcart waited for him, and he was informed that Mr. Dell
was gone to Hinton, and would be fetched so soon as the priest
reached home.

On the road to the house Dick was still pondering the amazing
news to which he had not yet become in the least accustomed.

Chris married to a girl scarcely more than half his own age was
an inconceivable picture, and for that reason neither ludicrous nor
impressive; it was only unimaginable. What in the world was Mrs.
Hamilton about? It was not quite so bewildering as it had seemed
at first, for it had appeared from a subsequent letter that the engagement was not formally recognized; he was only allowed to look
forward to an engagement on the conditions of a regular income
with a prospect of its continuance, and of both Annie's and his
own final perseverance at the end of the two years.

Still, it was bewildering enough. Annie was a Protestant heiress,
an entirely innocent girl, and of a very tolerable beauty; Chris was
a penniless Catholic vagabond, with a tarnished past; and they had
known one another for less than three weeks, and that, more or
less in secret. Dick had been aware of his friend's curious power
over women, but he had scarcely realized its full extent.

What, too, was Chris's own state? He certainly believed himself
in love, but, as the priest had reflected once or twice before, there

was a difference between sincerity and genuineness. Had the money really nothing to do with it? Again, Chris undoubtedly believed that it had not, but was he right? Dick smiled to himself as he wondered how Chris would pose in his new position; it would be surely difficult even for him to appear romantic and melancholy as the married master of twenty-thousand acres and eight-thousand pounds a year; he was cut out for tragedy, not domestic drama. He smiled also as he pondered Mr. Stirling's consternation at the prospect of a Romish landlord, and ultimately a Romish landlady too, for of course Annie would turn Catholic some day; Jesuits and seminary-priests would be in worse odor than ever at the Vicarage; no doubt the whole affair would be pronounced there to be an unusually flaring instance of Babylonish guile — the Vicar would never believe in Yolland innocence again.

Mr. Yolland was in the smoking room with a tea tray as Dick came in, having seen the dogcart whirl off in the dusk to fetch Chris.

"Well," said the priest, sitting down. "I'm —"

"Just so," interrupted his father. "I've been saying that too."

"Tell me everything."

"Well, first, he is very much in love."

"Really and truly?"

"I think I may say really and truly. In fact more than anyone I have ever seen. Of course he shows it more too, but he is simply a different person. He radiates light and sweetness. Breakfast is a new meal, and he is at Mass every day."

Dick helped himself to sugar.

"Of course," he said. "That is how he would take it. And does he go over there every day?"

"Well, no. Once a week is permitted. And she and her mother have dined here once."

"Why was it allowed?"

"My dear Dick, there was no question of anything else. Miss Annie is as mad as he is. And it isn't allowed; it is only not forbidden."

"And what does the mother think?"

"Don't ask me. I have no idea; and I think she has none either. She is simply marking time, to save a defeat."

"I see," said the priest musingly. "But isn't it very extraordinary?"
His father smiled.

"I have given up saying that. It is an inadequate word. But what
are you to do with a daughter who raves and has hysterics and
fainting-fits? And she had all that."

It was very much as the priest had surmised. The affair had
been carried through by violence, and there was undoubtedly
treachery too in the besieged citadel. Mrs. Hamilton had plainly
been very deeply touched by Chris himself even before the matter had begun.

The father and son sat together half-an-hour more before the
wheels of the dogcart were heard in the drive, and then Mr. Yolland
abruptly rose.

"I will be getting to my room," he said. "You will want to talk—"

Dick stood up, smiling in spite of his misgivings, as the door
burst open and a radiant vision dashed into the room.

It was undoubtedly Chris, but Chris transformed, who held him
by the hand and laughed for sheer love. A flood of words poured
out, but the priest heard none of them; he was looking amazed at
the change that love had wrought.

Even drama had forsaken the lover; he stammered, he trembled,
he made awkward gestures, he repeated himself. There were no
perorations, metaphors or shrugging of shoulders. He named the
Divine Name in the singular, unblenching; he cried the name of
his Love aloud without shame and without reason; he described
little pointless incidents, her looks, her words, her silences, her
movements. He exclaimed at his own unworthiness a dozen times
and in the same phrases; he poured out his gratitude, his passion,
his penitence and his hopes, in foolish and redundant language.
Yes; he was very much in love; his black eyes were candid and lam-
bent with it; the lines were gone from his lips, swallowed up in it,
the little furrow above his nose almost erased.

"My dearest man, what is the good of talking? God Almighty
Himself has no words for it!"

It appeared that Mrs. Hamilton had made an exception for Dick's
visit, and the two were to be allowed to go over to lunch next day,

and to pay their devotions at the shrine. But the visits were to end presently, as Chris had only ten days more at Amplefield, and there was to be no running down from town once a week. He greatly bewailed this.

"You can't understand, of course, old man; you are a priest and all that, poor devil; but you know it's a serious thing these two years. Four times a year is all that I could screw out. Oh! I'm sorry!"

Dick grinned pleasantly.

"I am certainly a priest and all that. But I have some faint glimmerings, — in spite of my denseness."

"Oh! My dear man, I didn't mean that. Good Lord! I can't explain. Dick, tell me again you are pleased!"

"My good chap, I haven't any words either."

"Now just sit down, and let me begin again at the beginning. Tea? No. Damn tea! Sorry, old man!"

They sat there till the dressing bell rang, and the eloquence was not exhausted. Chris drew the unwilling and splashed priest into his bedroom to hear really and truly what sort of a person Annie Hamilton was.

"You've only got a beastly soutane to put on; you can easily wait ten minutes while I change my studs. Well, look here — first of all—"

And then the tale flowed again.

Dick listened obediently enough, but he really could not attend. He knew perfectly well what Annie Hamilton was like. He had known her in long clothes. So he watched his friend instead, saw once more the marvelous underclothing, the sock suspenders, the thin virile arms all brown sinew and muscle, the scapular of our Lady of Mount Carmel; he observed the play of the silver initialed brushes, and the hair grow sleek beneath them; the profuse ablutions in stinging hot water; and heard the untiring song of praise sound thin and muffled from beneath a rough towel — broken and ejaculatory, as the tight shoes rose to their places on the slender feet.

Yet he was really impressed; it seemed to him a very marvelous miracle that love had achieved — no less than the conversion of a cynical, soured, ungenuine soul into a flame of simple devotion that had itself the nature of immortality. But he could not resist one slight attack.

"I say, here's your *Boccaccio*. I had quite forgotten —"

"Give it me," cried Chris, astraddle before the fire, manipulating a tie.

The priest handed it him, wondering what he wanted.

Chris released a hand, snatched the vellum-covered book and chucked it straight into the heart of the fire.

"There!" he said.

"Good Lord!" said the priest.

Dinner was a difficult affair; but it was really amusing to watch Chris striving to show a decent interest in Mr. Chamberlain and the situation in Russia. Mr. Yolland bore himself with a fine stupidity, and introduced the most astonishingly dreary subjects one after another; Dick obediently followed his lead, and Chris floundered, like a stout merchant out deer-stalking, endeavoring to keep up with the talk, and to avoid absorbed silence on the one side, and precipitous irrelevancies on the other.

But Mr. Yolland showed mercy after one cigarette, and mentioned an important letter that cried to be written.

"Dick, just come into my study for two minutes, and then you mustn't interrupt me again tonight."

When the door was discreetly shut, his father turned to him.

"Dick, would it be kind or unkind to release him from the library? It is, of course, the merest farce. I believe half the books are upside down."

"Unkind," said the priest decidedly. "First, it is a mechanical operation, and secondly he would have no excuse for stopping here. Do you mind?"

"Not in the least. Very well, then. But he must make a show of having finished in another ten days."

"It shall be done," said his son.

"I talked like that at dinner because I thought it wise. A safety valve you know. And now, as I said, you mustn't keep me a moment longer from my letter."

"Oh, yes! The letter!" said Dick, and laughed aloud.

A few more points had to be elucidated by Chris on the subject of the eyes and hair of his female friend, and these had not been properly dealt with until nearly half-past ten. Then at last he referred to himself.

"But you know, old man, I'm such an unworthy brute. When I think of that darling — and then of myself. Good God!"

"Oh, well —" said the priest vaguely.

"But I haven't told you half. I've been such an unreal devil. I've made excuses till I've nearly believed them myself. There was that thing in Paris, you know. I told you about it; I went wholly and unreservedly to the devil then. And that was only a year ago. Good God!"

He beat himself on the thighs with indignation.

"Well, it was a year ago, and you gave it up of your own will."

"Gave it up! I should think so! The things that fiend knew and did! Dick, I don't believe you'd ever speak to me again, if you knew all."

"You've been to confession?"

"I have. A week ago, to Father Maples. I tell you he had a time of it. I don't suppose he's ever heard such a tale in his life —"

"Don't, my dear man. . . Well, and you're sorry?"

"Sorry! Why, I'm nearly mad when I think of it. And yet I know perfectly well No, I won't say that; it's inconceivable. But I'll say this: I've regretted I gave it up — two or three times, when things were bad with me. My dear man, it's like a kind of madness; I tell you that I've always believed all right in the devil since then. No one but he could have thought of the things. Why —"

"Don't tell me!" cried the priest. "I don't want to hear! It's done with, thank God! And you're a free man."

"Well, yes; but —"

"There are no buts. I don't want to jaw theology; but have the goodness to remember Saint Mary Magdalene —"

Chris nodded.

"I know. She and our Lady together! Dick, what a thing it is to be a Catholic!"

They smoked a minute or two in silence.

"Look here, Dick, there's one thing I want to ask. . . I suppose I'm all right in not telling her all this?"

Dick had already anticipated this question, and reviewed his casuistical learning. So he answered instantly.

"Why, yes. Why should you? She takes you for better or worse — and it's you, not your sins, Besides, they aren't yours any more now."

"Except for purgatory?"

"Except for purgatory."

"Well, you're sure?" said Chris slowly. "I swear I believe I'd tell her if you think I must —"

"I'm sure you're not obliged."

"Well, it'd probably kill me, and it'd certainly kill her, or send her mad. But upon my word, if it was necessary I'd do it. . . . Dick — you'll swear on your oath that forgiveness is all right."

"I swear, on my oath."

Chris threw his cigarette end into the heart of the fire; a flame flickered and was gone.

"There, like that?" he asked. "Gone? Burned up?"

"Like that," said the priest. "Of course you've got to eat the ash some day, but it's only the ash."

"Only the ash," said Chris slowly. "I suppose I can stand that, in purgatory."

"We've all got to," said the priest briefly; "that is, if we're lucky."

"Oh! Dick! Luck! And think of mine —!"

Then he was off again on a torrent till after midnight.

(2)

It was an edifying experience next morning to observe Chris at his devotions.

He insisted on serving his friend's Mass at half-past eight, and went through his ceremonies with ardor. He kissed the priest's hand fervently at the taking of the biretta, ministered the cruets as if they contained liquid diamonds, put a restrained passion into the very ringing of the tinkly bell, sighed his *Amens* like love-words, cried "Holy Mary, Mother of God . . ." as if he had already entered heaven, and ended by kissing his friend's hand almost as if it were his mistress's.

Father Maples came out to greet them both when they passed the presbytery-windows half-an-hour later.

He was of the portly type, rosy, fair-haired, with shrewd gray eyes and a perpetual fat smile.

"Well, Father, so you've come to congratulate your friend," he cried. "And I'm sure we all congratulate him with all our hearts. Of course she isn't a Catholic, but that can be remedied some day, eh, Father?"

"We will hope so," said Dick coolly.

"Mr. Dell will do his best," cried the priest again. "What a thing it will be — Hinton Hall in Catholic hands! You will want a chaplain, eh, sir?"

And so on, and so on.

When they had got clear of the gate Dick turned round.

"Why did you call him *antipatico?*" he asked curiously.

"That was before," said his friend solemnly. "He is *simpaticissimo* now, in spite of everything. Dick! Why are priests such bouncers?"

"They aren't," said the priest, "they are nothing of the kind. Now Father Maples —"

"Father Maples calls himself a man of the world. Is more wanting? Besides he tried to tell me a *risqué* story one day; not really *risqué*, you know. Oh! You know the sort. He thought it would please a layman, and make me think him a fine chap."

"You are so confoundedly critical," snapped Dick, in defense of his order. "If he hadn't, you would have called him a solemn prig."

"I probably should," assented Chris. "That kind of man can't help being one thing or the other. And he is generally both."

"That is singularly untrue," began Dick in rather a head-voice.

"Oh, shut up!" bawled Chris. "He's an angel. I give in. Now about Hinton today."

Then he expounded an elaborate program for the isolation of himself and his darling after lunch for at least two hours.

"You will have such a lot to say to Mrs. Hamilton, you know And she's a very charming woman. You've often told me so."

"I see," said Dick, "and the morning room will be ours till four. Thank you very much. Where shall you be?"

"In the schoolroom. Jack is away, thank God!"

"The schoolroom," echoed the priest.

"Yes, the dear child!"

Chris's impatience was piteous to behold as the morning crawled by. He appeared, in the yellow coat, at the smoking room door shortly before twelve, and explained seriously that it would be a pity to keep the horse waiting on such a — such a windy day. It was impossible to call it cold. At a quarter past he entreated his friend to see that his hat was in the hall, and as the half-hour struck he uttered a loud profane exclamation and rushed from the room. By seven-and-twenty minutes before one, they were going at a canter up the drive.

Dick evaded the lovers' meeting on the steps, and fled to the morning room. Mrs. Hamilton looked up from her desk, smiled, said a word or two and finished her note.

Then she came towards him.

"We must have a long talk, Father Yolland," she said. "I knew you would be down here soon. Am I to be congratulated?"

"I think so," said Dick solemnly.

"Well —" She looked at him, still smiling doubtfully. "We shall know better in two years, or say three. Here they come."

Annie too was changed, but not in the same direction as her lover. But she looked alive, positively, not negatively. She did not look a woman, for that was impossible; but a woman's soul was in her eyes, and an extraordinary kind of awe. She behaved beautifully; she talked about the Indian famine and American beef-trusts, she sailed through the door without looking to see if Chris were following, and her deportment continued with scarcely an interruption through lunch.

But Dick heard her sigh suddenly, as he disappeared afterwards in her mother's wake in the direction of the morning room, and left the two alone.

Mrs. Hamilton settled herself in her upright chair by the fire, took a fan to shield her face, indicated the cigarettes and matches, and began as if she were dictating a letter: —

"My dear Dick Yolland, I have hitherto been considered a sensible woman. Please do not contradict me. I cannot bear much more opposition."

Dick smiled and said nothing. He saw that she was wound up.

"And now I really don't know what to think. You saw them at lunch. Very well, then.

"Now you need not tell me all the arguments against the arrangement. I suppose I have repeated them to myself, and to Annie, altogether between seventy and eighty times. I did everything. I said I would take her abroad for a year, like a mother in a book. I told her she was a schoolgirl and a baby, and that he was an adventurer and a scamp. I pointed out the religious difficulty, the financial, the social, and all the rest. I entreated, stormed, argued, ignored; I was pathetic, sympathetic, and antipathetic. I even cried a little one evening, and attempted to have hysterics myself. I knew that was my last card, and that I could never hold up my head again. And you see the result. My dear Dick, I cannot conceive what I am about. Can you explain it at all? I hold you responsible, you know."

Dick was intensely relieved that she took this line so vivaciously.

"I am not in the least responsible," he said. "You would have him here. Please tell me, don't you really like him very much?"

Her face grew suddenly grave.

"Ah! We are coming to the point," she said. "I do like him very much, though I can't imagine why. (I suppose I am a little unconventional.) But I am afraid that other people may have liked him very much too. Father Dick, I am going to ask a very wrong question. Can you tell me much about his past life?"

Dick grew grave too. He had not an idea what to answer. Fortunately she relieved the situation.

"He told me something, but of course I would not hear too much. I know quite well that he went wrong once. He tried to tell me."

"Well?" said the priest, with dry lips.

"I think you will believe me," she went on, "when I say that that weighed with me more than anything else. I didn't really care very much about the money and all the rest, but I did care about that. I am extremely conventional in those things — up to a point. This is what I want to know. Is he really all right now? Is he honestly and entirely free from — from all that? I know it happened some time ago."

Dick was conscious of the lifting of an immense pressure. The thought of Chris's sins, especially of that of which he had told him last night, had been a good deal of a burden. He knew him to be clean living now, but the question had been as to whether this was sufficient. But apparently he had really tried to tell Mrs. Hamilton. He licked his lips and prepared to answer. But again she was beforehand.

"I understand perfectly that it is extremely unfair to sound his friends, but it would be more unfair to sound his enemies. I know you will say the best for him that can be said. Now then!"

Dick shifted his feet.

"Well, then," he said, "I believe him to be all right. In fact I am certain of it, and if you had heard him talk last night you would be certain too. He was asking me about — about forgiveness. He said he felt the thought of it all would drive him mad, if he were not quite sure of forgiveness. He said something else too that I think settles the matter: he said he would be willing even to tell Miss Annie herself, everything, if it was the right thing to do. That means a great deal from a man of his pride."

Mrs. Hamilton murmured something, looking at him with interested eyes.

"And there was another thing too," went on Dick, encouraged. "You know his *Boccaccio* that he always goes about with? It has been a kind of Bible to him, but it wasn't anything more than a pose, really. Well, even that has gone. He chucked it into the fire last night."

"The dear man!" cried the lady.

"Yes, indeed; I am glad you appreciate that. It meant a lot to Chris. Well, and the way he talked about Miss Annie! I wish you could have heard it —"

"My dear Father Dick, I have. Again and again."

"Yes, I know; but to another man it means more. I have never seen such a change. He seems perfectly natural. It is a miracle."

"Then you really think —"

"I tell you, he has dropped even his posing, and that means everything. I think I know now why I always liked him so much. He is showing his face at last."

Mrs. Hamilton made an abrupt, uncharacteristic movement with her hands.

"I can't tell you how pleased I am, Father Dick. I was very uncomfortable — much more than I let anybody see. Lord Brasted —"

"What?"

"Why do you say that? Lord Brasted has written me such a letter! Of course he knew dear James very well, and all that, as he says, but I don't think even that —" She made a movement as if to get up, and then sat back again. "No. I won't show it you; it isn't fair; but he says the most dreadful things. . . Why do you look like that?"

"It's very odd," said Dick. "Chris's beastly intuitions seem to have been all right. He said that Lord Brasted hated him."

"He doesn't hate him. He only says that I am mad. Of course I had to write and tell him everything. He says he is coming down here after Christmas."

"But you won't listen?"

"I certainly shall not listen. Besides he couldn't tell me anything I don't know. You see Mr. Dell told me quite enough, and now you tell me all this. . . . Of course Annie may change — I have warned him of that; or he may himself —"

"He certainly won't. He may die, of course."

"Don't, Father Dick."

"Oh! I don't think he will," laughed the priest, "he's got something better to do."

"And about his income? I am going to be resolute on that point."

Dick explained the situation. The position on the *Saturday Express* was a certain hundred and twenty pounds a year, and implied a good deal more. Chris ought to be able to make at the very least another hundred by outside articles.

"And where will he live?"

"I think I shall ask him to come and live with me — as a paying guest."

"Oh, do! I should be so much happier."

"Very well, I shall be delighted."

It was very pleasant to the priest to sit there in that charming morning room, by the cheer of a wood fire, and spin plans for his friend. Things had straightened themselves with such miraculous swiftness, and a level plain road lay ahead, leading direct to the Delectable Mountains.

He understood everything now — Mrs. Hamilton's position, her pride in her own unconventionality, her double set of reasons for yielding, namely her daughter's obstinacy and her own affection for Chris. He had a greater opinion of Annie now than ever before.

He looked round the familiar room with a curious sense of novelty. There were the tables with their silver things and flowers, the inlaid spinet, the brown walls hung with watercolors, the pendant plasters on the ceiling. Outside there was the hall, the suite of rooms opening beyond, the court, the stables, the park; and Chris was to be master of all this. They would be neighbors one day; their estates would march together!

He laughed aloud suddenly in the middle of a sentence.

"Well," said the other.

"It is all so extraordinary — Chris living here! I can't see him in the picture. What in the world will be his pose?"

"I thought you said —"

"Oh! Of course all that posing is gone. But he must be allowed to strut a little sometimes. After all, he is Christopher Dell!"

"There is one thing I cannot face," said Mrs. Hamilton presently, "and that is Mr. Stirling. Are clergymen allowed to excommunicate?"

"I believe not."

"Well, that's a comfort. He came up here as soon as he heard. He said he was sure it was a malicious slander, and he said all the disagreeable things instantly, in order that I mightn't silence him by telling him it was true. He asked me then all the rhetorical questions that he could think of — whether I realized what I was doing, and so on. I told him I didn't, in the least, and that took the wind out of his sails. By the way, what about Mr. Dell's religion?"

"Oh! He's a — a Roman Catholic all right — particularly just now. I believe he always has been one at heart."

"But about Annie?"

"Oh! He'll behave perfectly well. He'll be far too honorable, I think; he'll absolutely forbid her to become a Catholic for fear that he should be thought to have influenced her unduly."

"Really?"

"Well, no; not really. In fact I shall be surprised if Miss Annie doesn't become a Catholic some day —"

"Of course if her convictions —" began the mother.

"Oh! Well," said Dick, "he won't bother her, if you mean that. He's the most individualistic Catholic I have ever known."

They went out presently and walked a while on the terrace in the gusty weather. Rooks fled across the torn sky to the tall trees in the front of the house seeming to balance themselves on the point of one wing; and the creepers on the south wall shivered and glanced as the wind struck them. It was a shouting day, and Dick's exhilaration rose with it. It was really true then that Chris would have all this one day, or rather hold it in trust for his children. Chris's children! How abominably he would spoil them! All that fat pasture land sprinkled with copses; those woods against the sky — he would go about them solemnly on horseback, and think himself very busy.

The two really important persons came out at the verandah door presently, and across the grass and between the flowerbeds. They walked a little apart, but their faces wore a subdued radiance. They looked almost like two children.

Dick stood with a smile all across his face like a fox terrier. He could not help it; it was so absurd and so delightful.

"Well?" said Mrs. Hamilton.

"Well?" sighed the two.

(3)

They could not talk much going home. There was a groom behind, and Chris was naturally melancholy. It would be six days
before he could traverse this road again.

Mr. Yolland too was at tea when they arrived, and it was not
until nearly six that Dick said all that he felt.

He ended by a word or two about Mrs. Hamilton.

"My dear chap, I'm delighted you told her what you did."

"Why? Has she been questioning you?"

"Of course. What else do you suppose she wanted to talk to me
for? She asked me all sorts of things."

"And you told her —"

"I told her what I felt."

"Dear man!"

"Well, but why didn't you tell me you had told her?"

"I didn't."

"How?"

"I didn't tell her what I told you. I only told her about my first
affair — you know — when I was at Oxford."

Dick did dimly remember some veiled confidence, but his jaw
rather fell.

"Then all this other affair —"

"Why, of course not. Why should I tell her? I was willing to tell
Annie, as I said."

Dick meditated a moment or two, rather uncomfortably. It seemed
that he had been under a small misconception, and that Mrs. Hamilton
knew nothing whatever about the affair of last year. He tried to remember what he had said. He had certainly been very emphatic, but
surely he had not said anything that was not true, viewed in this new
light. He had only insisted that Chris was all right now.

"What's the matter, old man? You don't mean to say I ought to
tell her?"

"No," said Dick slowly, "I don't see the necessity. After all —"

"After all, I'm forgiven, aren't I? And she knows I was a bad hat
once. It doesn't much matter how long ago it was, as long as I'm

not a bad hat now?"

"No — I don't suppose it does."

"Look here, Dick, I don't understand —"

The priest made an effort.

"No, you needn't; it's perfectly right. As you say, she knows quite enough to decide. And she has decided."

"Really? You're sure? You know I shouldn't like —"

"No — I'm sure. It's all right."

"Really *finito?*"

"Finito."

"Then for God's sake, let's change the subject. It stinks."

Chris was certainly very much changed. Three weeks ago, however severe his penitence, it could have taken no other form than that of an elaborate discussion of details, with many exclamations. Now it appeared that the whole subject was horrible to him; he had faced it in confession, renounced it and thrown it away; he didn't wish to finger the foul thing again even for purposes of contrition.

This was all very cheering to the priest, and the slight discomfort of his recent discovery presently passed away. He could say, with his hand on his heart, that his friend was straight now.

They talked of numberless things that evening and Dick opened the question of Chris's lodging with him.

"My dear chap!" cried his friend. "You know you couldn't stand me for a week."

"Shall I be frank?"

"Well, yes!"

"Well, I don't think I could have, a month ago, or you couldn't have stood me. But things are different now."

"How do you mean?"

"Good Lord! Must I tell you to your face? Well then, you aren't the same person. *Boccaccio* gone, and all the rest! You'll burn the silk pajamas next."

"Oh!"

"Well, isn't it so?"

"Dick, it is so — I swear it. I wish to wear a Norfolk jacket with the belt unbuttoned, and a twill nightshirt for the rest of my life."

"Well, then, will you come and wear them in Soho Lane? Twenty-five shillings a week. Accounts rendered and discharged every Saturday morning."

"Dick, do you mean it? Oh! You are a good chap. I'll come — I'll come and live in Brixton if you ask me. Or Little Tooting."

"All right then. I'll expect you on Tuesday week."

"Dick, must you really go back tomorrow?"

"Of course I must. I've got confessions all the afternoon and evening."

"I wish I was one of your people. May I black your boots when I come?"

"I shall be delighted. Six pence a week off for that!"

So they went on till Dick had to say his office. It was all rather frothy talk, and of no kind of value. Its only interest to the priest was that it was the symptom of an extraordinary convalescence. Chris had become a kind of boy again; he could give and take with good humor. Dick had not to guard his language.

He glanced up at him once or twice over his book, and found him once more more interesting than the fortunes of the holy person, related in the second nocturne. Chris sat poising a poker between his thin sinewy hands, staring, staring at the fire with the light on his chin and forehead. His lips moved now and again, he smiled irresponsibly once or twice, he sighed in half-content and half-melancholy two or three times. He hardly smoked a cigarette in forty minutes.

Dick shut his book as the dressing bell rang.

"There," he said, and took his friend by the arm.

Mr. Yolland introduced the subject of his friend, Mr. Rolls, at dinner.

"You met him, I think, Mr. Dell, didn't you?"

"At lunch in the cottage," said Chris serenely, "when I behaved so extremely badly."

Mr. Yolland glanced up from turbot, smiling.

"I went to see him today. You must go over to Foxhurst before you leave us. It is really an astonishing house; it has everything necessary for a story. You should write an article on it,"

"Do tell me, sir,"

"Oh! You must see it. It has galleries, a court, moat, a King's room, a Queen's room; it had a hall, but that's gone; and it has a ghost."

"Yes?"

"I don't know how long the Rolls have had it. One of them was a kind of *aide-de-camp* to Mary Stuart. They have always been Catholics."

"And he is the last?"

"He is the last. His wife died, and there are no children."

"And he himself?"

"Well, Dick calls him a mystic. And he is a superb gardener; and . . . and other things."

"Mrs. Hamilton told me some odd things —"

Mr. Yolland's manner changed a little, and his voice sounded cold.

"People will say anything," he said. "Yet I don't know that I am surprised —"

"I beg your pardon, sir; I did not mean that —"

"I know. You mean his guests."

"Who were there today?" asked Dick.

Mr. Yolland smiled a little.

"Well, so far as I remember there was a — a Presbyterian minister; a — a broken-down actress and, yes — he was there, I saw him in the garden — an ex-priest."

"By Gad!" said Chris.

"Just so."

"But what are they doing —?"

"They are his friends," said the other shortly "The actress poured out tea."

But Chris's eyes were already beginning to be vacant, and Dick switched the conversation on to another line. It was impossible to expect the lover to attend to any one irrelevant matter for more than three minutes.

The departure next day was a sufficiently cheerful affair. Senti-

ment was impossible in an open phaeton at a quarter past eight on
a rainy November morning, although Chris did his best. He insisted on breakfasting with his friend at seven forty-five, and sitting by his side all the way to the station.

"Ten days more," said Dick, turning towards him as he drove.

Chris sighed violently, and then abruptly smiled.

"Only ten days," he said vivaciously.

"You beastly hypocrite!" said Dick.

"Well, I am. But a man must keep his manners."

"And what time shall I expect you?"

"Oh! About dinnertime," said Chris vaguely, "or perhaps after.
Don't sit up. You see there'll be a lot to do on the last day."

"Of course."

"Dick, give me a poky room. No more spare bedrooms."

"I shall give you your money's worth, neither more nor less."

"What shall I do all day, till this *Saturday Express* business
begins?"

"Poems," observed the priest, "or articles. I should imagine
poems."

"By Gad, yes! And it begins at the New Year?"

"The Editor says so."

"Dick! What extraordinary luck the whole thing is! It's like a
conjuring trick. The omelet is positively in the hat, when expected."

"And without one broken egg."

"Exactly."

They were five minutes before their time, and Dick preferred to
sit under the fur rug till the signal dropped, while the groom dis-
posed of the bag and took the ticket.

"You travel third?" asked Chris.

"Where else?"

"By Gad! I will too, next time. I never thought of it."

"You will be back in time for another breakfast at nine," observed
the priest.

"I think not," said Chris. "To tell the truth, if you don't mind—"

"What on earth do you mean?"

"Dick, for God's sake don't laugh. But would the groom mind

taking me round by Hinton?"

"But you can't —"

"I know I can't. But I want to go past the gate. You can see the roof, you know. Oh, Lord! What a fool you must think me!"

But Dick did not in the least want to laugh. It seemed to him once more to be the most wonderful thing he had ever seen. And this was Chris!

"Well, I must go," he said, "there's the signal; and I've got to get to the other side. Goodbye, old man. Tuesday week."

"God bless you, Dick!"

Chris took the reins and watched him across the line; he saw him speak to the groom, but he could not hear what was said.

When the train was gone, and he had waved frantically to the silk-hatted head protruded from a third-class window, the groom came back?

"Mrs. Warwick's is the best, sir," he said, taking the reins.

"Eh! What?"

"For tobacco, sir. Master Dick said you wanted some tobacco in Hinton."

CHAPTER VI

A New Disorder

(I)

C hris paused with uplifted fountain pen, and looked at the
windows for inspiration.

It was the second week in January, and he was engaged on his
third descriptive article for the *Saturday Express*. He was conduct-
ing his readers through the year in Italy, a month late, and had
arrived at Christmas Eve in Naples. At this moment, before his eyes,
for he was an excellent visualizer, floated the forms of men clad in
sheepskin, marching with out-turned feet, legs wrapped in rags,
and felt hatted, playing upon little pipes through the streets in the
early morning.

There were few people about; a child or two stood in a doorway,
a troop of Satanic goats dawdled on the Rampe Brancaccio, and
two Englishmen, of whom he was one, invited the musicians to
come upstairs to the flat and play a little melody to an ivory statue
of the Mother of God. It was very charming he remembered; the
cold morning sky, the brisk air, the pale island across the Bay, the
solemn smoke-oozing mountain, all vast and violet against a rosy
dawn; then there was the climb upstairs; the odd contrast between
the tanned country-boys and the damask-lined walls, the shrill
sweet playing, and the delicate yellow image looking down from
its bracket between the windows. He remembered the curious thrill
with which he realized the splendid Catholic paganism of it all; it
was so that men had played twenty centuries ago before other statues than this.

Then as he stared and smiled the vision faded, and he saw the
heavy London fog (so fit an emblem of the character of the people
who made it) lying like a woolen bank against the panes. He sighed,
put down his pen, and went to the window.

He had been settled in now for six weeks, and better understood what it was that lay before him. Two years was a long time. He had returned a fortnight ago from his Christmas visit to Hinton, and his appetite was still keen. She had been so sweet! They had skated together one day on the Long Water; he had held her hands and looked into her face among the furs, rosy-flushed where warmth and biting air kissed one another. They had sat long evenings together over the wood fire in the schoolroom, listening to the deathly silence of the frost outside, watching the lilac flames lick the fragrant logs. The days had gone by like pearls, he thought, each perfect, no two alike, linked by a golden string of dreams and a half-conscious joy of being where he was. (That was a poetical thought, he told himself; he would see presently how a sonnet would frame it.) But the pearls had slipped through his fingers, and he was left now, empty-fingered and dissatisfied.

Two years! And Easter would be the next glimpse of paradise.

Yet he knew perfectly well that he was happier than he had been in the whole previous course of his life. The fever was gone, soothed away by coolness — the coolness of his love's hands. There was an object now, and there had been none; the dreariest details of life, the little journeys on an omnibus, the sulfur of the Underground Railway, foggy mornings like this — all were rendered less opaque by a distant light on the horizon; in two years he would say goodbye to all this.

At the same time he was occasionally conscious of a strain.

Before all this had begun and he had learned the ecstasy of innocence, there had always been the relief of the imagination; there had been districts of thought, visualized images, formed partly from retrospect, partly from anticipation, which had been open to him as a city of refuge from sordid facts. Now all this was closed; it was disloyalty even to look at the closed doors that led to this bewitched country. At first it had been an intense joy to know that he had looked his last on this realm; it was the happiness of coming out from an artificially lit, heavily-scented room into clean morning air. But now he was conscious that there were moments when the clean morning air struck a little chilly; when objects seen in the cold light of a pure dawn were less inviting; when the warm fancies of his old life beckoned him, as when an early riser in winter looks for a moment regretfully at the tumbled bed in a darkened room left an hour before.

But the attraction was not severe. After all the keen air is better, and pride at having been resolute compensates for lost comfort. There was not yet anything approaching to a struggle in his mind; he firmly believed that he would grow stronger every month, and that by the time that the two years were gone he would be free even from the perils of imagination.

He shivered pleasantly as he looked out at the smoky orange medium that seethed beneath in the street, listened for a moment to the solemn roar of the City, and went back to his place by the cheerful fire.

Dick looked in half-an-hour before lunch, with rather a pinched, tired face.

"Well?" he asked with an obvious attempt not to be peevish.

"Pretty fair," said Chris. "It will be Pompeii in a thunderstorm next week, and we shall spend Lent in Rome."

"Pompeii in a thunderstorm," observed Dick reflectively, sitting down and taking up the poker. (He felt rather dreary, generally, on Monday mornings.)

"Yes, the old and the new, don't you know. It actually happened to me. There wasn't a soul there besides myself. Vesuvius roared and smoked, and the rain came down in torrents. And then the sky cleared to a bright blue, and there was the — the vile place, like a sort of decayed roué, all dripping and shining."

Dick grunted.

"And then Rome in Lent. By Gad! I shall let the tourists have it. Baedekers and green veils, don't you know, at the giving of ashes in St. John Lateran!"

"Let them have it! Let them have it!" murmured the priest.

"You may depend on me. Look here, may I just read you my stuff?"

Dick did not attend very closely. He was thinking for the hundredth time of how very extraordinary and pleasant the whole thing was, and how very tired he was. They had got on admirably so far for six weeks. Chris was an ideal companion; he was always friendly and interesting, it was nice to come in from Mass on cold mornings and find him, brisk and clean looking, warming his hands over the fire, ready with short selections of news from the morning paper. During the day they did not meet a great deal except at meals, and at times like this when a solitary soul desires a relief. Chris was generally attentive and thoughtful. Once when the priest came back from a sick call towards three o'clock in the morning he found that his friend had made a fire and boiled cocoa. Chris had been greatly distressed when Dick had reminded him that it was after midnight, and that refreshment was not possible to a Mass-priest.

It was pleasant too in the evenings to go up to Chris's room and sit there for an hour before going to bed, listening to his compositions with more or less of attention, and conspiring inefficiently in plans for the screwing of editors.

But Chris's literary life was making good progress; there was no real need for conspiracy; his extra articles had a kind of sting about them that caused them to be accepted, and there was no more any cause for anxiety as to the necessary income of two hundred pounds a year.

There was therefore nothing to cloud the prospect. If Chris could only be kept quiet and busy — and there was no sort of reason to expect him to be otherwise — the two years would roll by, and the story would leave him happy ever afterwards.

Chris's voice ended, and the priest stood up, stretching himself and yawning.

"Excellent, my dear chap! Just a little pagan, you know, but —"

"Pagan! Why, of course it is. Catholicism is just that. That's why it's so obviously true; it's the sum of all religions, and the Queen of them. Why, if I didn't think —"

"Oh! Yes. I know all that. I suppose it's all right."

"Why, look at the Vestal Virgins! What are they but nuns? With the same virtues and the same sanctity! And incense, and lights, and flowers — all pagan, my good man — every one of them. And Catholicism has absorbed them all, just as it is bound to do. Why, it's the strongest argument of all."

"Yes, yes, I know —"

"And what are the old gods but attributes of the Christian God? Pallas Athene is His wisdom — Apollo His beauty, and so on. Puritanism is the Devil!, my dear Dick. It's just sectarianism, that rules off a little corner, and denies everything but itself. That's why I put up Hermes in my rooms at Oxford. By George! I'll put him up here."

"You mustn't. It would cause *admiratio* to Betty."

"What's that?"

"*Admiratio?* Oh! It's not admiration, it's a mild sort of scandal."

"It's a good word," said Chris fervently. "I must remember that."

"Oh! It's an excellent word. It meets a felt want," said Dick, yawning again.

"Give me another instance."

"Oh! It would cause *admiratio* if — if I smoked a pipe in the street, or if you said you believed in Pallas Athene."

"But I do."

"Very well, then. If you said that outside this room it would cause *admiratio.*"

"Then I've caused a lot in my time."

"Then you shouldn't."

"Why not? Look here, Dick, I'm not one of those people who can shuffle and act and pretend. If I feel a thing I say it. I can't keep back my real beliefs."

"My dear man, that's the sheerest nonsense. Of course we all keep back lots of things. We don't shout out in the morning from our windows that we've slept very tolerably, and are just going to have our bath."

"That's not fair; it's not parallel. You preach what you believe, don't you? Well, why shouldn't I? It's the creed that makes the man—"

"Bosh! Shut up. You're a heretic. Besides, it's time for lunch."

Chris followed, protesting.

He announced at lunch that he was going round to his old club to see about readmittance, and the payment of arrears. Dick felt rather annoyed at the news.

"Why do you want a club?"

"My dear man, it's necessary. One hears all the gossip there."

"Why do you want the gossip? Is it worth ten pounds a year?"

"That and other things, certainly. You don't understand a bit. It's necessary for a man of my —"

"Oh! My good man —"

"Well?"

"Can't you forget your everlasting temperament for ten minutes?"

Chris looked slightly annoyed.

"I wasn't going to say that at all. I was going to say profession."

Dick was rather tired with Sunday work, and his perceptions were just a little bit dull this morning. Besides there was a chilly round of pinkish beef, and only warmish potatoes. So he paid no attention to the symptoms of his friend.

"Don't take yourself so beastly seriously. You are always jawing about your profession. After all, it isn't such a —"

Chris whitened so suddenly that the priest stopped.

"Well?" he said. "I was only going to say —"

"Why do you always sneer at everything I do?" began Chris explosively. "You are always jawing and finding fault. Of course, I'm very grateful —"

"Good Lord!" sighed the priest.

"I will ask you not to interrupt. I was saying that of course I'm very grateful and all that, but that doesn't give you a right —"

"I know it doesn't," moaned the other. "I take it all back. Your profession is the finest on God's earth; we wouldn't get on a day without it. And you're the brightest ornament —"

Chris rose abruptly. His lips worked a moment.

"Look here, I'm not going to stand this. I'm doing my best to keep my temper; but, by George, there are some things —"

Dick was rather angry too. He had meant nothing seriously, and he was annoyed that the other should take it so. He looked at him between half-shut eyes.

"I've never seen such a man," he said. "You flare up at the least thing —"

Chris went out, banging the door behind him, and the priest heard his steps go downstairs. Then presently the street door banged too.

In ten minutes Dick had become rather angry with himself. He honestly had not meant to be annoying, but he was quite aware that he had tended that way.

He looked at Chris's half-emptied plate with a touch of real compunction; a piece of gristle, delicately severed, lay along the rim; the potatoes were half eaten, and even in that moment of anger, Chris had not omitted to lay his knife and fork neatly together. It was really rather pathetic.

But he ought not to have gone off like that. Dick hated rudeness like sin, and it was certainly rude of Chris to depart so swiftly, shutting the doors in such a way. He wondered where he had gone — where he would get lunch, and so on.

He determined to say a word of regret when his friend came back; he would not apologize — that would be so bad for Chris. But he would just say that he had not been talking seriously, and that he was always stupid on Monday mornings.

Then he smoked a cigarette, dozed a little, awoke with a start and a taste in his mouth at half-past two, and got up, feeling more irritable than ever. There was some visiting to be done; there was a fog, and he was very tired.

He came back about half-past five, and there was no Chris. But there was a note, brought, Betty said, by a messenger boy a little after four o'clock. He opened it and read it. It was scrawled on half a sheet of notepaper, stamped "Doric Club" at the top, and contained half-a-dozen words.

"Dining out. Don't sit up. In haste; C. D."

It was rather a dreary evening that the priest passed. He supped alone, dozed again, read his office, answered a couple of letters, and finally, about eleven o'clock felt really angry.

It was scandalous behavior on Chris's part! Here was a man to whom he had given shelter and food, to whom he had been the means of unheard of prosperity, over whom he had taken a great deal of trouble, with whom he had borne through every sort of annoyance, and, above all, whom he had taken into his house at ridiculously inadequate terms, and had treated in every way with affection and respect. And now, at the first slight misunderstanding, this man had gone off in a sulk. It was childish, babyish, unworthy of a grown man!

He went up to bed presently, crossing himself savagely with holy water at the door of his room, and in ten minutes was in bed, feeling particularly wide-awake. He heard the clock below strike the quarter, and the half, and then there were footsteps on the stairs.

The priest waited as usual for the minute tap on his door to see if he was awake; but, although he heard the footsteps pause, there was no tap; and a moment later, the door of the next room shut quietly.

Very well, said the priest to himself, there should be no apology, even of the most disguised nature next morning. He required to receive, not to offer, expressions of regret.

(2)

Dick felt a great deal better next morning.

He did not see Chris in the sacristy, so he vested and went in with the sacristan; but during the reading of the epistle he was aware that Chris was changing places with the server. He could not help reflecting that this signified that it was all right between them, and, as he bent over the altar for the *Munda Cor* he registered a swift vow to be natural at breakfast, and not to refer to the unfortunate incident of the previous day. It would be better so.

They both kept silence as usual during the unvesting after Mass; the priest washed his hands, and went back into the church for his thanksgiving.

He stayed a long time this morning at his prayers. The little grimy church, pleasantly dark and faintly redolent still with the Sunday incense, was like a caress to him. It was very quiet this morning; the fog still soothed the traffic outside, and only an occasional woolly rumble in the little side street broke the living silence within.

Dick pondered a number of things when he had said his more formal prayers, and chief among them were his relations with Chris.

He had certainly been trying to his friend the day before, and he
made an act or two of contrition for it. He did not know how he
had come to forget himself; it was the first touch of unpleasant-
ness that had come between them for over two months. He re-
solved to be extremely careful for the future, especially on Monday
mornings when the surfaces of the soul are a little raw.

What a curious man Chris was! Undoubtedly prosperity was
good for him; it had called out his virtues, not his defects. He was
more, not less serene than when he was in trouble. On the whole
he had really behaved not badly yesterday; perhaps it was not fair
to accuse him of sulking; it might well be that he had thought that
a few hours' absence would go further than any amount of explanation in the direction of healing the rift.

Dick made another act of contrition with his eyes screwed tight,
rounded up his devotions, and went out of the church, buttoning
up his long double breasted French coat.

He let himself in with his key, took off his coat in the hall, and
went straight on into the dining room, rubbing his hands with brisk
cordiality, and determined to be as friendly as possible. Yes, he would
presently say he was sorry.

Chris was not there.

For a moment he stood astonished. Such a thing had not happened once before. Then he saw the back of an envelope lying on
his plate, and took it up, wondering.

There was a line written almost illegibly upon it.

"Gone to catch the 9:10. There's something the matter at Hinton.
Just heard. Can't wait a moment. Will write or wire. — C. D."

As he still stood with this in his hand, not knowing what to think,
Betty came in.

"He's gone, Master Dick; he just put a few things in his bag and
went. He told me to tell you he couldn't wait."

Dick nodded.

"Was there a wire?" he asked.

"No, Master Dick; I think there was a letter."

Dick turned the paper over mechanically, and recognized Mrs.
Hamilton's neat handwriting.

He had an uncomfortably thoughtful breakfast. First he dismissed the theory of Annie's illness; if it had been urgent there would have been a wire. Secondly he dismissed the thought that she had changed her mind about Chris; in that case the rejected lover would scarcely have been asked to come down. Then he reflected that he was judging hastily; Annie well might be ill, and Mrs. Hamilton have written to that effect; and a man like Chris would, of course, have caught the nine-ten. Or again, it might be even the second theory, and Chris have gone without an invitation. Really there seemed to be no other theory; but whatever the explanation was, it must be connected with bad news of some kind.

Dick poured out a second cup of coffee, and sat stirring it till it was cold.

He could hardly have believed that he could have passed so uncomfortable a morning for so small a cause as the departure of Chris. But he sat before his fire, with a book taken up for a presence, while his mind trod the round. There seemed something sinister even in his last interview with his friend; they had parted hastily, with sharp words, nearly twenty-four hours before, and had not spoken since, except in the stately dialogue at the altar. What if this were some kind of omen that he could not interpret? He was terrified at the thought that there might be some real trouble at Hinton; he could not even picture what it would mean to Chris. If this new element were suddenly withdrawn from his life, he would be in far worse case than ever; the whole of his new and ordered existence would crumble back with a crash into the chaos from which it had risen, carrying with it even the flimsy crust that had begun to form, however slightly, before he had known Annie. As the priest contemplated this, it seemed to him that he was looking into a pit. . .

It was impossible for the most vivid imagination to construct any theory for the future, except the hackneyed suggestion of suicide.

A great regret seized him. If only he himself had been less peevish the day before he would not have suffered so much, but he felt that he had forfeited Chris's confidence; it was not to him that the other would turn now in the event of disaster.

Then he told himself he was a fantastic ass; that Annie had probably a cold on the chest; that Mrs. Hamilton had proposed the two years to be shortened; either of these things would be quite enough to make Chris catch the nine-ten.

He took up his book and read a little, but the dismay reasserted itself, and half-a-dozen times that morning he found himself reading the same page from which all interest had departed. Twice he started up, hearing a bell ring below, and waited; but silence followed, and the third ring he did not notice.

He had just stood up to poke the fire when Betty came in with an orange-colored envelope in her hand. He snatched it, tore it open and read; and so stood.

"Any answer, Master Dick?"

"No — yes."

He seized a pen, scribbled an answer and handed it to her.

"And — Betty — I shall be going down to Amplefield by the two forty-five; I don't know when I shall be back. Send round to St. Mary's to see if a priest can say Mass here tomorrow. If they can't, tell Jennings to put up a notice on the church door that there will be no Mass."

"Yes, Master Dick —"

"I will be back tomorrow night unless I wire."

"Yes, Master Dick. There's no bad news?"

"I don't know," he said. "Yes, there is; but I don't know what. Oh, no, it's nothing to do with my father."

When she had gone he read the telegram again.

"*For God's sake come down. Am meeting 2:45. Dell. Amplefield.*"

If the morning had been uncomfortable, the afternoon was ten times worse. He sat in the railway carriage, first-class, for he could not bear company, staring out through the streaming pane at the blurred streaks and colors that represented the landscape, at the whirling horizontal wheels that stood for plowed fields.

He knew now that it was bad news, and that it was news which in some way concerned him. Chris would scarcely have wired merely for the sake of receiving sympathy. And why was he at

Amplefield, and not at Hinton Hall? There was only one possible answer to that. And all the while one theory, that he had fiercely stamped upon in the morning, raised its head higher and higher, and sickened him with the malignant despair in its face.

He pulled himself together as the train drew up in the dark at Marlesdon, but there was no Chris on the platform. A groom only awaited him.

"No, Master Dick, Mr. Dell is at home. The master has sent the brougham, and here's a note from him, sir."

He stood under a lamp to read it.

"I cannot leave him," he read; "there is something the matter at Hinton; he will not tell me what. He is in a dreadful state. Come to my room as soon as you arrive."

The drive seemed interminable. Dick sat with clenched hands on the edge of his seat, hardly able to refrain from putting his head out of the window and shouting to the coachman to gallop. He watched the lights in the little village as he drove through, and then the red trunks of the pines and the heather patches, in the light of the carriage-lamps, as they passed through the lodge gates and began to go uphill, and he sprang out at last beneath the Georgian portico, dazed at the sudden change from darkness and with the violent torment of his own thoughts.

His father came out of the smoking room opposite, as his footsteps sounded in the hall, and the two turned and went into the study.

"Well?"

The old man looked at him, and then spoke with that hasty breathless voice that men use when there is sickness or death in the house.

"They have found out something at Hinton. I don't know what. I believe it's all over. Did you not see Lord Brasted at the station?"

Dick shook his head.

"He came by the same train as you. There is to be another interview tomorrow morning. That is why he wired for you."

"What is he doing?"

"He's sitting before the fire. I have hidden his revolver. My dear lad, he's nearly out of his mind."

"Let me go to him."

"One moment. Let me tell you. I tell you I don't know what it is, but it is something disgraceful. I think perhaps you know what it is. He wrote the telegram instantly when I mentioned your name. I had to rewrite it; it was scarcely legible."

"Has he had anything to eat?"

The old man shook his head.

"No, no. You don't understand. I tell you he is nearly mad."

"Let me go to him."

"Directly; there's no hurry. He's quieter now. Get quiet first yourself, dear boy. You mustn't be hysterical. . . . There, there; it's all right."

"His revolver?" gasped Dick.

"I've got it; it's all right. He can't hurt himself. But I thought I'd better not come to meet you. . . . There's no knowing, and I don't want the servants to see him."

"Ah! Let me go!"

Mr. Yolland went to the door of the study.

"You must use your discretion. I don't know what to advise. . . . Try scolding him. . . . I don't know."

Dick pushed past his father, crossed the hall, paused a moment at the door, and listened. But there was no sound from within.

Then he opened the door softly and stepped inside.

CHAPTER VII

A Relapse

(I)

Lord Brasted was finishing his cigar in the glazed veranda after breakfast. There was no sign of any tragedy about him. He was as pink and prosperous looking as ever, sitting now in a tailed gray suit with one stout leg crossed over the other, and a well-laced boot, of the color of a ripe horse chestnut, cocked in the air.

He was reading the *Standard* newspaper, and thinking about something else; the cigar, clasped by a capable-looking finger, protruded from the edge of that journal.

Yesterday he had received the wire which he had half-expected, and had come down by the afternoon train. There had been a long interview with Mrs. Hamilton, and a short one with Miss Annie, both of which had tolerably satisfied him. Of course it was a hard thing that had to be done, but he was pleased to observe their resolution, and to recognize that the elder woman at any rate took a sane view of the situation.

There had been a scene in the morning, he understood — the kind of scene that he would have expected from that dramatic young man whom he had met on a previous visit, and there would probably be another one in a few minutes. He was perfectly willing to confront him under the circumstances; he did not propose to spare him, and he was quite satisfied with the state of his own nerves. He had not driven a *Panhard* for nothing during the last eighteen months.

A door opened, and a footman appeared. Lord Brasted stood up at once, laying his cigar-end at the foot of a small bay tree that grew in a tub, followed the footman through the drawing room, crossed the hall, and went into the morning room, still carrying his newspaper.

"It is half-past," said Mrs. Hamilton, without looking up.

She was sitting in an upright armchair by the fire, with her back turned towards most of the room. Her ringed fingers lay along the arms of her chair and clasped the knobs at the end.

Lord Brasted parted his tails, drew up his trousers slightly at the knees, and sat down on the other side of the hearth.

"Yes, dear lady; I was just coming. . . . It is all very unfortunate."

She was quite silent for a moment, then she spoke suddenly, and with a curious hardness in her voice.

"I think it is disgraceful that he should ask for this interview."

Lord Brasted cleared his throat.

"It is very natural," he said. "I have the papers here. Do you think he will deny it?"

"Of course," she said contemptuously.

"And then?"

"I shall tell him what I think."

They sat in complete silence then; once the newspaper rustled as Lord Brasted shifted his position; once a log shifted with a soothing murmur on the hearth, and a little firework display of sparks flew up in the column of gray smoke; but outside all was still. The rain and wind of last night had dropped, and the world waited, poised in silence, bathed in clear sunshine, as if for some great movement of the elements.

The little morning room was full of the wintry light that shone through the small square panes and the new coats painted on them, and fell upon the inlaid spinet, the deep blue-bordered carpet, and the delicate spindle-legged tables loaded with dainty silver. It was a setting perfectly appropriate for a graceful little love scene, or the climax of a small comedy.

Lord Brasted rose at last, and went to the fire, lifting the tongs from the hearth to rearrange the logs, and as he bent forward the other sat up suddenly.

"There!" she said.

There came from outside the clear, spanking trot of a horse, suddenly echoing in the forecourt, the hiss of wheels on gravel, and then silence.

Lord Brasted, still completely self-possessed, continued his movement, propped a log end-wise, set back the tongs carefully so that
they should not slip, and turned round, drawing an envelope from
his breast-pocket as the door opened.

Even his nerves thrilled a little as he looked at the two men standing there.

Christopher Dell had the face of a dead man in which two black
eyes alone showed signs of life. His lips showed like a straight
gash in his face. He was perfectly dressed, and the contrast was
horrible. Beside him stood Father Yolland, buttoned up to the
neck in a clerical frock coat, with a suppressed kind of defiance
in his air. His chin was thrust out, his snub-nose resembled a
bulldog's, and his sandy hair appeared stiffer than ever. It was he
who spoke first.

"Mr. Dell has sent for me," he said. "This is my business too,
Mrs. Hamilton."

His voice too rang hard and defiant, and as the woman stirred
in her chair Lord Brasted saw that she was trembling a little. He
hoped that she was not going to break down. But she said nothing,
though her lips moved, and she made a little preconcerted gesture.
There were to be no formalities.

Lord Brasted cleared his throat, and glanced down at the envelope in his hand.

"Mrs. Hamilton has asked me to speak for her," he began, "and I
understand that it is what Mr Dell —" (he bowed slightly without
raising his eyes) — "it is what Mr. Dell wishes. Of course I have no
alternative, disagreeable as such a duty is! But — er — but I should
be ashamed not to say — under these circumstances — what I
have felt myself compelled to say — under other circumstances —
in fact —"

He broke off, drawing a long paper out of his envelope, and feeling a little dissatisfied with his exordium. He was also slightly disconcerted by the silence and motionlessness of the two figures
opposite him. Christopher Dell was like a waxwork image.

He cleared his throat once more.

"Here are the facts," he said.

He lowered the paper and folded his two hands on it behind his back.

"I will not pretend that the news of Mr. Dell's engagement to Miss Annie gave me any pleasure. I told Mrs. Hamilton so at the time; she knew what I thought from the beginning. It did not seem to me suitable. . . . Well, I happen to be a member of the Club to which Mr. Dell used to belong — the 'Doric ' — It was there that I first heard what I suppose I must call gossip. I do not excuse it. But it was more than gossip to me. I may remind Mr. Dell that I had been a friend of Mr. Hamilton for several years, and, I think I may say, a friend of Mrs. Hamilton, too. I have been allowed to regard this house almost as my own home. Father Yolland knows that.

"When I heard this gossip then, I felt it my duty to ask questions. It was, I may almost say, as if an uncle, or even a father, heard talk about a stranger who was to be admitted to a — to the family — er — towards which he stood in — er — that relation. I am quite aware what Mr. Dell may think fit to call this action on my part, but I think if he will consider the circumstances —"

The priest's voice suddenly broke in, harsh and brutal.

"Cannot you come to the point, Lord Brasted? We do not want to hear this kind of explanation."

Lord Brasted lifted his eyes without raising his head.

"Perhaps not, Mr. Yolland, but in justice to myself I felt bound to make this statement first. . . . Well, I said that I made these inquiries; I heard a good deal about Mr. Dell, and I wrote two, no, three days ago the result of my inquiries. . . ." (He lifted the paper and smoothed the creases.) "Here is a copy of the main facts. I will, for the present, reserve the names, but I am perfectly willing, if Mr. Dell desires it, to put this paper in his hands immediately that he may see the names for himself. I have not shown Mrs. Hamilton the names, and I do not propose to do so, unless . . . unless it is necessary."

He lifted the paper nearer his eyes, and fitted his gold pince-nez carefully on his nose The two figures before him, he perceived as he did so, were perfectly motionless still. Mrs. Hamilton was as she had been, in her chair, turned towards him, with her face away from the others, but it was downcast, and her hands lay together on her lap.

"I beg your pardon," he said, lowering the paper once more, "but I must add that it is not by my wish that I am here. Mrs. Hamilton telegraphed for me yesterday morning, when she heard that Mr. Dell proposed coming here, and I understand that it is by his wish too that I am here.

"Well, here are the facts."

The silence was intense in the sunlit room; the sputtering of the logs had ceased, and he perceived once more that the three figures had not stirred, nor was there even the sound of breathing.

"Four years ago Mr. Dell was in Italy. Here he made the acquaintance of — of two persons whom I will not name, but who are notorious for — for evil living. He was constantly in the houses of these persons. It was generally understood that he held with their — their peculiar views of morality, and identified himself with them.

"This, I am aware, is perfectly vague; it is no more than an introduction to the story proper.

"One of these persons, a woman, divorced from her husband, and — and a Roman Catholic by profession, has a flat in — in a certain street in Paris. Her reputation, my informant tells me, is the worst conceivable. I may say that that reputation had reached even my ears more than five years ago, in connection with a certain trial, and she has been before the public twice again since that date.

"A little less than eighteen months ago — or to be more precise, about last August or September year, Mr. Dell came to Paris, and took up his quarters in this woman's house. At this time Mr. Dell was believed to be penniless. He was constantly seen in Paris, in the same carriage with this woman. He was once seen in a box alone with her at the opera. (I can mention the name of the piece that was played that night, if necessary.) Twice he entertained, in the apparent position of master of the house, two persons in this lady's flat, both of whose signatures I have upon this paper.

"This state of things continued, it is believed, for not less than six weeks, and not more than two months, for towards the end of

October Mr. Dell was once more in London. Since that time I have nothing more to relate."

Lord Brasted paused, lowered the paper and glanced up for an instant.

"Now, Mrs. Hamilton wishes me to be her spokesman in this matter, so I will ask Mr. Dell to — to consider me in that light. Mrs. Hamilton desires me to say — she will correct me if I am wrong in any statement that I make — she desires me to say first that she does not consider a man who has lived in this way to be a proper husband for her daughter, and she wishes to know whether Mr. Dell admits or denies these statements that I have laid before him."

He lifted his eyes as he ended, and looked straight at the two men.

For a moment he was astonished at their motionlessness.

Christopher Dell, in his long yellow coat, stood like an image, his hands invisible at his sides, his face cut, as it were, out of yellowish wax, with closed lips, and bright, hard eyes like those of a mummy-case, unwinking and unflinching, staring straight upon him. The priest at his side was as still, with his hands clenched, and his face alive with emotion. It was he who was the first to break the horrible silence. He moved an inch or two forward, and his voice shook a little.

"Lord Brasted, both my friend and I decline to deal with you. I do not consider that you have acted properly. These things should have been laid first of all before Mr. Dell, if indeed you were justified in interfering at all. I say this to explain why I am going to address myself to Mrs. Hamilton."

"My dear sir —" began the other.

"You will kindly allow me to deal with this in my own way. . . . Mrs. Hamilton, I have this to say.

"I have known my friend here for many years. I know perfectly well — and he wishes me to say this — that his life has been gravely irregular. This story which Lord Brasted has gathered up so carefully is sufficiently true. He does not wish to deny it —"

"Well, then —" began the other once more.

The priest's eyes blazed, and he advanced a step.

"Have the goodness not to interrupt me again. I am speaking to Mrs. Hamilton. . . . He does not wish to deny it; it is sufficiently true, but I wish to add this: Mr. Dell repents more bitterly than I can describe. . . ."

Lord Brasted turned away with a little gesture.

"You need not sneer, sir," snapped the priest. "Mrs. Hamilton, I imagine, believes in repentance. I say that my friend repents bitterly, and as a proof that this is as I say, I will also ask leave to finish what Lord Brasted left unfinished. Mr. Dell left Paris without five pounds in his pocket. He deliberately, of his own free will, broke with the woman; there was no quarrel, but he left her and all that she had to offer; he made his way on foot to Calais, crossed over to England, walked up to London, and has been living there until last October earning his own bread. During this year he received more than a dozen letters from the woman in Paris begging him to return. He burned eleven of these letters unread. The first that she wrote I have brought with me today. Mr. Dell was often in want at this time. For eight days he was an inmate of the Marylebone Workhouse; this was in June last, and it can be verified by an application to the master. He was then paid for an article he had written, came out and took a room by himself. From this he was again turned out in October, and he came to me, after a night spent in the open — exactly as I should have come to him under similar circumstances.

"I do not know if Mrs. Hamilton desires, or can conceive, greater proofs of a sincere repentance than these. But I may add once more my own views. I thank God for the example of penitence that my friend has shown. Soon after his engagement was permitted I was with him, and he then professed himself willing to tell Miss Hamilton everything, if I thought it necessary. I told him there was no obligation to do so — that the past was past. It was by my advice, then — advice which I should certainly give again in the same case — that these facts were not made known six weeks ago.

"Also, for the last six weeks he has been living in my house, and I have nothing but good to relate of him.

"And I will add this last word. If it was my own sister that was in question, I should give her to be my friend's wife without an instant's hesitation."

His voice shook as he ended, and he fell back to his friend's side, trembling all over.

Lord Brasted turned back again from the fire and cleared his throat, but before he could speak Mrs. Hamilton by a sudden movement was on her feet, and facing the two friends.

As Lord Brasted looked at her, he had no longer any fear of her yielding.

She stood as taut as a steel rod, her hands clenched by her sides, her gray head upraised, and her face rigid and hard.

"Father Yolland," she cried, and her voice was as hard as her face, "Father Yolland, it is astonishing to me that you should dare to speak like this. I can only suppose you are blinded by your friendship with this man. I have always supposed that, as a clergyman, you had as great a horror —"

Dick sprang forward again and faced her.

"I have as great a horror," he cried back, "I loathe and detest it; but I have something else as well. Do you mean to say you understand nothing by forgiveness?"

"Forgiveness! I cannot understand you. If you mean God's —"

"I mean God's. I mean the Divine Charity that forgives you and me —"

"If you mean God's," she cried again, "I pray with all my heart that he may find it. He needs it."

There was a sudden movement, and Chris was a yard nearer, his hands upraised, his face contorted by something so frightful that the man on the raised hearth sprang off it to the floor believing that he was on the point of a spring.

"God's," screamed the convulsed man. "God's! Who is God? God?"

Then he dropped on his face, and a dreadful moaning began.

It was all done in an instant.

Even Lord Brasted felt himself thrill from head to foot; it was so appallingly unexpected and dramatic. He stood for a moment, trembling slightly, completely bewildered.

From the yellow heap on the floor by which the priest was kneeling came unintelligible sobs and moans. Thin hands snatched and tore at the blue carpet, and feet scraped on the floor behind.

"Chris! For God's sake. Chris! Stand up. What is it? What is it? Get something — run — get something; he is dying — Brasted, you damned brute!"

Then the priest was down again, talking rapidly, trying to lift the struggling thing on the floor,

Lord Brasted put a hand on the woman's arm, and tore at the bell with the other.

"Mrs. Hamilton, go away for five minutes. It's not fit. I'll come too. Father Yolland, we shall be in the dining room."

Then the two were gone, leaving the priest and his friend.

(2)

The two stood by the dining room fire without speaking for a full minute. Mrs. Hamilton was in front of the hearth, staring straight down into the red coals, her hands rising and falling mechanically from her skirt as if to catch the warmth. Lord Brasted leaned against the table, the paper still in his hand, wondering what on earth was the proper gambit. He was conscious that his hands were a little damp and slippery — no more.

She spoke suddenly, without turning round.

"Do you think we should send anyone —?"

He cleared his throat with a little effort.

"There is no need. I rang the bell. One of the men will be there. . . . You behaved magnificently my dear lady."

She said nothing to that, and after a pause he went on.

"It was very dramatic," he said. "We might have expected it."

"Is it a fit?" she asked in a low voice.

"Fit? No! He must have thought it out. He is a born actor. Didn't you notice that he didn't roll over? He was on his knees."

She was silent again.

"And then what he said!" went on the other. "It is all in keeping."

She turned a little, and glanced at him a moment; her lips moved, but she still said nothing. He was astonished by the pallor of her fine face, and the steady brightness of her eyes. Then she turned back, and so they stood.

Five minutes later the door opened suddenly, and Dick Yolland came in. He stood by the door, closing it behind him, but did not look at the two who turned to face him, and he spoke in an impersonal, passionless voice.

"He is better," he said. "He is sitting down. One of the men is with him."

"We will wait here," said Lord Brasted. "There is no need —"

The priest paid him no attention whatever.

"He says he will not go till he has seen Miss Annie," he went on, looking at Mrs. Hamilton.

"That is out of the question," she said sharply.

"I am giving you his message," went on the priest quietly. "He says he will not go until she tells him to go. Then he promises he will go quietly. Of course you can drag him out, but he will resist, and he will come back. He means what he says. He is perfectly desperate."

The woman turned to Lord Brasted.

"Well?" she said.

He laughed shortly.

"It is what I should have expected. You must not listen to him."

"For my part," went on the priest, "I will undertake that there shall be no violence. He will ask her if she agrees, and if she says yes, there will be an end. He will never trouble this house again. If not, it will be as I say."

Mrs. Hamilton looked at him a moment.

"You undertake that?"

"I undertake it."

"Very well —" she said, and put her hand on the bell.

Lord Brasted sprang forward.

"I implore you —"

She rang the bell.

"I cannot have a scene. You can trust Annie. You know what she thinks."

They stood without speaking until the man came in.

"Tell Jameson to ask Miss Annie to come down here — not to the morning room. Father Yolland, will you be so kind as to go back to your friend until we come in?"

Chris was as the priest had left him. He was in the upright chair now wheeled about where Mrs. Hamilton had sat five minutes before, his head thrown back against the carving, and his hands clenched, as hers had been, upon the knobs at the ends of the arms. His face was almost expressionless, except for his eyes that looked out unwinking and fixed as the priest came towards him. Behind his chair, greatly embarrassed, stood a footman holding a glass and decanter.

"You can go," said Dick briefly. "I will attend to Mr. Dell."

When the door had closed he laid his hand on one of his friend's, and spoke as if to a sick child, looking down compassionately on that mask of pain.

"She will be here presently. You must not frighten her. I have promised that you will not."

There was not a flicker of expression in response, and even in that moment the priest wondered how far Chris was genuine. His face was exactly that of an actor simulating splendid despair. His whole attitude seemed screwed into rigidity by an intense physical effort. There was no doubt that he was in agony, but it was doubtful how far the expression of that agony was natural.

The priest stood back and waited, as the minutes began to pass.

Dick had no theory at all as to what would be best to do when this last scene was over; he had not the smallest doubt as to what the answer would be. He only foresaw that he must get Chris out of the house and into the carriage; that they must drive home; that he must not leave his friend day or night till the crisis was past. Probably he would want watching for a long while

So he stood, listening to the tick of the French clock over the mantelpiece, staring at the sunlight that lay on the blue-bordered carpet, conscious of little but of an intense desire that all this should be over quickly.

Then the door opened; Chris rose to his feet, and stood first swaying, then motionless.

The three were in the room, not half-a-dozen strides away.

On the left stood the mother, who had entered first, and shrinking against her, with a face as white as paper, and eyes full of horror and misery stood the girl, in her dark brown morning-dress, her two hands held firmly by her mother's, and clasped by her other arm round the waist. Lord Brasted stood on the right, a little advanced before the others, a little pale too, but perfectly resolute and controlled; it seemed to the priest as if he were there for purposes of defense.

But Annie's face left no doubt as to what her answer would be. She was terrified beyond question, but there was something more than terror in her eyes; there was the kind of loathing there with which a timid child would look at a crushed toad, or a horrible crime. She stared so at the rigid yellow figure a moment, and then hid her eyes against her mother's shoulder.

So they stood in silence.

Then Chris's figure before the chair began to sway again slightly, and the priest moved out a step. But there was a swift gesture from the clenched hand in front, and the next instant his voice rang out, with an hysterical crack in it, but strong and virile enough.

"I will take my sentence from you. You are my only judge."

There was no yielding now in that voice, and it struck a note that lifted the whole affair to a less sordid plane. Dick was amazed at the sudden transition, and he saw that the three opposite were startled too.

Lord Brasted moved forward a half step and stood hesitating. Mrs. Hamilton lifted her head suddenly and stared, and Annie too was looking up now, with dilated eyes.

Chris straightened himself yet more, till his long coat hung in straight folds, and his head was up and defiant. There were half-a-dozen emotions in his voice, all at full stretch — passion, misery, fury, appeal, and a dramatic sense. Dick felt his hair tingle and the sweat prick his skin at the sound of it.

"You can save me or damn me," he cried. "But understand what you are doing."

"You blackguard," cried Brasted, all flushed with anger in an instant.

"Understand what you are doing!" rose the voice, shrill and shaking "I am either saved or damned. I wait for you to tell me which. Either I am your lover, or, when I leave this house, I go to hell."

Annie dropped her face again, and a long sobbing breath broke from her.

"Am I to go or stay?" he cried.

It was extraordinary how he dominated the room. To the priest's perceptions the three opposite seemed to shrink, to lose their significance. They were like dummy figures when an actor comes amongst them. They lost their semblance of reality. The room itself appeared no more than a setting in which the passion of one man alone lived; the sunlight, the sparkle of silver, the glow of color, were but accessories, stage-devices that had lost their point. He seemed to himself no more than a spectator.

"Am I to go or stay?" cried the hard voice once more.

A little movement broke out in the group opposite. The mother had dropped her head and was whispering in the girl's ear. Dick could hear the hiss of the sibilants. But the girl was sobbing violently, her whole body shook, and she could not speak.

It was surely some ghastly play, some over-realistic rehearsal. It was impossible that all those things should be true. This stiff, tragic figure in front, for these few instants the master of them all, could not be Chris who had laughed and posed and' pretended and laughed again with merry eyes a week ago.

Then the figure suddenly jerked in a spasm, as if it put out one more effort of energy, and as it did so, the girl, still with her face hidden, thrust out a thin repellent hand, and the moaning became intelligible.

"Go! Go! Go!" she sobbed, and sank into moaning again.

There was an instant, in spite of the low, piteous sound, when a hush seemed to envelop the priest. Then his ears sang and drummed, and a red mist blinded his eyes. . . .

Chris was speaking, and it seemed as if he was standing by the door, his voice was deadly quiet, and every syllable cut like a whip.

"I go then, where I have said; and I leave you and your God together. I would kill myself if I believed in Him, and tell Him what

I thought. You have done a great thing amongst you. You have damned a soul. . . . You, Father Yolland . . . I have no more to say to you. . . . — You have lied to me about God, and there is no more forgiveness for that than for anything else in this world. . . ."

The door was open now. Dick through a mist of tears could see a blur of light, and the yellow figure dark against it. He was aware that the other three had shrunk away to let the man past, but he could not move or speak.

. . . "I am thankful that I know the truth at last about God and man."

Then he was gone.

End of Part I

Part II

CHAPTER I

The Consulting Room

(I)

M rs. Hamilton sat out on the lawn beneath the great striped umbrella.

It was a really hot July day, and the sun was still high. Below the terrace the park fell away in a long smooth sweep of pale green and gold, broken by railed plantations, down to the cool shadow of the tall woods. All about her the flowerbeds murmured with bees, and butterflies like settling scraps of white and colored paper dipped and curtsied above the geraniums and mignonette. The long stately house had put out awnings like sleepy eyelids, and beneath them the windows were wide. A pigeon cooed from the roof, and a small fat dog snored on a promontory of the lady's dress.

Mrs. Hamilton looked very content and rather sleepy too, and she was expecting tea to make her more of the one, and less of the other. She would drive a little afterwards; the pony carriage was ordered for half-past five. She and Annie would drive together without the groom, and by the time that they got back Jack would have arrived from the station. It would be very nice to see Jack again; the poor boy needed some rest too. She had seen him last week, and he looked thoroughly tired.

She was extremely glad that the season, for her at least, had come to an end, although she had had a satisfactory two months of it. Annie had come out wonderfully. Last year there had been the unfortunate incident of that Mr. Dell who had behaved so badly, and Annie was listless and unintelligent in consequence. That first season had not been a success. But this second one was a very different affair; two or three younger sons had been very attentive, besides poor Mr. Summerfield, the minor poet, whom Annie had treated so cruelly. But then Annie had had enough of that kind of thing, and a burned child fears the fire. Next year they would do better; it was not to be a question of younger sons then; she would take a larger house, there would be four balls and perhaps a piece of red carpet at one of them.

Of course Mrs. Hamilton did not care in the least for that kind of thing she told herself; she only wished to see Annie married to a good man, not positively penniless, and a title would add grace — it was not at all essential. These things were very empty; the real thing was the dear child's happiness, as she had assured Mr. Stirling when he came to call yesterday; she could not understand how mothers could plot and scheme like poor dear Lady Scrymgeour. The season, balls, German princes, and so on, were no more than the unfortunate accompaniments of a necessary process. She would far sooner live in the country — God's country — in a simple way, and leave all else to guidance. Yes, Providence was very kind. He had intervened almost miraculously eighteen months ago, and, through Mr. Rolls' extraordinary tact, had succeeded in restoring Annie's equanimity. That September week over at Foxhurst had done wonders. What a very clever and good man Mr. Rolls was! She would never feel anything but gratitude towards him.

How sweet the country was! — (God's country.)

Mrs. Hamilton sighed contentedly, looking with half-closed eyes across the terrace down to the rolling park. She never felt so happy as when at home; things were so simple there; there was just the pleasant little round of duties, the company of her daughter, peace and prosperity. And she had undergone a great mental conversion during the last few months. Unconventionality seemed unsafe when put into action; it was all very well in thought, in fact it was the spice of life; but it must be a philosophy to think by instead of a rule to act by. Even for thought too there was something pleasing in a wholesome normality acquiesced in not because of a lack of personal originality, but because it had been deliberately discovered to be the highest art of living — it resembled the verification of a platitude. The little country-church for example — how sweet that was! — She had grown really fond of it. Of course Mr. Stirling was rather tiresome sometimes, but then he had been remarkably sensible in their great trouble. He had pointed out to Annie so clearly that sometimes great difficulties were permitted only in order to strengthen character — a kind of inoculation, he had said almost apologetically. He had quoted a little Tennyson, too, with fervor and felicity, about "dead selves" and "higher things." Yes, his influence had been wholly good, if somewhat trite. When the first shock was over Annie had found refuge in religion all through the spring; she was at church morning and evening, and there was a dreamy introspective look in the dear child's eyes that had promised great serenity to follow. Of course she did not like to talk about Mr. Dell — it had all been so painful and shocking — but she had come to her mother at last, after a week at the seaside before going up to town, and had said, with such a beautiful look, that she had found herself at last able to pray for him, and Mr. Rolls had completed the cure.

His treatment had been very different to the Vicar's, but of course he could not be expected to be as highly trained. He had just told Annie to leave the past alone — that the future was her business — that people were intended to develop along their own lines, and not along those of others — so Annie had reported. She said that he had not been at all brutal, as she had half-feared. Of course he was unconventional, but Mrs. Hamilton liked that. Conventions were so dull and tiresome she told herself. That was the one blot on Mr. Stirling, though a blot that had served her well last year. They were the garments worn by common sense, and, like all garments, serviceable enough when used as clothing, utterly irritating when paraded without their proper body. Mr. Rolls lacked conventions, but he certainly had a naked kind of common sense, sometimes disconcerting but always reliable.

She was rather interested in this train of thought, and believed it to be epigrammatic; she had been told more than once how sharp she was, and how incisive, and, in a well-bred sort of manner was pleased to be told so. That was exactly what she wished to be, unconventional in thought and word, but positively rather than negatively, sensible, stately, friendly, and incisive.

So she did not notice Annie following the man who carried the tea-urn on its tray, until she was close upon her.

"My dear child," she said, "how well you look! I have had a meditation."

Annie smiled contentedly, sat down, and began to tickle the inside of the fat little dog's hind leg with the end of a lace-fringed parasol.

She did look extremely well in her white cotton dress, marvelously innocent and fresh, with sufficient pallor to imply a soul, and sufficient warmth to demonstrate a healthy body. She had been in the country just a week, and a charming freckle or two proclaimed that she had spent her time suitably

"What was your meditation, Mamma?"

"Only how nice everything is, and how pleased I am!" murmured Mrs. Hamilton.

Annie nodded gravely, and withdrew her parasol as the fat little dog kicked and grunted.

"I entirely agree," she said. "I love it more than ever."

Then the cucumber sandwiches came out.

"What about a call on Mr. Rolls?" asked her mother presently. "I think it would be graceful."

Annie smiled again, very prettily.

"Yes, I do like him," she said. "He is such a sensible man. I shall never forget what he said last year. I can't think why people don't like him."

"Of course he is very odd," went on the other, "and some people can't see below that. He is entirely unconventional, as I was thinking just now."

"But that is what is so nice. You know I am sure he doesn't care for that lovely old house; he never says anything about it, and hates to show people over."

Mrs. Hamilton sat silent.

"Mamma, do tell me. Is all that is said about him true?"

"What is said about him, my dear?" asked the other a little coldly.

"Oh, you know — about his gambling, and his breaking his wife's heart and so on?"

Her mother sat silent again a moment before she answered.

"I don't know, my darling," she said at last. "I know it is said —
I should think it might be possible. I — I don't know what to think."

She spoke with such an odd hesitation that her daughter looked
at her surprised.

"Mamma, are you — are you at all afraid of Mr. Rolls?"

"Of course not," came back rather sharply.

"Oh."

Annie sat still, looking out along the length of the lawn and
flowerbeds, but she did not see them; she was wondering whether
her mother's last words were quite true. For herself, she was afraid
of him. He had not said a word last year that was not perfectly
courteous and kind; more than that, he had really soothed away
her terrors and quieted her, telling her that she must not fret about
what she could not help, and somehow making that platitude appear both true and new. But she had an odd feeling that there was
a great deal behind all this, and she could not imagine what it was.
He lived a very ordinary life, writing a good many letters, walking
alone for the most part, never seeming in a hurry. She had walked
with him a good deal in the gardens — knowing quite well that she
was there for the purposes of a nerve cure, and being rather pleased
with the fact; and her life had never seemed quite the same since
that week. Things appeared more real, small things more large, large
things less significant. He had neither cut nor untied the knot; he
had touched it only, and it had fallen apart.

It was all very mysterious.

"What's the matter, Annie?"

"Nothing."

"Are you thinking about Mr. Rolls?"

She smiled, showing a double line of very white teeth.

"Yes, Mamma."

"Well?"

"I don't know, Mamma. Who are all those odd people who stay
with him?"

The elder woman looked at her daughter doubtfully.

"His friends, I suppose," she said shortly, and stood up. "There
are the wheels."

It was a delightful drive through the lanes to Foxhurst in the evening sunshine, and the two talked comfortably of small things — the new pony that went so well with the old one that Annie wished to have a pink ribbon on one and a blue on the other; the new curate who, Mrs. Hamilton remarked (and noted for use on another occasion) had all the qualities of a poker except its occasional warmth; the leak in the hot water cistern; a question of tulle; an entirely new and subtle interpretation of a text by Mr. Stirling on the previous Sunday, that hitherto had appeared to bear a crudely obvious meaning — until at last Foxton village was traversed, a vast yellow brick house on the right was passed, and Foxhurst towers appeared at the end of the short lime avenue.

An elderly man took off his soft felt hat to the ladies as they wheeled in.

"That's the new chaplain," whispered Annie. "A monk, I think. He doesn't look like one. . . . Oh! What a place it is!"

Two slender old brick towers showed before them like a castle in a tale, linked by a battlemented room over a wide high arch. To right and left looked stately rows of windows, diamond-paned, barred, out of a high wall once red, now nearly a pale orange with time and lichen. Through the arch as they approached the bridge now welded for ever by peace and civilization, showed a wide graveled court with a great lead pump in the center.

As the ponies' feet rang hollow on the bridge Annie looked to right and left at the wide deep moat as still as a mirror — a mirror of bewildering green and blue and rose, from the heavy elms and the evening July sky, itself clear brown water, lying fifty yards to this side and that, and turning in a broad angle at the outward sloping corners of the house that ran down into it.

Within the court, as they crossed it at a trot, the great house rose high against the sky to right and left — the same rows of windows, all open, through which looked the upper half of portraits hung in the shallow corridor beyond, dark oak, gorgeous paper; while in front lay the long low red brick entrance corridor, broken by a squat tower, where the great hall had once reared its lantern. Over the parapet to the left rose up the western window of the old chapel, surmounted by a small Latin cross.

"I had forgotten," murmured Annie again, as the ponies wheeled and drew up. "It is like a dream."

"Yes, Mr. Rolls was at home," said the grave man at the door; "would the ladies come in?"

A second man appeared, to hold the ponies' heads, and the two went in up the steps and turned to the right through the little parqueted entrance hall — absurdly new, for it was only built in the days of the First George — and so into the older part.

It was a long, uneven corridor through which they went, carpeted with some heavy stuff, unnoticeable to both sight and touch; a row of windows on the right looked directly into the court, while on the left a door or two and a flight of old steps with slender carved banisters, gave entrance to the living rooms and first floor. There were portraits everywhere, ecclesiastics, kings, great women, children, each looking out in the fashion of his day, and three or four great old chests.

Then a door was thrown open before them, and their names were called out.

Annie looked again with interest, as she always did, at the tall lean man, brown-faced and gray-haired, who pushed aside his chair, and came towards them.

He was already half dressed for dinner, wearing a velvet coat over his evening clothes, and appeared to have been writing letters, for his table was covered with paper, and an unfinished sheet lay on his blotting book.

He said nothing at all as he shook hands, but that, Annie remembered, was his way; she rather liked it. But her mother began at once a murmur of general talk.

"It was such a charming evening. We were obliged to come. We only came down last week. I hope we are not disturbing you at this time."

"Indeed, no; I am always at home in this room."

The girl remembered then the little mysterious room upstairs which she had never entered, whence twice only during her visit her host had been summoned. She had learned after a couple of days that he was officially not at home when he was there; but that he was always accessible here.

How pleasant his voice was too! It was always a delight to hear it; it was rather low, and particularly virile, and seemed very slightly to affect the throat of the listener. Yet it always gave her a sense of security and strength.

Annie sat down, and looked cautiously about her, as her mother began the proper kind of conversation.

There were the four portraits that she remembered; the bearded man in the ruff over the fireplace, the stout ruddy Georgian woman between the bookcase and the door into the corridor; the boy, killed at Naseby, on the wall opposite the fire, and the fair-haired girl in mid-Victorian dress over the writing table whom she understood to have been this man's wife. Yes, she looked innocent enough to have her heart broken.

The rest of the room too had a mysterious interest, for it was so little modernized; paneling ran from floor to ceiling on all sides, covered, as were also the two doors, with linen pattern, the ceiling was crossed by a couple of great beams; a low bookcase ran along from the hearth to the old press, all black wood and scroll-work that stood opposite the window. The writing table too was attractive; the edges were long worn into bluntness; it appeared to be supported by about seven legs. The floor was polished, with three or four mats lying upon it; there were half-a-dozen tall-backed chairs besides those in which she and her mother sat. It was certainly a perfect room of its kind, and its perfection was enhanced by the square-paned window hung with painted coats, beyond which lay the nearer trees of the park, a stretch of grass and the mellow distance.

And the owner of it all seemed appropriate, in spite of his apparent detachment from it. There was an air of age and carved oak about his thin brown sharp-profiled face and gray hair, of stateliness and strength about his upright attitude, his immovability, his slow virile voice; and with the gossip about him still before her mind, there was a pleasing parallel between the house that had passed through such storms of history, and the man about whom floated such rumors.

Her train of thought was suddenly broken.

"Annie, my dear, you would like to go round the house again, I am sure. Mr. Rolls, might she —?"

The girl knew perfectly well that she was to be under discussion, but she did not mind that; it was interesting, so she stood up cheerfully.

"We shall all go?" said the tall old man standing up.

"No, no, if you please. I want to talk to you. Annie, my darling, you will find your way, won't you? May she, Mr. Rolls? Come back in a quarter of an hour."

When the door had closed, the elder woman turned again, determined not to be garrulous.

"I am so much satisfied," she said. "The child is perfectly herself again. You did wonders with her last year."

Mrs. Hamilton was fully aware that she was not at her best with this old man. It was easy enough to be incisive and authoritative and unconventional in her own house, but it was not so easy here. She found herself anxious to please, deferential in her manner and just a little timid.

Mr. Rolls bowed a little.

"I am so thankful you told her what you did; it was just what she wanted," went on Mrs. Hamilton, struggling for complete self-possession.

"She is happy, then?" asked the man quietly.

"She is perfectly happy, and as simple as a child still. That trouble last year seems to have left no mark on her; she is as natural as ever."

"I understand."

"You do think it would have been the greatest mistake to have allowed the matter to go on? Of course it was impossible."

Mr. Rolls dropped his eyes,

"It would have been — the greatest mistake."

"I am so glad you think so. Of course there was only one opinion. And she felt as strongly as I did."

The other nodded meditatively two or three times.

"And as for Mr. Dell —" she went on. "I simply do not know what to say. When I think how I was taken in!"

Mr. Rolls looked up.

"I beg your pardon?" she asked.

"Taken in?" he said.

"Yes, you know he told me a great deal about himself; I thought him very — very frank and all that, and then I found out he had not told me a hundredth part —"

"I see. But surely you would have known that."

"I'm afraid I don't understand."

The other leaned back in his chair.

"A spendthrift, Mrs. Hamilton, never reveals all his debts."

She shifted in her chair.

"Of course —"

The other went on as if she had not spoken.

"We must not expect people to do what they cannot; neither Mr. Dell, nor your daughter."

It was said so quietly that she did not quite understand.

"Nor yourself, nor myself, Mrs. Hamilton," he ended.

She was completely bewildered. But it was a comfort that he had included himself.

"Then — then what happens to responsibility?"

"We are responsible for doing what we can," he said gravely.

This was very odd conversation; it was either the deadliest platitude, or the most startling novelty; and she was not sure which.

"Then — then what is the proper treatment?" she asked vaguely, hoping that she was making the right shot.

It seemed that she had; for the melancholy eyes instantly turned upon her full, and the drooping eyelids lifted. There was a new ring in his voice too.

"Ah! One must be nurtured and encouraged; the other must be broken to pieces. One is weak and another deformed."

"And how are we to know? And — and what am I?" she added on a sudden impulse.

She felt that she was being intelligent, but the feeling waned a little as he turned full on to her.

"Do you wish me to answer, Mrs. Hamilton?"

"Why, yes, of course."

When Annie came back from her wanderings ten minutes later she perceived that something had happened. Her mother's eyes were very bright, and her cheeks flushed, and she was sitting very upright indeed on the edge of her chair.

The tall old man was very grave opposite her, leaning his head on his hand; but he stood up alert and upright as she came in, and asked her courteously how she had fared.

Her mother was certainly cold at her goodbyes, and a little defiant, and said nothing at all until they were clear of the park.

"What were you talking about, Mamma?" asked the girl curiously.

Mrs. Hamilton whipped the ponies briskly, and set her lips tight.

"Nothing at all, my dear."

(2)

When the ladies had gone, John Rolls turned to the butler.

"The dogcart is gone?" he said.

"Yes, sir, half-an-hour ago."

He nodded and went back, walking very slowly through the hall, turned to the left, passed along the corridor, and pushed open one leaf of a heavy door. He closed it behind him, genuflected, and sat down in a chair to his right, laying his hands along his thighs, and so remained motionless.

The chapel was full of the soft evening light streaming from overhead through the west window and falling on the square-cut granite altar, the bronze door of the tabernacle and the round apse behind. It was dead silent within here, and the chirp of the birds without and the distant cries from the village seemed to be a separate affair altogether.

The man himself sat like an image, his hatchet face lifted, his lean brown fingers reaching to his knees, and his feet together. And so he remained.

At the sudden echo of hoofs from beneath the arch on the other side of the court, half-an-hour later, he moved and drew a long

breath, rose up, genuflected once more, and went out, signing himself as he did so, and he was on the steps as the dogcart drove up.

"Come in, Father," he said.

Together he and Father Yolland went along the corridor, wheeled
to the right, passed along again, still in silence, and went into the
sitting room Mr. Rolls shut the door.

"Now," he said, "give me the fact; we will talk after dinner."

The priest looked worn and anxious, and his snub nose added
pathos.

"Dell is in London," he said.

"Have you seen him?"

"No."

"Very well." He looked at his watch. "You have twenty minutes
for dressing."

Dick gave him a quantity of small news during dinner, of not
much importance to either of them; and the men came and went
behind their chairs like intelligent shadows.

At the clink of coffee cups in the doorway, Mr. Rolls stood up.

"You have finished your wine, Father? Coffee is in my room."

There was no appearance of haste or interest in the old man's
face as he sedately took a cup of coffee, and pushed the little spirit
lamp over to the priest. Then he stood up and went to the hearth,
holding his cup and saucer, and facing the other as he sat in the
chair by the writing table.

"Now, if you please —"

Dick sighed, looked straight in the other's melancholy eyes a
moment, and then began.

"It was this morning I heard. I met Brandiston — you don't
know him, sir, I think? He told me that he had seen Chris go into a
boarding house in Westminster — I've got the address. He let himself in with a key, so I suppose he lives there. That is absolutely all.
So I sent the wire, as you told me, and followed it up."

"Did Mr, Dell see this man?"

"No."

"How was he dressed?"

Dick smiled wearily.

"Oh, smartly. That proves nothing."

"Ah! And his writing? Have you seen any of his work in the papers?"

The priest hesitated.

"I don't know. A fortnight ago I thought that perhaps one article on the Olympians might be his. I wrote to the editor; it was the Westminster, I think, and was told politely that there was no information for me."

"Yes?"

"I dare say it wasn't his, either. He writes just like — like everybody else of his sort — purple and scarlet, you know."

"And that's all?"

The priest nodded.

"Absolutely all. I haven't heard a word since. I told you how he disappeared."

"I remember."

"I wrote to the address of the woman in Paris — three times altogether, I think — and got no answer."

"Yes."

Mr. Rolls emptied his cup, set it on a chair, and turned again to the priest.

"Shall we go out? It will be very pleasant out of doors, I think."

Between the entrance-corridor and the moat lay a broad, sloping strip of turf, and at the edge of the water ran a long gravel path, closed by a seat at either end, set in a recess of laurels.

They walked up and down here two or three times before either spoke, under the radiant evening sky in which glimmered half-a-dozen tiny jewels; the air was full of the clamor of rooks, and the scent of miles of grass and flowers. On one side rose up the house, the line of red brick corridor pierced with windows, and finishing in the chapel at one end and the corner of the great salon at the other running down into the water below and rising to a square tower above. On the other side lay the moat, an oily mirror of rosy sky, broken only by the cautious circles of the fish sucking down supper. Beyond that again stretched the flat park, rising a mile away with the slopes and woods of the Amplefield estate.

Then suddenly the elder man spoke.

"I supposed it was this," he said. "The Hamiltons were here this afternoon."

"Yes?"

"Those things always fall together, if you watch. You must go and see him."

"He will refuse me."

"Your name is not necessary. Ask for his room."

"And then?"

"That is all for the present."

"But we must be prepared —"

"Certainly. That is why you are here.

Dick was silent. He still felt rather bewildered with the rush of town, the sudden shock of the news, and the anxious journey. But the country air and the evening, and above all the presence of this curious old man, so extremely quiet and strong, who walked and talked so precisely — all this was beginning to soothe him. He waited confidently.

"Well, Father?"

"I was waiting for you, sir; I thought you said —"

"Have you any proposal?"

Dick shook his head.

"And you wish me to make one?"

"If you please."

The old man was silent for a moment.

"This is a tentative offer then. But I do not make it positively."

"I understand, sir."

"It is that you should bring him here, and leave him — leave him entirely to me."

"I suppose I may come and see him?"

"No, Father; you are not the man for him."

It was so brutally unexpected that the priest winced, audibly.

"You are wounded, Father? But remember you have failed."

"But was it my fault then?" asked the priest piteously.

Mr. Rolls indicated a seat with one hand.

"Sit down, Father. Light a cigarette, if you please. . . No, it was not your fault; nor was it Miss Annie's. It is chiefly a question of temperament. Innocence and love are not sufficient."

Dick sat still, strangely moved, but he scarcely knew why. It was partly the intoxicating evening air, the fresh scent of rushes and water, the mystical light. Partly too it was the presence of this man — so true to type in his clean-cut, well-bred face, his precise clothes, his attitude as he sat easily back; so peculiar in his deep, steady eyes, the rigid, down turned mouth, and his odd vibrant voice. And then those words — "Innocence and love are not sufficient" — Dick told himself for the hundredth time that this was his superior in everything except matters hierarchical.

"Please tell me, sir," he said at last.

"You really wish it?"

Dick nodded, horribly afraid.

"He needs one thing, just as you and I do, Father. I need not tell you what that is. But the way by which Grace comes, is another matter, and in our hands. That way may be Love or Wrath. And I think it to be wrath here. Remember he has lived a gross and filthy life."

"Well, sir?" Dick's voice trembled as he spoke.

"This man must be broken to pieces, I think."

Dick half-rose and sat down again.

"Ah!" he cried.

The other turned his face questioningly.

"Yes, Father? You wish me to say what I think? Is it not so?"

"Yes," whispered the priest.

"Well, then. We might give him a child to care for. With some I should do that. But not for him. It is too late for that."

"May I speak, sir?" asked the priest breathlessly.

"It is what I wish."

"My dear sir," began Dick volubly, with a sensation that he was pleading for his friend's life. "He has had a terrible time. I can't explain how much he has suffered — he is as sensitive as a child! His soul is. . is bleeding. I — I swear that it is! That is his excuse. I never meant —"

The other looked at him with steady melancholy eyes, and Dick stopped.

"Yes, Father?"

"Mr. Rolls, I should never have wired today, if I had thought —
if I had dreamed you would think all this. . . He — he needs love
and . . . and tenderness — and — and building up. Of course I
don't forget his sins: but for God's sake don't say —"

"Yes, Father?"

"Oh, my God! Don't you understand? Don't you understand?"
cried Dick passionately.

Dick could see his profile, thin and severe against the evening
sky, the chin a little tilted, the heavy brows like thatch over the eyes,
the tight, down-turned lips together. It looked utterly heartless,
and he repented with all his might that he had come down here
tonight. Why had he not gone to Chris as his heart told him? He
felt helpless in this presence.

Then the thin lips opened.

"This is my suggestion, Father. It is the best I have to make. Do
you wish for my reasons?"

Dick swallowed in his throat.

"If you please, sir."

"The man is *poseur*," said the other serenely. "I mean by that
that his character is encrusted. That then must be all broken
away. It cannot be melted now; it is too late. It has been fused,
and has hardened again. It cannot be fused again. Do you follow me, Father?"

Dick laughed without merriment.

"Breaking, sir! And who will do the breaking?"

The sharp profile turned into a thin, full face, and the melancholy eyes were on him.

"I will do that," he said.

"How? How?"

"You can leave that in my hands."

"But he will not stay?"

"I shall make him."

"How?"

The other was silent a moment; then he turned.

"I shall first appeal to his pride," he said.

Dick felt utterly helpless before this unsmiling, unfrowning, courteous cruelty. He sat paralyzed as regards actions or words, and his thought ran round like a mouse in a cage, seeking escape. The darkness seemed to have fallen very quickly; it was coming on, veil by veil. There were a dozen stars out by now; a window in the corridor brightened suddenly as a lamp was lit. It was all as inexorable as this cruel, tranquil atmosphere that had closed so quickly on him. He felt himself shivering a little. Then a night-insect blundered, humming, against his sleeve, and he started violently.

"Well, Father?" said the quiet voice.

"Give me time," whispered Dick. "I must pray; I don't know what to say. . . . It's impossible — impossible."

"Shall we say tomorrow morning then, after Mass? When must you leave, Father Yolland?"

Dick stammered out that he must lunch at Amplefield, and go up to town in the afternoon.

"Very well then. You will allow me to serve you?"

Dick bowed.

"It is a semi-double, I think. May I recommend a Mass of the Holy Ghost?"

CHAPTER II

A Hospital Letter

(I)

B olton Street, Westminster, looked at its very worst when the priest turned into it about eleven o'clock in the morning. Behind him lay the unlovely thoroughfare through which he had come, swept by a dry, hot, unwholesome air, full of the smell of cabbages, fried fish, and unclean humanity, clamorous with shrill children and abusive women — (all as has been told a hundred times by as many chroniclers); and here was Bolton Street, as stagnant as the Pit, in the blaze of the July sun, glaring with white pavements, airless and dreary. Tall house-fronts rose against the sky on either side, set with square windows, suggestive of nothing but conventionality and a terrible kind of social pride, as of a retired tradesman striving to conceal his past. It had not even the grace of bare poverty.

This ambition was more than apparent in the front of number three where the priest presently found himself. From the two windows on either side of the front door looked out lace curtains pinned together; in one was a chessboard table, half covered by a wool mat; in the other the back of a mahogany chair allowed a dining room table to be seen, where no doubt the boarders sat three times a day, in the solemn gloom beyond. There was a brass plate on the door, inscribed with the name "Mrs. Perch" in elegant italics.

Dick pulled the bell, and turned round to wait, listening to the jangle in the area below, and aware that a face crowned by a cap had peeped instantly from the first floor window. He stood staring out disconsolately at the houses opposite, the hot, empty pavements; half hearing the broken murmur from Great Peter Street, and trying to rehearse what he was going to say.

There had been of course no resisting the imperious man. Yesterday morning the priest had said Mass, as he had been asked, and had yielded helplessly half-an-hour before the dogcart came round. He had yielded, he told himself, because there was nothing else to do; it was impossible to leave Chris in London, yet he could not go to him without a proposal ready.

He had determined to be friendly and natural, to refuse to see any significance in his friend's silence and avoidance of his company, to ask no questions beyond those generally necessary to sociability, and to meet any dramatic poses by an inability to understand them. He would not play dominoes any more with this man; he would disregard openings and play his own game. He would even refuse to allow his own pity to dominate him; pity would come later and in private. John Rolls must be trusted utterly for the present.

There was a sound of footsteps within and the priest turned round.

"Mr. Dell?" he said interrogatively.

The shabby maid looked at him doubtfully, and Dick was aware that someone was listening from overhead.

"I don't know —" she began; "he said?"

"That's all right," said the priest mounting the step. "I know all about that. Which is his room? I'll go up."

"Name, sir, please."

"Oh! I'm an old friend," said Dick decisively. "Which is his room?"

He had pushed past her by now, but she still stood looking dubiously at his long coat and clerical collar. Dick put his foot on the lowest step of the interior staircase, half-conscious through dazzled, sun-tired eyes of the dingy, genteel hall, its marbled walls, its linoleum carpet, and the glass of dusty birds on the mahogany side table.

"Third floor front — opposite the stairs," she said hesitatingly.

A capped head protruded over the banisters as he went up.

"If you please, sir," said a sharp voice.

The priest went on until he faced the speaker, and saw, beneath a bracket holding an Infant Samuel, a lean old woman, with magenta ribbons in her cap, eyeing him severely.

"Mr. Dell," he said, conscious of the advantage that the three steps gave her.

"He can't see no one."

Dick attempted geniality.

"I'm an old friend," he said. "Er — and a clergyman."

This went home to some extent, and the old lady drew back a little, though not enough to let him pass. In the pause he was aware of the sound of frizzling far below him, and the pungent smell of burned fat.

"He can't see no one," she said again. "He's a writing gentleman, and is not to be disturbed before dinnertime."

"I'll take the risk," said Dick pleasantly.

"D'you come from St. John's, sir?" she asked sharply.

"No, no, Mrs. Perch. I'm an old friend. Which is his room, please?"

Her lips pursed themselves.

"Name, please."

"Father Yolland," said Dick desperately, trying to speak low; he was terribly afraid Chris would hear his voice.

The words went home like a bullet, and Dick instantly perceived the advantage in her aghast face. He tried to look sacerdotal, and she shrank back yet further as he came up.

"I'll take the risk," he said again, and went past her, delighted at the conservatism of the lower middle classes; no doubt the old lady expected an explosion, or at least a whiff of sulfur. He could see her through the banisters eyeing his legs.

There was an indescribably dreary view from the landing on the second flight, of pale brick house backs discolored by smoke, an invalid tree or two below him, and, above, an array of chimney pots, all sordid and unsuggestive against the hot, glaring sky.

The interior of the house, too, showed a diminuendo of gentility as he went up, yet it was no nearer to graceful poverty; the marbled walls had given place to a material resembling gray blotting-paper divided into Cyclopean blocks, the mahogany banisters to others composed of deal that hardly did more than pretend to the illusion that they, like the walls, were cut from expensive Italian quarries. There were no dusty birds here; there was not room for them. It was really incredible that Christopher Dell should be the minotaur of this labyrinth of hideousness; it was the kind of place, rather, where professors of phrenology should live.

The priest's head turned the last corner, with the smell of burned fat rising like incense about him, and the last landing became visible. There was a door on his left, the foot of the attic stairs on his right, with a table, a tin candlestick, and an enameled slop-pail on the floor, and immediately in front the second door.

Dick was astonished at his own excitement. He had not seen Chris for eighteen months, and until two days before had not known whether he were alive or dead. He had vanished after the last interview at Hinton Hall; Dick had followed him out too late, and had seen him disappear into the woods without turning his head; and the next news he had had of him was at a little station five miles away. There had been no trace of him in London; the letters sent to Paris had been absorbed there into silence; there had been no answer to advertisements. That was absolutely all that he knew for certain.

And now here he was within five yards.

The priest crossed the landing almost on tiptoe, and stood an instant listening before he tapped. There was no sound from within; only a faint whiff of tobacco-smoke stole out to mingle with other smells. It reassured him, and he tapped.

There was no answer; and he tapped again.

"Avan-ti-i," sounded in a head-voice; and then, "Come!"

Dick could not restrain one large quivering smile; it was certainly Chris; no one but he could pretend to be so denationalized. Then the smile died, as his heart began to rap imperiously at the base of his throat.

He opened the door, and went very softly in, smiling tremulously.

"Well, old man?" he said.

(2)

It was a dismal little room by nature, but grace had informed it. Dick was aware of a bed on the left covered with a creaseless red blanket, a chest of drawers at its foot ranged with shining instruments and a looking glass — on the right stood an easy chair without an antimacassar with its back towards him; there was a square of carpet in the middle of the room, and a table in the window. Sitting at this was the figure of a man in shirtsleeves, who turned round with uplifted pen as the priest spoke.

There was one moment of complete silence. Then Chris pushed back his chair, and stood, one hand poised, with the pen still in it, on his writing table, the other ready for gesture, with outstretched fingers.

He was certainly older; his hair had retired a little on his temples, and on the left side above his ear where the light fell on it, it was slightly streaked with gray. But his poise was the same — perfectly upright, with projecting chin thrown up and forward, and a severe cynicism in his eyes. His trousers fell from waist to ankle without a wrinkle to break the perpendicular; his waistcoat was unbuttoned, and showed a neat clip holding his tie to the edge of his shirt front. He wore exactly the air of an actor confronted with a mysterious and sinister stranger who arrives in a snowstorm.

The priest shut the door.

"Well, old man," he said again, "how are *you*?"

Chris cleared his throat.

"To what may I attribute —" he began.

(Yes, Dick reflected, that was precisely the expected opening.)

"Brandiston told me you were here. I thought I'd look you up. May I sit down?"

He advanced towards the easy chair, and Chris turned stiffly, still facing him.

He was obviously thinking how it was possible to assault a friend who would not cross blades or cry "on guard."

Dick did not venture to put out a hand; he felt as if he were treading on eggs; so he parted his long coattails, sat down, laying his hat on the floor, and took out a pocket-handkerchief to wipe his face.

"My word! Chris, you are hot here."

The other stood as still as an image. Dick understood that the attitude represented the paralysis of astonishment.

"You look surprised," he said. "What's the matter? Why didn't you —"

"Matter!" cried the other. "I am amazed at such — such —"

"Such what? Didn't you know I was in town still? Why didn't you look me up?"

Chris laid his pen down deliberately, and Dick thought he was on the point of folding his arms; but he only clasped his waistcoat convulsively with one hand.

"You come here —" he cried.

"Why not?" asked the priest. "I'd have come sooner if I'd known—"

"You come here?"

Chris licked lips supposed to be dry, and swallowed noisily in his throat.

"Look here, old man. Have you got anything against me?"

Chris sat down heavily and passed a hand over his brow.

"Against you? Against you?" he began; but the dramatic energy was waning; it needed the deliberate spur of the will. The other saw that.

"May I smoke?" said Dick abruptly, drawing out his case; he thought that for very pity's sake he must allow his friend an interval for transition. He struck a match thoughtfully on the fender, trying to prevent his hands from trembling, lit his cigarette, and drew a long breath or two of smoke. He adjured himself vigorously in his heart not to give in; he must refuse every cue.

"Now then, Chris, for the Lord's sake tell me what's the matter. Why didn't you answer my letters? I suppose you were in France, weren't you?"

"My God!"

"Yes, I thought so," went on the priest, carefully looking out at the chimney pots through the window, and affecting to watch the movements of a cat amongst them. "And when did you come back?"

There was no answer to this. Chris's cry upon his Maker had been uttered with a sudden gesture of both hands; now he was grasping the knobs of his chair-arms, and staring severely upon the friend who would not meet his eyes.

"Look here, old man. Are you very busy? I've got an invitation for you."

Chris's lip "curled" again.

"Say that again," he cried.

"Certainly. An invitation."

"Well?"

"From Foxhurst. Old Rolls wants to see you."

There was a silence.

Dick was aware that a pair of glittering eyes were supposed to be reading him through and through; so he contemplated the imaginary cat with even greater zeal.

"Well? What are your engagements? Are you on the *Saturday* still?"

Dick knew perfectly well he was not; he had received an indignant expostulation from the editor, eighteen months before, asking where Mr. Dell had hidden himself; but it served its purpose of giving him something to say.

Chris rose with great dignity, and regarded him piercingly.

"Look here. I don't know how you got here, nor what the devil you came for. I thought I was explicit enough last time. Shall I say it again?"

The priest stood up abruptly too; he knew that his self-control was ebbing like a spring tide, and he felt he must meet his friend before he lost it altogether. The other's voice had a crack that was not all art.

"No, Chris, for God's sake, don't."

There was one instant of silence. Then Chris wheeled about, dropped upon his knees and burst out sobbing, his face hidden in his hands.

For a moment the priest hesitated, looking at the shaking shoulders, the neat waist, and the beautiful trousers. He felt the shock of antipathy at this exhibition break on him like a wave.

Then he drove it back, summoned up all the sentimentality he possessed, and with one step was on his knees by him, his arm across the heaving shoulders.

"Dear man!" he said, hearing his own voice break, partly with shame, partly with real emotion, and his eyes filled with tears.

It was three or four minutes before either spoke. Dick watched the chimney pots against the glaring sky swim into clearness again, heard the chatter of sparrows beneath the eaves, and smelled the vapor of burned fat ooze through the door; and every one of the details was incalculably more distinct and objective than this thin body beneath his arm, gradually sobbing itself into quietness. Then it made a movement, the arms writhed out from beneath the bent head, reached across the table and hung limp appealing hands there, and the forehead rested on the sheet of half-finished manuscript.

Yes, that was a pose too — the attitude of weary and contrite exhaustion; yet the priest knew that if he allowed that fact to influence even the tones of his voice, all would be to do over from the beginning.

"Dear man," he murmured again, and pressed the limp shoulders.

Then a soft moaning began.

"*Confiteor Deo omnipotent), beatae Mariae semper virgin) . . . et tibi, pater . . . tibi pater. . . .* Oh! Dick! I'm a devil, a damned soul . . . in Tartarus . . . in Tartarus . . . *mea culpa . . . mea maxima culpa . .* Oh! But the gods have been hard — hard! . . . I've had no chance . . . no chance. . . . I'm a weak fool . . . no better than a woman . . . went back to her, Dick . . . I went back to her. . . . I burned your letters. . . . I've been with her for a year . . . more than a year — God damn me! — can't I speak the truth even now? . . . Sixteen, seventeen months . . . and . . . and in hell all the time. . . . Oh! You dear man . . . you angel of God! But it's too late . . . I've gone too far . . . the dog . . . I returned to his vomit again . . . there's no hope. Oh! But poor dog . . . poor little dog . . . poor devil . . . he knew no better. . . . Oh! Dick, don't leave me . . ."

The shoulders shook again with passionate self-pity, and the

priest's eyes were blind again. The chimney pots appeared to tot-
ter, to dissolve. There had been an instant just now when loathing
had gripped him like a wrestler — a loathing that was almost physical nausea at the thought of this man's life. But it was gone again in
a flash, engulfed in a sudden flood of emotion. Yet he knew it was
rank sentimentality, and he recognized again what a fool he had
been not to understand that sentimentality was the only way. And
he a priest!

"Oh! Dick — *confiteor tibi pater . . . pater amantissime . . .* how
good you are! How pure and good!

. . . But there's no hope. . . . I'm broken this time . . . broken this
time for good and all. . . ." (A hand stole back falteringly, and Dick,
lost to all self-respect, seized it tight with his own disengaged hand
and held it.) "Broken this time . . . There's no health in us . . . erred
and strayed."

Dick bit his lip fiercely, but he had to say it.

"The Good Shepherd, Chris, old man!"

"Ah — h! *Bone Pastor, nos tuere . . . in terra viventium.* . . . But
even He can't bring a soul out of hell. . . . I went back to her, Dick .
. . and . . .Oh! . . . I've lied and pretended too long. . . . I didn't break
with her this time . . . she turned me out . . . sick of me . . . she gave
me five pounds . . and . . . for God's sake, wait a minute . . . and I
broke with her last month. damn me! what a brute, what a brute. .
. and I took it. . . . Dick! Dick . . . I took it. . . ."

Dick patted the shaking shoulder softly.

"There, old man! you've made a good confession. . . . Come
now. . . ."

"Oh! Dick! . . I took it. . . I took it."

Dick thanked God fervently under his breath. It was this last
thing then that accounted for the collapse. Nothing short of that
would have done it.

"Now, Chris, old chap, you're worn out. Sit down again. We'll
have a long talk."

He rose to his feet, softly unloosed the limp hand and stood
looking down at the graceful contrition. Again he had to remind
himself that sentimentality was the only way — for the present, at

least. He put a hand once more on the neat shoulder, but it was an effort. It was all so sickening.

"Sit down, old man! You'll feel better directly."

He went back to his own chair and waited.

After yet another half-minute's pause, the figure too rose with an exquisite weariness, passed a hand over its eyes, and sat down too, exhausted.

The priest took out his cigarette case, leaned forward and held it out.

Chris looked at him an instant with tear-stained cheeks, and then, with a kind of reverent solemnity, as if he were taking some great sacrament, detached a Smyrna cigarette. A match was struck, and handed to and fro, and Dick crossed one leg over the other and began to look at the chimney pots again.

"Now then, the first thing is, can you come away this afternoon?"

"Where to?" asked the languid voice.

"Foxhurst. Old Rolls wants to see you."

Chris smiled pathetically, and Dick felt himself bound to observe it.

"I can come — yes. But *ad quid bonum?*"

"Country air," said the priest mendaciously. "You want picking up. What's that you're writing?"

Chris closed his eyes for a moment with a faint angelic smile.

"A little sketch," he mewed. "I don't suppose it will be taken."

"Have you had much accepted?"

"One thing, a little dream I had, of Olympus."

"I saw it —"

"Yes?"

"Oh! I thought it very nice — very good indeed," he added hastily.

"Well, that's all. All the others returned. I write what I think now, not what others would have me think."

Dick nodded sympathetically.

"Ah! Dear man!" sighed Chris. "Of course you understand. But who else would?"

Dick smiled with an effort.

"Well, but — I suppose you are hard up."

Chris's wan smile became really saintly.

"It was one and nine pence that I had this morning when I looked at my treasury, and seven pence of that went for cigarettes."

Dick ventured on a grin, but let it fade into sympathy as he saw the other's face.

"Of course — I know. Then old Rolls is just the thing. We'll go down this afternoon."

"I'm afraid my landlady —"

"Oh, yes! I see. Well, we'll settle that. Now how about lunch?"

"Will you lunch with me, dear fellow?"

Dick's snub nose wrinkled. There was abundant excuse.

"No, no. You must come with me. Pack first; there's lots of time, and we can catch the two forty-five."

Chris leaned forward suddenly with elbows on knees, and face in hands; the cigarette smoke rose gracefully from his hair.

"No, no, dear man! You are too kind. But I can't come. But how heavenly!"

Dick repressed a sigh. He knew perfectly well that the other consented at heart, and it was tiresome to have to repeat the formulas.

"My good chap! Don't talk rot. There's no kindness at all. I simply long for an excuse to leave town for a night. I've only slept away one night this year."

Chris was silent.

"Look here! You needn't refuse the first thing I ask you. I tell you honestly . . ."

Chris lifted his face and looked at him emotionally.

"Dear old Dick. I can't refuse if you put it like that. . . . I . . . I will do anything you tell me. . . I tell you I'm broken . . . broken this time for good and all."

Down went the face into the hands again.

Dick was relieved, but astonished, at the swift capitulation. He had expected at least five minutes' resistance. He threw his cigarette away and rose briskly.

"Well, that's first rate. But we mustn't lose any time. . . . Look here . . . sovereign." He fumbled for his purse.

Chris threw a swift glance at him, and then dropped his head still lower.

"I'm ashamed, ashamed! The second time!"

"Don't talk rot. Here! Go and settle up. I'll wait here."

When Chris was gone at last with many gestures and cries, Dick let his face relax into a large, contented smile. But he felt abominably tired too. It had been a considerable strain.

He stood up to look round the room with eager zeal.

Really, Chris was an artist! There were the shaving things, the initialed brushes, and the nail instruments in beautiful parallels on the chest of drawers. Silk socks depended from the bed-rail with suspenders attached. There were four books by the head of the bed, and the priest sped across on tiptoe to look at them. Omar Khayyam, a Horace, a novel by Pierre Louys and another by Jean Lorrain. It was a perfect selection.

The table too was as it should be.

A little pile of manuscripts, each clipped, lay on the left-hand corner. Dick lifted them carefully to look at the titles.

"*The Three Dread Sisters.*"

"*A Soul in Suffering.*"

"*Tartarus.*"

"*Renier de' Calboli.*"

His eyes, too, caught patches of purple epithets. Waters were "murmurous with melancholy," it seemed; "her eyes were full of limpid light, shot with silver gray," and "her hands seemed formed to twine themselves with amaranth and asphodel." Cerberus also "uttered a rumorous roar"; the "dread ferryman lifted the penny from the eyes of the sleeping boy," and so on, and so forth.

There was a revolver, too, lying convenient to the hand on the right side. Dick looked at it gingerly, and perceived the copper caps of the cartridges in place. It was a detestable habit, he told himself.

On the marbled mantelpiece too were objects of interest — a calling card, rather yellow, face upwards, inscribed "Christopher Dell, Brasenose College, Oxford." A rosary, a diamond-type Dante, laid face open at the Inferno, of course, and, what touched him more than all else, five cigarette ends in an odd ink stand. He touched them almost reverently, and turned away abruptly as

Chris's hand fell on the handle outside.

Chris gave him one indescribable look, and poured a quantity of loose silver into his palm.

"Dick!" he said.

The priest watched him as he packed. A tidy Gladstone bag came from under the bed, labeled, and directed in fifteenth century handwriting. Then clothes appeared from the chest of drawers, were shaken, re-creased and refolded, each suit separated from its fellow in whitey-brown paper; then three shirts, probably the survivors of the shining regiment, eighteen strong, of a year and three quarters ago, and two sets of pink-striped pajamas. Then the books and papers, the dressing case — each thing in its place, a couple of pairs of boots, one of pumps, and a little leather box of handkerchiefs, a small bottle of violet scent, and when all was done, the revolver.

Chris held it up.

"Dear man," he said, "an hour ago I thought this was my only friend in the world."

Dick tried to respond with a suitable expression of countenance.

"Dick! Twice this has been at my head in the last month! And every time something — something restrained me. Was it your prayers, dear man?"

Then the revolver slid into a side pocket of the bag, the straps were fastened, and Chris stood up.

"Oh! Dick!" he cried again. "My good angel! And to think of the country!"

He caught the priest's hand, and kissed it passionately.

(3)

Dick woke up early at Foxhurst next morning, and lay long, staring out at the morning sky through the open window. He was sorely puzzled, and not a little apprehensive.

Last night had been uneventful. They had seen little of their host till dinner, and he and Chris had walked long in the golden sunshine under the trees. Chris had been what he had promised to be — subdued when he remembered it was his selected pose, as if emotions were for him exhausted; he had said as much with an appealing pathos, half-a-dozen times, but there had been feverish fits when he cried out against the hardness of the world, the inexorableness of fate, and his own wretched weakness. He was born under Gemini and Mercury, he said; that accounted for all. Then he had gone to confession.

At dinner, briskness was uppermost. Dick perceived that his friend thought it proper then to affect a cheery manner, with occasional glimpses of a world weary heart, and that presentation had continued interspersed with eulogies on country life till eleven o'clock, when Mr. Rolls retired. Then Chris, with a loud sigh of relaxation, had allowed himself to talk a good deal, to sit with his head in his hands, and to smoke four more cigarettes with an air of a saint's detachment. He had also taken a little whisky after the manner of one who needed support, as he related his adventures in the boarding house, and described Mrs. Perch's attempts to make him drink liquorice water on Saturday nights.

Mr. Rolls had made no sign. He had been perfectly courteous, as he always was, and apparently unconscious of any situation but that of two guests enjoying his hospitality. Once only had he mentioned Mrs. Hamilton's name, and his eyes never wandered off his plate as Chris snarled noiselessly like a foiled stage villain. It seemed to Dick incredible that it could be the same man who, only two nights before had sat in the twilight and dissected living souls so unflinchingly. He felt a great deal reassured. Chris would surely be safe in such hands.

He was contemplating getting up to go for a stroll before Mass, when a tap came on his door, and Chris came in on tiptoe in pajamas and slippers.

"Dear man! Did I awake you?"

Dick protested he had not. He had been awake an hour.

"What a brute I am! May I sit down a minute or two?"

He sat down delicately on the edge of the bed, and began his tale.

"Dick! What a place! Why did I never see it? It is Paradise — Paradise for a sick soul! I have been awake since dawn . . . listening,

listening and thinking! ... Breathing God's morning air!" He sighed musically.

"And Rolls! What a man! What a *grand seigneur!* I love him, and he terrifies me too! He is a man!"

He began to swing a foot.

"Why didn't I know him before? His very presence is soothing. I think — I think that if anyone on God's earth could heal me it would be he! How does he get his peace? But it is too late; too late!"

He looked out of the window with eyes intended to be full of a dreamy pathos.

But this was a great deal better, thought Dick.

"Don't say that, old chap," he said vaguely from his pillows.

Chris looked at him emotionally.

"You good man!" he exclaimed. "I wish to God . . . But it's no good. I'm broken for good, this time."

"Chris," said the priest with a sudden resolution.

"Well, dear man?"

"I've got to go back to town, you know. But —"

"Go back! Why, I thought —"

"No. I must go; but Rolls wants you to stay on a bit."

"My dear chap — I can't!"

"Look here, Chris! I want you to do something for me. I really mean it." (The priest was speaking quickly and warmly now; it struck him that it would be a good opportunity to take the first step.) "I really mean it. I want you to stay on here a bit. Let Rolls look after you: he wants to; he is wonderful; he is a real mystic, you know. . . . Do you know what an Irish priest said of him once?"

Chris looked up inquiringly.

"'As good as God and as clever as the Devil,'" quoted Dick.

The other smiled doubtfully.

"Look here, old man," went on the priest, "do stop."

"Dear man — it's no good."

"I don't mean about religion particularly," pursued Dick incoherently; "I mean about everything. Don't think I'm a — a jaw bags. I'm not jawing. But you know, you're all broken to bits; you said so; you want mending. Now don't you? Very well. Stop here and look about you; you can write, you know, just as well here as anywhere . . ."

"But my good chap, I can't possibly —"

"Oh! That's all right," cried Dick vehemently. "Old Rolls knows all about that. He's not a bit like other people, you know. I've — we've arranged."

Chris's foot was still now. He was staring at his friend.

"You must forgive me! I had to tell him about your writing, when he asked me to let him know when you got back to England —"

"How much does he know?"

"Why, he knows all about the row last year. Of course he does! Oh! Chris, don't be a fool."

Dick knew he was talking a little hysterically; but he couldn't help it.

"And you mean to say he knows all?"

"Why, I suppose so. Of course everyone does about here."

"And he asks me to his house? And to stay?"

"Yes."

Chris got off the bed, and began to walk up and down the carpet, to the window and back again. Then he stopped at the window, and stood staring out.

Dick had not an idea what he was feeling. It might be anger or gratitude or shame, or all three. All he knew for certain was that Chris was meditating the most graceful attitude to adopt — it might be that of injured pride, furious righteousness, or a becoming contrition. It was surely impossible to pretend that the invitation was anything but convenient! But Chris managed it.

He turned round at last, holding out a hand.

"Dick, old man. I don't know what to say! God bless you! God bless you! I did not know there were such people in the world!"

"You'll stay?"

"I'll stay. For as long as you tell me. I trust you utterly."

After Mass and breakfast, the two went out into the moat-garden. But they had hardly set foot there, before their host appeared in the doorway.

"Father Yolland, may I interrupt? Might I have a word with you?"

Dick followed him in, and the two went up the corridor into the sitting room.

"Sit down, Father."

Dick went to a chair feeling like a schoolboy. He had a half-hope that this shrewd man might have changed his mind; even as he looked at his face in the light from the window, he was not sure. It seemed wholly emotionless.

"Father Yolland, Mr. Dell has told me he will stay. That is very satisfactory."

"Told you, sir?"

"While you were at your thanksgiving. He professed himself very grateful. I wish to tell you my proposal."

Dick licked his lips, staring at the rigid face. What was he going to hear?

"Mr. Dell will not be able to write while he is with me. I shall provide him therefore with all that he requires. I propose that he stays six months at the least. After that, I shall put at his disposal two hundred pounds a year for five years."

Dick gasped.

"That meets your views then? It is only fair. I do not think he will wish to write for some while after he has left me."

"Why not, sir?"

"I think not, Father. I may be wrong. But there is my intention in any case. But I shall prefer that it comes to him from another hand, and he must not be told of it, until he leaves me. My proposal will not hold good if he remains with me less than six months."

"And — and what will he do here?"

The other looked him straight in the eyes.

"I shall not tell you, Father. And I beg that you will not inquire. I shall inform Mr. Dell this afternoon."

"It — it will not —"

"It will be what I believe him to require. You must not write to him. We will make that plain presently. Have you anything further?"

Dick drew a long, trembling breath.

"Mr. Rolls, do you still think what you thought on Tuesday?"

"Yes, Father."

"You — you are sure?"

"I am quite sure."

There fell a silence between the two men. Dick felt torn with doubt; but he dared not put it into words. The presence of the other dominated him entirely. This hatchet-faced man was so cruelly certain — and he so hesitating. It was no good — he must trust utterly.

"Well, sir?"

"Well, Father, that is all. He is your friend. Will you commit him to me?"

Dick drew another long breath.

"I will, sir," he whispered.

Mr. Rolls stood up. He paid no attention to the emotion of the other; he remained, with his fingertips on the table, looking steadily down at the papers that lay before him.

"You must pray," he said, "with all your might. Remember that all is under God, absolutely. . . . I know you love him. . . . Will you ask him to come this way? We will arrange the first step now."

Dick drove away an hour later, alone.

CHAPTER III

The Hospital

(I)

Chris went about the house and grounds that afternoon in a passion of melancholy romance.

He had lunched with his host and the Benedictine chaplain, a little prim brown old man like a clerical monkey, and nothing had been said beyond generalities. At the end Mr. Rolls had told him that he would be obliged if the other would amuse himself that afternoon, and that he himself would be back to tea. Meantime he would find the keys of the whole house in the porter's lodge.

It was an astonishing house. The three original sides of it were pierced by corridors above and below that corkscrewed, climbed and dropped in an entirely unexpected way. Out of these opened rooms on the outer side of the court.

There were numbers of old bedrooms, approached by descending steps, each containing an ancient bed hung with curtains, a couple of chairs or so, one or two black tables. There were curious portraits in some of these rooms, and Chris passed a very pleasant time looking into the eyes of these, marking their dress, peering at the little coats in the corners, even once or twice adjuring them in pathetic language to tell him the Secrets of Life and Death. His eyes filled with tears three or four times at his own earnest pathos.

In one room he found a tall mirror, iridescent and dusky with age, and posed before it for a few moments, advancing first one foot and then the other, folding his arms, letting them drop languidly, staring with an infinite variety of expressions into the eyes of his own ghostly replica.

"Who are you?" he cried softly at last. "You stranger from the land of dreams! From where do you come? whither are you going? What is the true soul — the very self — behind those — er — those shadowed eyes?"

He leaned forward till the melancholy face touched him with the icy smoothness of old glass; then he grew slightly ashamed, and just a little frightened.

The King's Room delighted him — a paved floor, an oriel window, linen patterned walls, a high stone fireplace with dogs, a long hanging of fourteenth century work beneath the oak ceiling, a great low bed, nearly square, with twisted columns at head and foot, voluminous curtains, valance and counterpane embroidered all over with huge roses and medallions. He climbed gingerly on to the bed, and lay there in an ecstasy of melancholy, thinking himself an exiled and ruined king, but with a yet undaunted princely heart.

Towards four o'clock he came to the chapel, and stood there with the air of a high-minded infidel who had outgrown the childish illusions of faith and regretted them. Yes, there was the bronze tabernacle above the altar with its strange Contents lying quiet within in the silver cup. It had meant so much to him once; it meant so little now, except that it represented the center of the world's faith. He reflected for a while on Pallas Athene, the mysteries of Mithras, the death and resurrection of Osiris, the strange colored romance of medieval days. . . It was very beautiful, he thought; perhaps it might make an article — "Considerations in a Catholic Chapel." Then he unfolded his arms, reflecting that he had gone to confession last night, hesitated, and with a sudden impulse genuflected and went out.

He would go to the garden, he thought, that beyond the moat where he had walked with Dick yesterday evening; there was an hour yet before tea, and he would like to get his ideas ranged in line, dressed and equipped in a suitable uniform, before he encountered his host.

He found a retired seat, placed in a recess of shrubs, whence he could see the old towered house, sat down, and began to roll cigarettes and thoughts together.

First there was Dick — the dear man who meant so well and who understood so little. He was like a child in his simple affection, his warm impulses, his lack of resentment; he was like a child

too in his lack of discernment, of real intelligent sympathy. He
would never understand — how was it possible that he should? —
the heart of one who had eaten so freely of the Tree of Knowledge,
who had drained the dregs of sin, who had lived, suffered, aspired
and agonized, as he himself had done.

No, this courteous old man, John Rolls, was a fitter companion.
That old man had suffered too, he was sure; it was in his face; perhaps he too had sinned!

A pleasing prospect began to unfold itself before Chris. He was
here as a patient, he told himself, a psychical convalescent like the
others of whom he had heard before, but more deeply interesting;
but he would not be that long. He was sure that the other understood. For a while perhaps he would accept the new *rôle,* acquiesce
in a sweet melancholy in whatever was prescribed, and little by
little he would win this old man's heart by his touching contrition
and languor. Then he would be appreciated; he would become in-
dispensable; he would find himself in the position of an intimate,
and a far more intelligent one than that old Mr. Yolland who, Chris
was sure, was a most conventionally limited person without perceptions or insight. . . .

He began to wonder what his treatment would be. He was sure
it would be a very beautiful and delicate one; had not Dick said
that the physician was a mystic? There would be some exquisite
old world conversations; perhaps a course of meditation would be
exhibited, daily Mass, the rosary each evening, readings from French
dévots. Yes, he would submit to all; he would even go to confession
once a week if he were desired to do so; and to Communion — yes;
his faith was equal to that, as he had said last night; he could take
the Mystic Bread, Delight of Gods, Food of Angels, in the true in-
ward spirit of religion. It was all one, after all. And the Church
knew what she was about.

It would be a kind of aristocratic Retreat, he thought; he would
be quite willing to walk a little in the park at sunset, with his finger
between the leaves of a pious book; he could even pluck and press
a flower at moments of emotion. He could do it all, admirably.
Perhaps it would indeed be balm to his wounded soul.

And meantime he would also enjoy the luxury of tragic remembrance.

There would be no lack of somber background to this delicately vivid foreground; his last year had touched in the dark washes that would take long to fade. His life at Paris had taken care of that, and the color of real heavy squalor had been supplied by his recent month in London.

It was a great change for the better, he told himself. Here was this exquisite house and park with its old world atmosphere, his own paneled room with the deep window seat in which he could dream with his cigarette; the chapel, which perhaps might come to mean more to him in a few weeks' time; his courtly, impressive host; even the monkey-chaplain was not without a suggestive significance.

What articles he would write! Polished periods, fragrant like wood carving, similes like silver point vignettes, allusions like the note of flutes and ancient strings, with a world weary note sounding through all like the throb of a distant organ heard through paneled passages! . . Chris positively writhed on the seat with pleasure as he pictured himself writing them.

Yes! He had composed his new attitude at last; it all fitted in beautifully; he was to be an exquisite recluse, speaking in a low voice, looking with deep regretful eyes, understanding men and things, realizing the hollowness of life and the joys of the interior spirit; a silent intimate of this distinguished old man; pointed out to visitors as a man with a history, — a history preserved as it were in lavender — whispered about in corners, perhaps even at Hinton — Then he writhed again with other emotions, and for a single instant a crack opened and he saw himself as he had once hoped to be, a simple-minded man living on his estate with his children about him — bright with cleanly joys, serving God and man, and loving a dear wife with all his heart. Then the crack closed. No, this was better; a melancholy and distinguished recluse was more beautiful — far, far more beautiful.

A clock beat five from the stable-turret across the park, and he rose, throwing away his last cigarette among the bushes. He walked very slowly back to the house, with his eyes downcast, and a careful melancholy in his bearing.

(2)

"It is a superb place, sir," said Chris again, setting down his cup for the last time.

Mr. Rolls bowed gravely.

They were sitting in the parlor in which the master of the house usually wrote and worked, for the whole house, with the exception of the few necessary rooms, was altogether unlived in. Chris was in the window seat, posed as for the photographer, one knee clasped in his hands and his head slightly thrown back; and his host was, as so often, upright on the hearth with his hands behind him. He was a magnificent *grand seigneur,* thought Chris once more, noticing how his head overtopped the high mantelpiece, and marking his long, thin limbs, his gray hair and his keen profile, and just a little formidable, as a *grand seigneur* should be.

Chris sighed heart-brokenly.

"Nature!" he said. "O great god Pan! What a healing touch! I almost forgot myself for a while in the gardens this afternoon."

He turned to see the effect, and saw the other looking at him.

"You find that too, Mr. Dell?"

"Find it? I live in the country; I exist only in town. You cannot conceive what a pleasure it is to me to be here."

Mr. Rolls was silent a moment. Then he came across from the window seat and sat opposite him.

"Mr. Dell," he said, "may I say something?"

Chris was a little startled by his movement and his words; he seemed to be looking at him out of those odd thatched eyes with a very real interest. Chris felt flattered, "What you will, sir!" he said, smiling.

"It is this. I wonder how far you mean what you say."

The sense of flattery vanished like a pricked bladder. He half thought he must have misheard. Yet those strange eyes showed no confusion. He unclasped his knee and sat up.

"I do not understand, sir."

"About the country. . . . Will you tell me what it is you want, Mr. Dell?"

This was very disconcerting; it was so entirely unexpected. It seemed that the situation had shifted from arm's length to hand grip. But his pride awoke fully armed at the suggestion of insincerity, and his face arranged itself defiantly.

"This is what I want, Mr. Rolls; it is not much. I ask a simple room — not even a house — simple food, a little wine — a bed to sleep in — hard work to do: God's country and God's silence about me. No more than that."

He made an eloquent little gesture. But the other neither moved nor spoke.

"I am weary of artificial life — false friends — smiles and presences — all the hateful conventions, all the shallow protestations! I thought once — I thought differently, but I understand now. I ask so little! And the gods deny it me!"

He felt really warm with eloquence, with a passion for simplicity.

"And your writing?" asked the other softly.

"Bah!" he cried. "What is that! A wretched quill-driver! It is nothing to me. I would not write another line if I were not driven to it."

He looked up again at the watching face; it was perfectly passive, and there was something in it almost like incredulity.

"You do not believe me, sir? You think I am bragging?"

The grim lips smiled.

"I believe you think so now, Mr. Dell."

Chris was stung. His whole body stiffened with resentment.

"What is the good of talking, sir? I cannot prove it, but I swear to you —"

"Well?"

"I swear to you that I am like that! Not one man understands me! All the world thinks me shallow and superficial, because I smile and laugh. They little know. Even you, sir."

He was flushed with conviction; his sallow cheeks showed a tinge of pink, his black eyes were bright with passion.

Mr. Rolls lifted a hand deprecatingly, still watching him so intently that Chris was forced to stare back with defiant pride.

"Tell me, Mr. Dell! Tell me exactly what you want. You mean, I suppose, that you want a pleasant little house — with servants —"

Chris broke in indignantly.

"Good God, sir! Do you think I mean that? I mean that I envy the farm laborers in this place — that I envy Dick and Bill trudging to work early and late, with God's sky over them, and mother Earth beneath their feet, and peace and simplicity in their hearts. I mean —"

"Mr. Dell, why have you never tried that, then?"

The tone of that odd vibrant voice cut him like a knife. It was incredulous, contemptuous, sneering.

Chris sprang up, in a beautiful attitude.

"Try it, sir? Why, who would take me? What experience have I had? What do I know of manual work? Could I cart dung, with these hands?" He flung out thin sinewy fingers. "And what else can I do? I am a cracked vessel, sir — fit for nothing but the dust heap."

His voice shook with conviction, and that sneering face whipped it into enthusiasm.

"Before God, sir, it is true," he cried. "But what is the use? Who will believe me?"

"You would tire of it in a week," said the contemptuous voice.

Chris's mouth worked, his hands clenched.

"I believe you believe what you say," added the other with a horribly courteous emphasis.

Chris froze with white fury, and sat down deliberately. It was abominable he should be insulted like this.

"Very well, sir," he hissed. "You do not believe me then! Then I think it is time —"

The tall old man suddenly leaned over to him, propping himself on one hand.

"Mr. Dell, I offer you all that you ask. You shall have a fair trial."

The catastrophe was so sudden that for one moment Chris sat bewildered, with open mouth. He ran his eyes over the other's face, but it seemed perfectly serious.

"You shall have what you want," went on the other, as serenely as if he were proposing a walk in the park, "and you shall have it for as long as you like. I will provide a room — in the village. You shall live with my Scotch gardener, in all respects as you said. You shall receive the wages usual and necessary. I suppose they will be about fifteen shillings a week."

Chris swallowed in his throat; his hands felt limp and moist. Then he cleared his throat to answer as the other leaned back.

"Mr. Rolls —"

"Of course if you were — if you did not mean what you said just now," observed the other, "you have only to say so."

"I did mean it," snapped Chris. "I mean every word! For how long?"

"For how long?" asked the other in apparent astonishment.

"For how long will you give me work?" Chris explained hastily, with cold dismay at his heart.

"For as long as you will," said the other slowly. "I should think myself —"

It pricked him cruelly. But he had plenty of spirit.

"Well, sir? What do you think?"

Mr. Rolls looked at him.

Do you wish me to say?"

"Of course —"

"Well, I should think it might last a month, possibly two — certainly not more than six."

Chris stood up. His face was white, and apprehensiveness tugged at his heart strings, but he was brave enough in his words.

"You shall see, sir," he said, looking without a sign of fear into the other's steady eyes. "You shall see whether I am a mere *flâneur* as you think me. What I said, I said in haste, but I repeat it at leisure. It is the dearest desire of my heart. I have nothing to live for."

"You understand that you will be a servant — not an eccentric guest!"

Chris whitened yet more.

"I understand perfectly — a farm laborer —"

"No, not that, an under-gardener."

Chris bowed.

"You will be under Mr. Whalley's orders; you may appeal to me if necessary exactly like the rest. You will wait in the hall then, like the rest. You will sit with the rest at Mass on Sundays."

Chris licked his lips with the tip of his tongue. He wished he could check the trembling that shook him.

"I must tell you, Mr. Rolls, that I do not believe —"

The other checked him with a movement of his hand.

"That is nothing to do with it. You are a professed Catholic; you must do as the rest."

"Very good, sir. . . . And I may worship my own gods —"

"You may worship what you like. But you will be at Mass on Sundays."

It was too much. The tone and the words flicked him like a whip. His lips snapped together and opened.

"Mr. Rolls, I must beg —"

"Well, Mr. Dell."

"I must beg you will not speak to me in that manner."

The grim, lean face smiled.

"So soon? But I beg your pardon. You are my guest still."

Chris flushed, but he caught at the straw. It did not matter; he would keep his head up an hour longer.

"I am sorry I was forced to remind you of it, sir."

Mr. Rolls bowed from the waist, and Chris found himself wondering whether the elaborate comedy were worth while. He sat down again.

"Of course it will finish me as a writer," he said.

"Surely not, Mr. Dell," said the motionless figure that had become now really terrible. "You will have new experiences such as few writers —"

"I shall lose my little connection, I mean."

"But I understood you did not intend to write any more."

"Of course — until I — I am an old man. And what then?"

"I pension my servants, Mr. Dell, when they are past work."

Chris swallowed again.

"Er — that is a great relief, Mr. Rolls."

There was silence then for a while. It seemed to Chris that the whole of life was utterly changed; it was as if he had seen the world

turn blue without any premonitory symptoms. Ten minutes ago
he had been talking and drinking tea, lounging in the window seat,
drawling effective sentences to a courteous old man who had smiled
and assented and been apparently impressed. Then the clock had
chimed the quarter before six; he remembered that distinctly —
and he had said another graceful word of appreciation of the beauty
of the place. Then it was as if the ground had begun to move; he
had been forced to step this way and that to prevent himself from
falling; Mr. Rolls had come across from the hearth and sat down,
and after that there had been no escape; each sentence that he was
forced to speak, in order to justify his own words — in fact in order not to appear a bragging fool — had taken him stride by stride
into mire. Now here he was, planted to the neck, apparently by his
own consent, and with no kind of prospect of escape.

To change the metaphor, he had been trapped. Yet he had walked
into the trap with his eyes wide open; there had been no conceal-
ment of the noose. He had said that kind of thing so often before
with impunity!

There was only one thing to be done. He had already tried one
or two plunges, and had been met by a steel point. He must learn
to remain where he was with dignity, unless indeed he could arrange a satisfactory quarrel; and even as he sat there, with his trapper opposite, there began to reform faintly before his mental vision
the lineaments of a new pose. He caught glimpses of himself, in
fact and not in theory, as a mysterious, highly-bred under-gardener
who would move about clouded with sorrow, illumined with romance. He would be pointed out to visitors as a man with a past;
he would occasionally, with a wan smile, communicate an enno-
bling thought to Mr. Whalley — some delicate mystical fancy about
Pan in the thickets; he would pause with uplifted spade as if he
heard the hoot of a distant flute; he would . . . .

His train of thought suddenly stopped. Mr. Rolls was standing
up looking out of the window.

There was his trapper! Chris watched him for a few seconds with
growing dismay. There was no doubt about it that this was a real
man. But how bitterly he had been deceived. He had thought him

half-an-hour ago an amiable, courteous, bland and picturesque *grand seigneur,* full of delicate instincts and manners; and he had turned out to be something else. What that was Chris could not yet perceive; but it was as if he had looked into a child's face, and found it a monster.

He spurred his pride, and stood up too. He was not going to be mastered, and led like a bear; he would conduct his own degradation and thereby deprive it of its sting. He was not going to be managed!

"I should like to see my new room, Mr. Rolls." His voice rang high and insincere.

The other turned round and eyed him mildly.

"Certainly. I had thought that perhaps tomorrow —"

"I should prefer tonight, sir," said Chris stiffly.

The other made a little inclination.

"Then if you will come with me —" he said.

(3)

Chris went to bed that night in his new rooms.

It was a little yellow brick house, outside the park, standing back from the road in its own kitchen garden, and was tenanted by three persons besides himself. Father Baynton, the chaplain, occupied a bedroom on the first floor, and the two front rooms on the ground floor. The Scotch gardener and his wife used the rest of the house, a kitchen and scullery at the back, and the two other rooms above; but one of these had been given up to the visitor.

It was a small square room with a door on to the landing, and a window looking out on the open country at the back. It held an iron bedstead, one cane chair beside it, and one Windsor chair with arms. There was a small chest of drawers, and a row of pegs upon the door. A pair of green serge curtains hung at the window, the upper panes of which had been removed, and there was a small square of carpet before the fireplace, convenient to the feet. A cheap crucifix of black wood and plaster hung below the ceiling against the chimney. There was nothing else at all in the room; no table, no easy chair. But there were four books on the mantelpiece: a Bible, a Penny Catechism with morning and evening prayers, Abbot Blosius' work on Mental Prayer, and "Kidnapped," by Robert Louis Stevenson.

Further instructions had been given him. It appeared that his work was to begin at half-past six. At eight he would return for breakfast, and at half-past eight he was to be back in the gardens until twelve, when dinner would be ready. At one o'clock work was to begin again, and continue till six, when he would go home to tea. At half-past eight there would be cold meat and beer provided, and he was to go to his room at half-past nine. The Whalley family retired at that hour.

He was to do this every day in the week except Sunday.

Chris got into bed in a twill night-shirt, threw off the red blanket and lay staring round the room — and particularly at the corduroy trousers and gray flannel shirt hanging behind the door, and a pair of immense boots by the chest of drawers. It was these he had to put on in the morning.

Every one of his possessions, even to his books, had been pronounced unsuitable for an under-gardener, and in a passion of pride he had consented. He had even thrust his own clothes, down to his silk vest and gold links, just now outside the door, for removal in the morning. He did not wish to see them again; he could not bear it. No! he was to show that cynical man that he too had a will of iron; that he was not one who promised without performing. He was to be an under-gardener? He would be an under-gardener. And he would be a remarkable one.

For a little while the flush of pride possessed him. There was the knowledge, almost unknown to him hitherto, that things were genuine at last. He understood perfectly that he was not playing a game; but he had too the quality of romance that gilded even the sordid facts that faced him. He would work — yes, till the honest sweat poured from him, and his hands were properly horny; but he would not lose for an instant his own splendid individuality. It was this capacity alone that had enabled him to meet the proposal so steadily. Like certain sea creatures, no food was amiss to him; he coated all alike with his own effusion before swallowing.

It had been pushed so defiantly before him too, at the very moment when his characteristics were flushed with energy, and it had
been done with a certain effectiveness that he did not yet fully understand.

From the contemplation of himself he passed to the contemplation of those with whom he would have to do, and began to
rearrange the grouping.

First, John Rolls.

Towards him his attitude was clear. He would touch his hat to
his master, secure in his own superb dignity of labor; he would call
him "Sir," with the most gorgeous irony as his protection. He would
never appeal to him; he would bear, if need be, the most cruel in-
justices. . . . How long would that have to continue? He had no
idea; but it could not be long before his own worth and determi-
nation were recognized. The first advances would surely have to
come from the other, and they would not be long.

Secondly, Dick Yolland.

He would hardly ever see that priest, but yet his attitude towards
him must be arranged. It would be one, of course, of immeasur-
able superiority, with a pathos of isolation in it. His eyes pricked
with tears as he contemplated a little scene of Dick's wistfully looking from a richly hung window at the poor, proud under-gardener
wielding his spade. He would refuse all entreaties to return to luxury
and comfort. No! he would tell him that he had found the joy of
labor at last, that Mother Nature had medicines that art and plenty
could not bestow.

Then he would shoulder his spade and tramp back to his lonely
cottage with a halo of virtue and dignity beaming round his head.

Thirdly, other acquaintances — such as old Mr. Yolland — the
same would do for him; the Hamiltons — Chris bit his lips fiercely;
he could not at once articulate a description of his attitude towards them. A broken heart, a biting scorn, a fierce white-hot indignation, a dramatic pose so perfect that it merged in nature.
Visions of a rich carriage — a white-faced girl, a worldly mother;
and of himself, foot on spade, pulling his forelock with a face of
stone. It was superb, complete, indescribable. Perhaps Jack would

be sent to him as ambassador — that generous, simple English boy. Oh! The words in which he would answer him! The wan smile that would linger long in the memory, the set determined face in which he would once more set foot to spade and drive it home.

Chris's face twitched with emotion, and he drew a sobbing breath. He was enjoying himself enormously.

The blind flapped suddenly in the night-breeze, and Chris came down with a run. This twill nightshirt was coarse to the skin, and how dismal the little room was with its crude furnishing, its uncarpeted boards! And it was to be his home for — for months — possibly years.

Then he began to review the last few steps again that had brought him to this; but with a lower elevation of mind. He began to consider at what point he had given himself away, and was unable to understand it. It was this horrible man who had entrapped him. He began to consider the horrible man.

What in the world was he really? Chris summed up the evidence. Facts: — a rich man, an old Catholic, well-born and well-bred, living alone, religious, mystical, philanthropic, brutal. Gossip: — wild in his youth, having broken his wife's heart, suspected of having extraordinary friends. There was not much unity to be brought out of this chaos; it was a figure that appeared if not self-contradictory, at least unintelligible. When he had first met him he had thought him to be a distinguished-looking man of the world — and he was that; but he was a great deal more besides. And what did all these maneuvers mean? It was very odd treatment to deal out to a brokenhearted blasé sinner! The actress had been requested to pour out tea; the brokenhearted man to dig in flowerbeds. One had been comforted, the other snubbed.

Then for the first time it began to dawn upon this dense creature that possibly there was some method in this distinction — that John Rolls, in his eccentricity, believed that digging in flowerbeds had a redemptive value — that the whole affair was prearranged and determined upon. But that was impossible — Chris had said what he had said of his own free choice — he had run his own head into the noose; Rolls had merely asked questions; he had not made one suggestion; it was from himself that the suggestion had come.

Ah! It was puzzling, puzzling. But how hard the world was!

So moods surged and chased one another through his brain. He experienced pride, resentment, curiosity, pathos, dignity — one after another; and as the series rose and sank like waves, his consciousness grounded now and again, like an imprisoned boat, upon the brutal rock of fact beneath them all. Here he was, here he would have to remain, with the flapping blind, the uncarpeted boards, the corduroy trousers, the gray flannel shirt. He was no longer Christopher Dell, Esq., author and journalist; he was Dell, under-gardener at Foxhurst. That was all that there was to be said about it.

He woke half-a-dozen times that night, and the situation asserted itself almost instantly, sometimes dreamily, sometimes dramatically. But all his prancings and attitudes did not prepare him for the clump of boots outside at half-past five, and a voice, with a strong Scotch accent, telling him to make haste.

CHAPTER IV

Quackery

(I)

I t was Jack who first brought the astounding news to Hinton. He had heard it from the Vicar, and he conveyed that obliging ecclesiastic with him from the village to announce it at home.

It was shortly before lunch that they arrived; Mrs. Hamilton saw the two from her morning room coming across the lawn, and rang the bell to order another place to be laid, with a sense of suitability. Yes, how pleasant the country was! — with the Vicar dropping in like this occasionally to lunch with the Lady Bountiful, in company with the children. If it was tiresome, it was suitable; and she was thinking a great deal about suitability just now. She was tired of her essays in heterodoxy.

Jack, too, looked entirely suitable, as he came in without knocking, and held the door aside for the clergyman to come in. He was in homespun with gaiters; and his upper lip was mildly fringed with fair hair; he certainly carried himself very well, and his face had exactly the air of detached superiority that is proper in a well-bred young man of nineteen.

"Aunt Mary," he said as soon as was decent. "Have you heard that Mr. Dell is back?"

She instantly ceased to attend to Mr. Stirling.

"What do you mean, Jack?"

"Tell her, Mr. Stirling."

"It is quite true," said the Vicar in a tone in which interest, pain and excitement fought for expression. "I had it from the Vicar of Foxton this morning. He is at Foxhurst — and this is the most extraordinary part of it all — he is working as under-gardener for Mr. Rolls."

Pain was certainly the predominant emotion now in his rather long face. He looked as he would have looked if he had heard that the man was in a workhouse or a prison, but the pain did not reign alone; it rendered his satisfaction melancholy without obliterating it. He had always known that the young man who had opposed him on the subject of Harvest Festivals would come to a bad end; besides, what could the Romish religion do for its votaries in the hour of affliction? He was grieved to think of the terrible state in which Chris must find himself.

Mrs. Hamilton looked at him a moment with a tight mouth, and a face a shade paler than usual. Her lips opened and closed; then she rapped out a sentence.

"It is thoroughly suitable," she said.

"I thought perhaps that Miss Annie —" began the Vicar tactfully in a head-voice.

"I will ask you to say nothing at all about it," whipped out the other; "nor you, Jack. I will tell her myself. . . You mean he is just an ordinary gardener?"

"I — I regret to say so," said the clergyman in trembling triumph. "He was in corduroys, I understand, and touched his hat to my friend."

Mrs. Hamilton's eyes wavered a moment. Then she drew a slow long breath.

"I hope it will —. Come in to lunch, Mr. Stirling."

She found it curiously difficult to behave suitably, and the stress of it made her rather silent as she sat at the head of the table with Jack opposite, the Vicar on her right and Annie to the left. There were half-a-dozen problems in her mind.

Annie looked particularly virginal and innocent in a large straw hat with pink roses, as she ate mutton delicately and refused potatoes, and gave them short and simple annals of the farm from which she had just returned. It appeared that all was as it should be there, flowing with milk and honey and young ducks and a new collie dog; while the Vicar listened with priestly approbation to the interests of his young parishioner. It was very wonderful, he thought, how this dear child had been preserved in all her unstained simplicity, and had come through the fire of an attachment to a dangerous adventurer without the least taint of the smell of it upon her soul.

How greatly his efforts had been blessed in her regard! It must be made a matter of thanksgiving, as it had been one of intercession.

He led the conversation round presently to a more definitely sacred line and introduced the subject of altar flowers.

"I was so grateful, Miss Annie, for the lilies on Saturday. Mrs. Stirling placed them herself in water. We thought them so very teaching."

Annie murmured melodious deprecation.

"They remain there, of course, until the end of the week. I cannot understand how some priests can remove them to their own houses when they become a little faded. Surely they are consecrated by their sacred use! But I know an excellent priest who takes another view; he distinguishes between those placed upon the altar and those beside it. We had a long discussion in the railway carriage the other day upon the point."

Annie looked greatly interested.

"Yes, Mr. Stirling?"

"I thought it such a good opportunity to teach our fellow passengers that we clergy too had our affairs to think of, and to make them think a little for themselves as well. One dear fellow next me laid down his paper to listen, as I raised my voice for his benefit. I am afraid we got quite warm upon the point."

"Then when they are faded —?" began Annie eagerly.

"They are laid reverently upon the little heap under the yew tree. I would not even take them out of the churchyard."

"But what about the cotton wool at Christmas?" put in Jack a little gruffly.

"That is burned by my own hands," explained the Vicar gently; "that is, if it is not worth preserving for another year."

He was greatly pleased that Jack had responded; for he had thought sometimes that the young man was a little thoughtless. Of course young men would be so, occasionally; they must not be pressed too hard; but at least he had the satisfaction of knowing that this one had received an abundance of Church teaching ever

since childhood, and surely it would tell in time. Priests had a difficult task, he often told himself; guidance must be so tactfully given
in this lawless, materialistic age; there was so much insensibility
and carelessness to be overcome. It was better done, he thought, by
a few bright and careful words dropped like this, at least in the case
of intelligent listeners, than by more definitely authoritative pro-
nouncements.

Mrs. Hamilton was not particularly interested. Of course it was
right that clergymen should talk and think like this, but she was
wondering how Annie would take the news after lunch.

"Are you riding, Jack?" she asked suddenly.

The boy nodded, with his mouth full.

"At what time?"

"Three o'clock."

That would do very well, she reflected. She could have a couple
of hours with Annie alone, and could take her time. But she did
not have the least fear as to the result; probably Annie would be
even relieved by the news. There was no possibility now of ever
coming across Mr. Dell again in social life. He had committed the
most satisfactory sort of suicide — extinction without tragedy. She
too almost thought that the matter was one for thanksgiving.

Half-an-hour later when the Vicar was gone she strolled as if
purposelessly into the smoking room.

Jack was in a deep chair with a sporting novel and a cigarette,
and by the way he looked up at her she saw it was no good pretend-
ing that she had not come for a reason.

"Yes," she said. "No, don't move; I'll sit here. Yes, it's about Mr.
Dell. Tell me what you think, my boy."

Jack shut his book.

"I don't know," he said.

"You don't think he'll come here, do you?"

He laughed shortly.

"Of course not, Aunt Mary. He's not a cad."

"But you don't like him, do you?"

Jack was silent an instant before answering.

"No, I don't. Though I'm beastly sorry for him. I did like him at first, you know. But I know better. That sort of chap's not good form at all."

She felt pleased at this.

"I know," she said. "That's just it; and I don't like him either. He behaved very badly about Annie, as I told you. Does she ever talk about him?"

He shook his head.

"We never talk about that sort of thing; and I think she's rather ashamed of the whole affair. But I was just as bad, in a kind of way. I did like him most awfully at first. . . I . . . I feel rather a brute."

"That's nonsense," she said decidedly. "Of course we're all very sorry about it. It's very sad and all that. But he was abominable," she ended vindictively.

Jack sat musing, with an unheeded cigarette in his fingers.

"What made you begin to dislike him at first?"

"I think it was the way he talked here one night — I thought it all splendid at the time, you know. But it was so beastly theatrical, you know —"

"It wasn't bad talk?" she asked swiftly.

"Good Lord, no — at least not that sort. I can't even remember what he said, but it was all about Italy, you know, and Johnnies in Florence, and so on."

She nodded two or three times.

"But I think it's awfully hard luck he's got to be a gardener," he added weakly.

"Nothing of the sort," she said. "I think he's very lucky, and it's very satisfactory, though I wish he wasn't quite so close. Why do you think he came so near Hinton?"

"Old Rolls asked him, I suppose."

"And you're quite sure he won't come over?"

"Lord! No. What should he come for?"

"And you won't go over and see him, will you?"

He shook his head.

"Because that might stir it up again, you know," she explained. "Besides, he wouldn't like it himself."

"I know."

This was very satisfactory, and she stood up as the gong sounded in the hall.

"There's your horse," she said. "Have a good ride. And don't bother about Mr. Dell. If he was worth thinking about Father Yolland would have done something for him. It just shows, doesn't it?"

"I suppose it does," said Jack, taking up his gloves.

(2)

The lady felt rather like a plate-juggler as she turned away from the steps whence she had seen Jack ride off, and went upstairs to Annie's little sitting room.

The male plate was all right, at any rate, and would go spinning comfortably away in its own plain orbit without any more attention; but this other delicate piece of porcelain must be handled more carefully. It was all perfectly right, of course, and needed nothing but tact, but Mrs. Hamilton was conscious of a slightly painful interest as she tapped at the white-and-gold door.

Annie had been promoted to the possession of two rooms, besides the schoolroom downstairs, but had chosen to move her bed next door, and to continue to live in her bedroom. She had really made it charming. The panels had been painted cream-white and the whitewash had been brought down a couple of feet to the broad ledge from which her water colors hung, and on which rested a row of blue plates and cups. There was a little blue Florentine carpet square, with a beautiful border all curves and petals, and delicate white furniture with gilded legs. It was just a trifle too expensively simple, but it was a most suitable setting to herself, who was sitting now in the window seat in the most natural attitude possible. Beyond her lay the rich summer sky and the green tumbled masses of the woods rising from the park thirty feet below her window.

"Yes, Mother?" she said.

Mrs. Hamilton came across to the window seat and sat opposite her.

"Nothing, dear. What are you going to do with yourself?"

"Rest till tea," said Annie decidedly.

"And the pony carriage afterwards?"

"Very well."

Her mother leaned forward and took the book gently; it was Keats' sonnets, she perceived, bound very nicely in olive and gold; and she turned the pages mechanically, wondering how she would introduce her news. Then she determined on abruptness.

"I have heard some news about Mr. Dell," she said, in a wonderfully natural voice. "He is at Foxton, I hear."

She perceived an instantaneous cessation of movement at the other end of the long seat, but took care not to look up. Then she thought she had better have done with it at once.

"Mr. Rolls has given him some work in the garden, I understand. He has been there more than three weeks."

"Yes?" came a very carefully natural voice. Mrs. Hamilton affected to pause over a line.

"How charming!" she said, and smiled deliberately. There was an instant's silence.

"And Mr. Dell?" said the girl again.

"Oh, Mr. Dell? That's all. Of course it's very kind of Mr. Rolls, but I wish he had given him work somewhere else. It would be very uncomfortable if we met him now. . . . Listen to this, Annie." And she read a verse or two.

She felt she was doing it quite beautifully. The swinging of the little white shoe had begun again, and Annie was looking out of the window. Really, this boy and girl were very satisfactory. They knew so perfectly how to behave, and no one could accuse them of being heartless. Their fine instinct had come to the rescue so unerringly, and they had responded so gallantly. Mr. Dell's significance dwindled to puny proportions. He was as a fish that had leaped dazzlingly for a moment in the sun; then he had vanished again into the depths, the ripples had dispersed, and the stream flowed on as serenely as ever. His reappearance further down had done nothing to trouble this peaceful reach.

"'. . . When some melodious sorrow spells mine eyes,'" she ended.

She glanced up at her daughter, and saw a pensive profile framed in coils of black hair looking out at the summer air.

"Yes, dear?" she said.

Annie turned, dropping her eyes.

"Mother, tell me!" she broke off. "How did you hear?"

"Mr. Stirling told me before lunch," said the other, watching the girl carefully, and wondering what she had meant to say.

"Why didn't he tell me, too?"

"My darling, of course he wouldn't; he left it to me."

"Did you tell him to? I really want to know."

"Why?"

"Of course you did. I meant to tell you; I wanted to before. You won't think me silly, will you?" She slipped nearer her mother and put out a hand. The other took it, a little uneasily, looking at the black dewy eyes and red mouth.

"It's this," she went on. "I know now that I never cared for him. I was just like a schoolgirl — you know, Mother!"

Mrs. Hamilton drew the girl towards her, conscious of an immense relief, and put her arm round her neck.

"My darling, of course I know. And I am so glad that you know it too. It was all very natural, and entirely my fault. We all must go through that kind of thing once. It's nothing to be ashamed of. That kind of man —"

"Oh! Mother, that's it. He's just that kind. Lots of girls at school used to talk, you know, and it was always that sort of man. It's horrid!" she ended vindictively.

Her mother kissed the black hair softly.

"My pet, it is horrid. I quite agree, but girls can't help it always; their mothers ought to look after them better — oughtn't they?"

"No, no; it was my fault. I was silly and sentimental. I can't bear that kind of thing now. I'm quite changed. You know that, Mother, don't you?"

"I know that my little girl is a very sensible, wise woman," murmured Mrs. Hamilton, trying to forget her own attitude towards Chris twenty months ago. "That's all the sham and glitter of life; — and it's good to find it out for ourselves. We have got to be just simple and straightforward."

"Mother dear, it's not wrong to pray for him sometimes, is it?"

"Oh, of course not, my dear," said the other, wishing to goodness she had the courage to say that it was.

"Because I do, you know, sometimes. I am so very sorry for him still, you know; not as I was when I cried, and was so silly, but, but a kind of quiet sympathy. Oh! I can't explain."

"I know, my pet. But you know —"

"I feel I must sometimes, when I think of all that happened. I do want him to be good."

"Just leave him to God, Annie dear," murmured her mother by a brilliant inspiration, — "in God's hands. I wouldn't think about him too much. Of course I'm not the least afraid —"

"Mother! Of course I couldn't ever think of him like that again. But how dreadful that he has come down to be a gardener. Just think! And he used to write, didn't he?"

"I expect he's lost all his positions. You know what happened when he went away from here?"

"I — I'm not sure."

"He went back again, you know — straight to Paris."

Annie drew a swift breath and sat up.

"You mean —?"

Mrs. Hamilton nodded.

"How horrible! How horrible!" said the girl.

"That just shows, you see," went on her mother comfortably, drawing her daughter's head back again, and beginning to stroke her hair; "that just shows that he never was really changed at all. It was all a presence, I expect. He was a poor man, you see, and you, my darling — well, you will be rich some day."

"How dreadful!" sighed the girl once more.

This was all a great deal more satisfactory than Mrs. Hamilton had dared to hope. Not only had the news been broken without the trace of a shock, but she had learned that Annie's conversion to what she would have called simplicity had been more thorough than she had dreamed. And now she felt that she had put a stone on the whole affair that would satisfactorily hold it down till the Judgment Day, and by that time Mr. Dell would be beyond the reach of her fears.

She felt she could not improve upon the situation, so she switched off the talk on to another line.

"What will you do with yourself this autumn, my pet, when Jack's gone back? I thought of asking some men down for the shooting. Jack can get leave to come down for a week, I should think, or Lord Brasted could come. I see he's been opening a Church bazaar at Esher."

Annie murmured that that would be very nice, lifted her head, and moved back to the other end of the seat.

"And we'll have some other people — some girls. You must see more of people, dear. It's very nice, all this going about with Jack; and he's a dear boy; but you see he must go back to town."

"Yes, some girls," said Annie absently, beginning to play with the window-tassel.

"Well, make a list," said her mother standing up. "We must write at once, or everyone will be engaged."

She came up to the girl.

"Give me a kiss, my pet. I'm very much pleased with you."

CHAPTER V

A Sight of the Knife

(I)

M r. Yolland moved his chair towards the burning logs, at his host's invitation, and drew thoughtfully upon his cigar.

He had written three days ago in compliance with a miserable letter from Dick, and had asked whether he might come and have a talk with his friend. Mr. Rolls had answered by a suggestion of dinner. They had talked of irrelevant subjects as long as the servants were in the room, with long silences, and now the guest was wondering how in the world he was to introduce his question.

But there was no need.

"Well then — about Mr. Dell?"

The other looked up in astonishment at his host who stood by the hearth. It was a wet evening, and a little chilly, and a fire had been lighted in the dark dining room, in spite of the fact that it was still August, and that daylight still lingered outside the windows. Mr. Rolls was standing warming his hands behind him, with his face scarcely visible in the soft gloom.

"You want to know everything, I suppose?" he said.

"Well — what you can tell me. Dick has written in alarm."

"Of course," said the other, and paused. "There is not a great deal to tell. He is working very hard, naturally. He has not been to complain yet. I gave him a fortnight, but he has been a month."

Mr. Yolland, shifted a little in his chair.

"John," he said, "I need not say that I trust you. But may I know why you have done all this?"

The other paused again, as his manner was.

"He is a *poseur,*" he said briefly; "a sentimentalist; he needs facts."

"But has he not had them? I understood from Dick that he has had a hard life."

The other sighed softly. His manner was very different in other company than this.

"In one sense, yes; but he has not profited by them. He is in plate armor. That must be broken; and I see no other way."

Mr. Yolland blew out a cloud of smoke.

"John," he said, "I wish you would preach me a little sermon."

There was again a pause.

"Well, I will tell you what I think. First of all, everyone who meets him either loves him or hates him. Those that love him spoil him, those that hate him he avoids."

The other nodded.

"Those that love him encourage him; he has, what one calls, a way with him. I know that you are fond of him; so am I, so is your son, so was Miss Annie, and her mother and Jack; so are the servants here. We all like him extremely, in spite of his obvious faults. So do a great many others whom we do not know. We are all very sorry for him. It follows that we are apt to give him his own way, and what he requires is another way. Miss Annie nearly succeeded, but she was not strong enough —"

Mr. Yolland interrupted.

"One moment, John. It is not my business, but can you tell me why Mrs. Hamilton is so angry with you?"

"I supposed she would be. She asked me what I thought of her, and I told her."

"Yes?" said the other smiling.

"I told her she was perfectly conventional, and that her mistake was that she thought she was not. Richard, I believe that those people do more harm than any in the world. They think they have no limitations, and there is nothing more limiting."

"Go on."

"No, there is no more to be said. But the first condition of broad-mindedness is to recognize that one is narrow; if one does not, one omits the most crucial fact of all. Now, see what that good woman did to this young man —"

He stopped abruptly.

"Yes?"

"No, I will not. I should say too much. And it is done now; she will not meddle again. Well, then, to return, this man's soul is at stake — no less. If he has sufficient will left, he will be saved. There must be a response, you know. At present he is living on his pride, and it is windy diet. I expect that this rain — Listen."

In the silence of the room there sounded the beating of another heavy summer shower against the windows.

"He was wet through at five o'clock. I saw him in the garden. Tomorrow he will be wet through again, and I shall expect him to come to resign his place in the evening."

"And then —?" asked the other, leaning forward a little.

"He will not resign it. He daren't. He could never brag again if he did. He has sufficient pride still to be wounded. I shall tell him the truth again and again till he knows it."

"Have you any fear —?"

"Fear? Yes. That is why I have put him with Whalley and Father Baynton. They both know enough about him; they are both on the watch for any attempt; and I have his revolver."

"Why do you fear that?" asked Mr. Yolland softly, aware of an odd dryness in his throat.

"Because he must learn soon the truth about himself and God Almighty. If I see any genuine signs, I shall encourage him; if they are insincere, I shall continue my old plan."

"And when he is broken?"

"When he is broken he must be mended. That will be a short matter; he has plenty of vitality left. I am sure of that, or he would have collapsed before now."

In the silence that followed, again came the furious rain upon the darkening windows.

Mr. Yolland leaned back in his chair with half-a-dozen emotions.

It seemed to him that he was looking on at an extraordinary drama. He knew all about this man whose thin outline he could discern against the ruddy chimney; he knew how he had treated scores of cases before, and nearly always with success, but his heart sank at the thought of Chris Dell in his hands. He had become, as his friend had said just now, really fond of this absurd young man; his very poses were so piteously appealing; there was a melodramatic gallantry about him that touched the heart to laughter and tears all at once. And now he was seriously wondering whether John Rolls was using the right treatment. It sounded brutal beyond description, and yet the physician was not brutal.

He had known him for over twenty years, ever since the other had come back from foreign travel after the death of his wife; he knew quite well that the stories told about that contained sufficient truth, though he had never heard the details; for with all the friendliness on either side John Rolls was an unapproachable person; there was always a certain stiffness on both sides; it had been with a certain timidity that Mr. Yolland had probed even as far as he had ventured to do this evening.

Suddenly the other broke silence.

"Father Maples has been here. He came to call at the cottage as soon as he heard. He told me he was sure that Mr. Dell would like to see him. Can you use your influence to keep him away?"

"I will try."

"We must have no interference. He will not stand it just now; it will distract him; he must be left to the earth — to the earth, and to large facts. Above all he must have no sympathy — or patronage. I have been asked by a priest to undertake him. That is enough for me."

"I understand."

"Your son too must remember that. He is not the friend for him at present. Besides, he has handed him over."

Mr. Yolland nodded; he began to understand that now. Dick took it all too personally to be effective.

"They had at least one quarrel, you know," he said.

"Of course. And with such a man you must not quarrel. You must either yield to him or break him; you must not coincide; you must not meet him for more than an instant on his own ground. You must attack or retreat."

Mr. Yolland was rather puzzled by this, so he changed the subject.

"John, you have never told me how you began all this."

"All what?"

"This — this doctoring."

The other paused again.

"I began it," he said without a tremor in his voice, "when I came home after I had killed my wife. It seemed to me that I must do something. . . . Then a poor brute came in my way, and I brought him here, and it succeeded. Then others came, I do not know how, and I did what I could. . . . I read a good deal then . . . oh! Mysticism, mental diseases, nerve diseases. I also tried to understand what the laws of nature were all about. And so it went on."

It was horrible to observe his composure, and his listener was conscious of a touch of fear that was never very far away. But he tried to answer in the same tone.

"And — and your principles?" he asked, intent on carefully breaking off an irregular promontory of cigar ash.

"Do you wish to know?"

"If you can tell me."

"Well, the first thing is self-detachment. I need not say I do not practice that, but I try. This house, for example; I thought I could not resist it at first, but — well; and the second is to pray a good deal; one must be supple; and the third is to treat no two cases alike, for, after all, no two cases are alike. And the fourth — yes, the fourth is to imitate Almighty God's methods — I mean, to shrink from nothing — to be prepared to be absolutely brutal sometimes. I think that is all; I have formulated no more."

Mr. Yolland compressed his lips, and for a moment wondered whether there was any self-consciousness in this relation of principles. Before he had time to answer his own doubt, the vibrant voice went on.

"You think me fatuous? Well, you asked me."

The other almost jumped in spite of his years. His thought had been dragged out and stabbed. He felt very unimportant in the presence of this alert intuition. It was all so extraordinarily simple, and he had thought it to be so elaborate.

"There is nothing more?" asked the dispassionate voice.

The other shook his head.

"Then may I ask you a question or two?"

"If you please."

"You have seen the Hamiltons. Well, is there any news about Miss Annie?"

"I have heard nothing."

"If you hear anything, will you kindly let me know immediately?"

"Certainly. But what kind of thing?"

"Any rumor of a marriage. She will certainly marry soon."

"Why do you think that?"

The other paused.

"This affair will have coarsened her; I have seen that. She is less tender; she will despise tenderness after this; she will be practical; though, of course, always sentimental too."

Again the guest was aware of the atmosphere of simplicity; that was surely very obvious, but he had never thought of it before.

"I will tell you if I hear anything," he said. "But tell me this: how did you learn all this — this —"

"There is nothing to learn, only to unlearn. Conventions are what are puzzling; there is so much to disentangle. If you wait and pull gently and watch, things are very simple. We are all very simple; it is when we forget that that we go wrong."

Mr. Yolland laid down the butt of his cigar; he had smoked all that was possible.

"Thank you very much, John," he said.

(2)

Father Baynton was checked next morning by a finger on his sleeve, as he passed through the chapel on his way to the sacristy to vest for Mass. He looked down, bowed slightly, and passed on, followed by the tall man with his head bent.

Arrived at the sacristy, he drew out the pierced door that moved on hinges, set a chair behind it, and sat down, slipping on his purple stole, and murmuring a blessing.

Then the voice began through the opening, quite cold and quite matter of fact.

"Since my last confession four days ago, I have sinned through pride; I have spoken of myself in such a way as to make an impression; I am not sure whether I could have avoided speaking so, but I took pleasure in it — during the conversation — at least once. . . .

"I wish to renew my resolution against this. (I mentioned the resolution before, Father; I am sorry I have failed to keep it on this occasion.)

"I have sinned once through despair. I did not trust God sufficiently in my thoughts, and I think therefore that I must have trusted previously too much to my own efforts; but I was not aware of it at the time. . . .

"I have sinned again through despair. You remember, Father, you spoke to me before about that. I am very sorry, but I have deliberately played with the thought that I was not forgiven for the great sin of my life — that it was past forgiveness. . . .

"I have also sinned through pride of birth and wealth. I took pleasure in the thought of who I was and of my possessions — once. . . .

"I have been slothful in prayer two or three times. Once I neglected through forgetfulness to perform a mortification I had intended. I renew my contrition for the sins of my past life — especially for my great sin against charity and piety."

The monk drew a breath.

"You will say for your holy penance once the *Anima Christi*. . . . You must remember our Lord's generosity. . . Say your penance with that intention in your mind. . . . Now make an act of contrition. . . . *Misereatur tui omnipotens Deus.*"

It was a pouring wet morning as Mr. Rolls sat down to breakfast three quarters of an hour later; the windows streamed; the moat outside leaped at a thousand points as if minute fish were rising at a multitude of flies.

As one gust more violent than the rest broke shattering against the glass he looked up from a plate of porridge and stared a moment against the dark morning sky.

Then he ran his eyes over the letters laid at his right side, pushed two or three away, and began, between mouthfuls, to open the rest.

But he had not looked at more than two before the butler came in.

"I beg your pardon, sir, — the — the under-gardener is here. He wishes to speak to you, sir."

The master did not look up.

"Ask him what he wants," he said. The butler disappeared, and the other lifted his eyes and looked mournfully again out of the window.

"If you please, sir," came the careful voice again a minute later, "he says he must see you. He will not say what he wants."

"Tell him I am not accustomed to receive such messages. He must either say what he wants, or he must come again this evening when I am at liberty."

"Yes, sir. At what time?"

"After he has had his tea. About half-past six."

"Yes, sir."

"Wait a moment, Simmons. Just bring me a sheet of paper and a pencil."

He wrote a line or two, folded it and held it out.

"Let Father Baynton have that if he has left the house. If not, send someone to wait for him outside the chapel, and beg him, with my compliments, to step here a moment. Let the note go immediately — as soon as Dell has gone — if Father Baynton has left already."

"Yes, sir."

The butler was back again five minutes later, and held the door open for the priest to come in.

"Good morning, Father. I am so sorry to have disturbed you. But it is only about Mr. Dell. I have just sent him his first unpleasant message; would you kindly make an opportunity for him to speak to you, and if you are afraid, let me know?"

The priest bowed from his chair.

"I am not at all afraid," went on the other. "But we must take no risks; and you were so kind as to say you would help me. Have you anything to report?"

"No, Mr. Rolls, I think not. He was up late last night."

"How late, Father?"

"His light went out a little before half-past eleven."

"It is the first time?"

"Yes."

"I expected it would happen soon. He is beginning to be rest-less. And he was wet through at least once yesterday. I have told him to come again this evening at half-past six."

"Very good, Mr. Rolls."

"Perhaps you will be on the watch, then, when he comes back. I shall do my utmost tonight. That is all, Father. Thank you very much."

He held the door open as the little wise-looking chaplain went out.

Then he went back and rang the bell.

"What did Dell say when you gave him my message?" he asked, when the butler reappeared.

"Mr. Dell said — I beg your pardon, sir — he said, that he had come to give notice, sir, but that this evening would do."

"Thank you, Simmons. Let me know as soon as he comes this evening. I will see him in the entrance corridor. He might wait there."

He passed one of his usual days, writing a number of letters for the twelve o'clock post, interviewing his agent, going into chapel for his prayers. Then he lunched, and rode out in the afternoon, returning a little after five. Then, after a cup of tea, he again went to the chapel. . . .

At half-past six the butler came to his sitting room to tell him that the under-gardener was waiting in the corridor. He nodded and said nothing. When the door closed he lifted his book again and went on reading, after a glance at the little round clock on the mantelpiece.

When the hands pointed to ten minutes before seven, he laid his book down and stood up. Then, after a pause, he went to the bell, rang it, and sat down again.

"Tell the under-gardener to come here. I have changed my mind; I will see him here instead."

When the door had closed he set an upright chair in such a position that the fading light would fall full on the face of any who sat there; but he was not contented with the result, and lit a couple of candles on the mantelpiece. Then, as steps sounded on the flagged passage outside, he sat down quickly and took up his book.

He paused an instant before answering the tap.

Then he called out to come in.

(3)

Chris was so angry as he walked across the floor in his corduroys, and stood by the chair, that for the moment he could not trust himself to speak. He was shivering slightly from head to foot, partly from cold, partly from anger, and partly from taut, over-stretched nerves.

This day had been the climax of his misery. For a month, by spurring and lashing his own pride, he had kept his resolution, and had gone about his work with an austere dignity of bearing and a kind of lurid fire in his heart that had kept his will warm and active. Then, yesterday, the weather had broken; he had been wet through twice, and the physical misery struck inwards to meet the despair that awaited it. He had passed a restless night, going softly up and down his room till nearly midnight, and then lying in bed, turning from side to side, rehearsing the two alternatives between which he had to choose. It was either the old squalid life in town, with some self-respect yet not that on which he most prided himself, or this coarse manual work with its endless discomforts, and its hopeless vista of day after day stretching into what appeared to be infinite.

As he had lain there last night, he asked himself how in the world he could ever have been fool enough to commit himself in this way. Pan was a charming god to adore in dreams, but he was rank and wet and loathsome in reality; he trampled his devotees instead of caressing them.

This was an amazing discovery. He had honestly believed hitherto that he himself was a child of nature, spoiled by the miserable conventions of an artificial society; he had traced all his misfortunes to this clash of discordant notes. There had been a number

of phrases that he had believed applicable to himself — or redolent of what he desired — "a simple, strenuous life," "naked and
unashamed," "cultured simplicity," "a man's a man," and the rest of
the journalistic jargon that had appeared to him to embody not
only profound truth in general, but the secret truth that lay at the
root of his own nature. He had woven so many dreams of Olympus,
and Olympus had disclosed itself as a wet uncomfortable mountain; the forms of gods were only mist wreaths, chilling the traveler
who clasped their knees.

But he did not so formulate these things; he had discovered that
dreams were not the same as reality; he had not yet made the same
discovery about the dreamer. He only perceived that there was a
hitch somewhere, and that he himself was at this moment cold
from having to wait twenty-five minutes in the hall, and extremely
angry at the indignity of it.

He looked at the long man in the chair with a bitter gaze.

"Well, Dell, what is it?"

Chris licked his lips.

"I have come to give notice, sir," he said.

The other paid no sort of attention to the tone of his voice.

"Why?"

Chris drew a long trembling breath through his nostrils.

"The place does not suit me, sir."

"Is it too hard?"

Chris made no answer, but stood rigid in the attitude of sarcas-
tic deference that he had selected as appropriate, eyeing the other
with a venomous viciousness that came very oddly from this brown-
faced figure in corduroys.

"Have you anything to complain of?" came the question again.

Chris clenched his hands and drew another long trembling sigh
of fury.

"*Oh! Mon Dieu!*" he whispered softly.

"I beg your pardon?"

Chris could bear it no more. That unconcerned voice was more
brutal than scourges.

"Good God, sir! Do you know what you are doing to me?"

John Rolls turned his face full on him for the first time, and let his melancholy eyes run up and down his figure and Chris's fury condensed into a kind of essence of hate as he was aware of it.

"I do not know what you mean by speaking to me like that. You will be good enough not to swear in my presence. You are my servant remember."

"I am not!"

"At this moment you are. You will not be so five minutes longer if you behave like this. What is the matter?"

"Matter!" echoed Chris softly.

Rolls lifted himself a little in his chair by a swift, smooth movement, and his eyes met the other's full. Chris stared back, his fury sustaining him.

The master sank back again.

"I thought you were a man," he said softly, taking up his book. "Of course you can go if you wish it. I have no kind of power to keep you. But I should have thought —"

He stopped, and although he was perfectly grave and controlled, Chris saw some faint emotion of humor shine for an instant on that lean face.

Chris sucked in his lips fiercely; he was astonished that he should feel so furious; he had prepared himself so carefully for sneers. He could not help it.

"What would you have thought, sir? That I was made of wood?" he asked, throwing all the spite he had into his voice.

The other laid down his book; if there had been the faintest sign of triumph Chris would have lost all self-control; but there was nothing but a direct simplicity in his manner.

"You wish to know?"

Chris nodded, knowing that he was risking everything, but unable to help it.

"Sit down then."

Chris shook his head.

"Very well, then. Now listen. You came here, ruffling and bragging —" he lifted a swift hand. "If you come an inch nearer I shall put you out of the window." (He rose so quickly that Chris started back, amazed and frightened by the great height that suddenly towered above him, and the fierceness of those mild eyes, and the sense of enormous strength, bodily and voluntary, that blazed out on him.) "Sit down this instant. You shall hear the truth now, anyhow."

There was one moment of suspense. Then Chris sat down suddenly.

The long figure sank back too, relaxed, and the purring voice went on as if nothing had happened. . . "You came here, ruffling and bragging, saying that you needed nothing more than Mother Nature and all the rest of that cant." (He was carefully picking his phrases, and they hurt all the more from their cruel deliberation.) "They were just sayings you had heard men use, but you nearly took me in. I almost believed you sincere; I did not quite, as you will remember I hinted. Then you said your piece over again; you were indignant at not being believed. So I gave you your chance to prove it. And after one month you come here, and tell me you have had enough of it! . . Do you want my comments on that? You shall have them whether you want them or not. I will tell you what you are. . . You are a sham, who has learned to talk; words mean nothing in your mouth. I have never met a man like you before, and I wish to meet no more. I am extremely vexed and disappointed." He eyed the stiffening, whitening face, piteously drawn and lined under its tan in the mingled day and candlelight, then he struck harder yet.

"You had better go back to your women and your beast's life, and forget that you ever thought yourself a man. It is probably the only thing you can do now. Perhaps you will have learned not to brag; that is one lesson at any rate. You can go back and write your stuff, if you want; but you will not forget this — that you are not man enough to hold a spade. Or you may blow your brains out and go to hell; I should expect that of you. It would be characteristic; I wonder you have not done it before; I should have thought you feeble and stupid enough for it. You can take your choice."

The stream of scorching words ceased abruptly.

There was complete silence in the room; the two figures remained motionless; one long and relaxed in the deep chair with outstretched legs; the other strung up, shaking from head to foot, bowed forward, with elbows clasped in either hand.

So the moments passed, marked only by the tranquil tick of the little clock on the mantelpiece.

Then the figure in the corner stood up, trembling violently, and the melancholy eyes of the master without a trace of emotion in them rose with it, watching the white face, the mouth that opened and closed, the fingers that clasped and unclasped the elbows.

Then Rolls spoke again, and his tone was exactly the same.

. . . . "Or you can have another trial here. You may do as you please. I shall send down to know presently. That is all, Dell."

Still the shaking figure stood there, and again and again the pale lips opened to speak, but there was silence.

"Very well, then; I shall take it that you will remain. Try to remember that you are a man. I suppose it is possible that you may be one some day. Goodnight, Dell."

The figure stood a moment longer, the light from the candles cutting across that drawn, inhuman face, throwing the long nose and sharp chin into clear prominence, and falling on the rough clothes that fell so grotesquely about the thin limbs; then it moved, swaying slightly, across the room. The door opened, and it passed out.

John Rolls waited to hear the uncertain footsteps cross the flags. Then he covered his face with his hands.

CHAPTER VI

A Nervous Bystander

(I)

The autumn weeks passed for Dick in London like a burden almost too heavy to bear. His work moved before him, unreal, as against a stormy background which would neither break nor clear. Over there to the northeast not a hundred miles away a process was taking place, of whose details he had no knowledge, and of whose result he was frightened to think. He told himself again and again that he was a fool to care so terribly — that, in any case, nothing could be worse than Chris's former condition — that the man who had charge of him was infinitely more strong and experienced than himself; in fact he brought every reasonable argument to bear upon his emotions, and each in turn fell back vanquished. All that remained was that he might be a sentimentalist and a fool, but that he did care, so that his work was irksome, his prayers except on one subject without savor, and his entire outlook on life colored by a thing which he could not help and which was no longer his business. He sent Chris's name to the Carthusians and the Carmelites; but it did not comfort him for more than a day or two.

He became a little superstitious, and more than once looked round him with a touch of apprehensiveness as he sat late at night over his office. He reflected that if ghost stories were true, and Chris were to kill himself, nothing would be more likely than that — at that point he called himself several kinds of a fool, and looked sternly again upon the printed Latin.

His anxiety was not lightened by encouraging news.

A day or two after he had written to his father, unable to bear the silence any longer (for he had promised not to write to Chris direct), he had an unsatisfactory answer, stating that Mr. Rolls knew what he was about, that he quite realized the seriousness of his task, and that any developments should be reported immediately. From the letter he gained only one grim solace, and that was the thought that his father also was as uncomfortable as he well could be.

It was piteous to think of that broken, dissolute shadow of a man in those hard hands. Surely Rolls' standard was too high; he did not condescend enough; mercy and not judgment was the way of salvation. Of course it appeared to such a man nothing less than deplorable weakness to meet such a poor broken creature as Chris on his own ground. There were no doubt plenty of wise saws about the bracing effect of adversity, and the enervating action of tenderness, but saws did not apply to exceptional cases. A broken heart needed something else.

Of Chris's attitude towards Annie Hamilton he had no very clear idea; but that there was a good deal of revulsive hatred in it he had no doubt. He had not dared to ask. He had so completely accepted Chris's poses in the place of Chris's soul, that he did not dare to inquire after the latter. They were as formidable footmen who always said *Not at home* with an air of personal grievance. All that could be done was to treat them with a dignified deference, and go away.

But he minded, cruelly.

It was not till halfway through October that he received further tidings, and they came in an abrupt and unpleasant form.

He had been out visiting through all the dreary afternoon, and let himself in by his latch key just as the lamps were beginning to glimmer through the faint town-fog as through a solution of badly frosted glass. He noticed almost mechanically that his usual peg was already occupied by a coat and hat, but was too tired to draw any conclusions from that fact.

He went upstairs to his own room where he hoped tea would be waiting, and opened the door.

His father was standing there, warming his back at the fire.

For a moment he felt physically sick with fear.

"It is nothing serious, my dear boy. Don't look like that."

"Is it Chris?"

"It is Chris, but nothing definite."

Dick shut the door, came forward, and sat down heavily.

"Father, for God's sake, what is it?"

"My dear boy, I tell you it is nothing definite; but I thought I would run up and see you. Can you put me up?"

"Of course. But what's the matter?"

"That's better. I'll just sit down. . . Yes, two lumps please, and a slice of that cake."

Dick made an effort, handed his father what he wanted, and took a cup for himself.

"Now then," he said.

"Well, it is nothing very definite. But I have heard some news that I thought you ought to know — Miss Annie is to marry Brasted."

Dick's spoon jerked out of his saucer with the twitch of his fingers, but he made no movement to pick it up. He stared straight at the ruddy, troubled face looking at him.

"Stirling told me. He was beaming. He told me it was a secret."

"When?" stammered Dick.

"When did he tell me? This morning. He was coming out of the park gates as I passed. It had just been arranged — or rather, I suppose, he had just been told."

"Does he know?"

"Who? . . . Oh, no. How could he? It is a secret."

Dick stooped and picked up his spoon; he was horribly frightened, but he made another vast effort to behave naturally, and apparently succeeded, for his father after another look went on quietly.

"I thought I might as well come — Dick, I'm fond of that young man, and I can't bear to think. . . Is he fond of her still?"

Dick shook his head.

"I haven't the least idea."

"But he will think he ought to be. Just so, and that comes to the same thing with him. I suppose he may do anything. He must be told."

"Yes."

"I think you're the man to do it. You have known him a long

time, you see. That's why I came up. Can you come back with me tomorrow?"

"I must — I can arrange it. But — but will Rolls —"

"Ah!"

The priest looked up again at his father, and saw a shadow on his face that was strange to it.

"What do you mean?" he said quickly.

Mr. Yolland stirred his tea thoughtfully with pursed lips.

"I wanted to see you about that too. I don't understand him in the least. He told me more the other night — just before I wrote to you — than he has ever told me in the whole course of his life. I thought I understood it too, at the time, and I find I don't."

"What did he tell you?"

"Oh, about his methods and so on. It seems that he has none — that he just waits to see what will happen. He has no plans beforehand. It's a kind of fatalism, as far as I can understand it. I've been thinking over it a lot — but really —"

"I thought you knew him so well," interrupted the other with a touch of bitterness

"So did I. But I don't."

"Have they had any rows?"

"At least two, if not three. One was next day. And he dropped another of his odd hints a week or two afterwards, and there was some gossip too in the village, but that may have been the same. Dick, I'm really rather frightened."

The two men looked steadily at one another, and neither found any comfort in it. Dick stood up suddenly, and went across to the fire.

"Oh! My God!" he murmured. "And it's all my fault."

The elder man rose too, and put his hand on his son's shoulder.

"My dear boy, you mustn't talk nonsense. It's my fault as much as yours. We both did what we thought best. And perhaps it may be the best, after all," he ended feebly.

After a minute's silence the priest turned round with a white, steady face.

"Sit down, Father, I'm all right. I'm not going to make a fool of myself. But we must put an end to this."

He poured out another cup of tea for his father, and one for himself.

"Now then," he said, "let us go through this carefully. What was it you heard in the village?"

(He was speaking now as an equal to an equal. His father recognized it and responded.)

"There was a scene in the street. It began in the King's Arms. He was there apparently — and the worse for drink —"

"One glass does that," slipped in Dick.

"I daresay. Well, there he was; and it seemed he was talking a lot about — about France, and so on. Whalley came and ordered him out, and he wouldn't go; so Whalley went up to the house. And in five minutes Rolls was there, with a horsewhip."

A swift hiss of pain broke from the priest's lips.

"No, it didn't come to blows. There was no need. Rolls said a number of things in the bar — before them all — at least that was what I heard; he told them everything pretty well, and he lashed the poor devil with his tongue until — until — well, they said it was awful to see the poor brute's face. He turned whiter and whiter. He tried to go for Rolls, but Whalley and the others held him back. Then he began to scream, and Rolls waited till he had done, and then went on again, and — and the poor devil collapsed at the end, and was carried home."

"Well?" came in an almost soundless voice from the priest.

"Well, he's there still. That's the extraordinary part. How in God's Name Rolls keeps him there —! Why the man doesn't bolt?"

"Is he working still, do you mean?"

The other nodded.

"He was yesterday. Father Maples saw him from the drive."

"When was all this?"

"About a fortnight ago."

"Why didn't you tell me?"

"What was the use? He's a free man, I suppose — he isn't tied there."

Dick drew a long breath and leaned back.

"I'm not so sure," he said. "In fact I'm sure he is. I think Rolls is — is —"

"I know. . . . Well, perhaps. But now this last thing is too much. Why couldn't the girl wait a bit? It isn't decent. And as for Brasted —"

"It's not Brasted's fault. It's that infernal mother. Well, what do you propose?"

"I propose that we should both go down there tomorrow. We'll just walk in and tell Rolls what we've come to do, and insist upon it. Then you shall tell the poor chap, and see what he wants to do."

There was a long silence.

Then the priest got up.

"I must go away by myself," he said. "This wants thinking about. Dinner at half-past seven, if I don't come back before. I haven't the faintest notion —"

His voice broke and ceased, and he went out, shutting the door behind him.

Mr. Yolland sat five minutes longer, staring at the fire, with his head on his hand. Then he too got up and went out.

Five minutes later as he passed in from the street to the church, the first thing that he saw among the gloom of the seats was his son's head bowed in his hands.

(2)

It was a curious journey that the two had next day. On both brooded the coming interview with unbearable foreboding, and they were silent as men are silent when they approach a crisis at forty miles an hour.

Dick sat in the corner of the carriage, his head propped on his hand, staring out of the window, conscious of the occasional crackle of a newspaper in the diagonally opposite corner, and also of the fact that his father was not reading it.

He had learned last night, as they sat together till nearly midnight, how extraordinarily that queer emotional unsatisfactory friend of his had affected the elder man; it was as if he had come across a child that had fallen in the mud and hurt himself; there was pity, anger, impatience, and tenderness all at once — pity at his state, anger at his culpable folly in falling, impatience with his refusal to be helped, and tenderness at the whole miserable affair. It was a crumb of comfort to know that his father felt like that; hitherto he had thought himself merely a weak fool; now it appeared that others drew the same emotions from the contemplation of Chris. But it was not much more than a crumb, for both were helpless, and each knew it of himself and guessed it of the other. It was not just money that Chris wanted — that could be supplied; it was readjustment, a clean spirit, a purged imagination, humility in the place of despair, self-respect in place of self-regard — a hundred virtues in place of a hundred vices.

Dick gave it up; they must leave miracles to God Almighty. But what could perhaps be done, and had to be done, was the breaking to him of the news, the preventing of his putting an end to himself, and his rescue from the hands of the man who was beginning to wear, to Dick's eyes, the appearance of a heartless demon.

If there was any sort of depending on Chris himself there might be a hope of this last detail, but there was no certainty that he would respond. He might be either completely cowed or completely reckless. The fiendish brutality that had held him so long might hold him still, indeed it probably would.

Dick ground his teeth in a kind of sympathetic agony as he pictured all that must have happened and especially the horrible little scene in the inn — the grinning faces of rustics, the sneering brutality of the big man with the horsewhip, the dreadful details poured out one by one like molten iron on to the raw flesh. No doubt Chris had been bragging — bragging in a kind of despair at his own isolation, desirous to wake some emotion, even the vilest and the feeblest, after his experience of that stone-wall man — bragging mysteriously of his life in Paris, of the splendid creature who had adored him, all full of rich epithets and hints and allusions only half understood by his listeners, but pitiably enjoyed by himself. And that dry, unbreakable brute had come in and told them all the facts, the sordid beastliness, Chris's relations with her, his dependence on her, her parting gift of five pounds — the price of shame. He had done it no doubt, as he had promised, to "break him," he had "met him on his own ground," as he had boasted to his friend, and driven the attack home, till the wretched sinner writhed and struggled and screamed, as the cruel point turned and twisted in his heart. Ah! Dick's nails pinched his own hands in shaking fury and compassion. . . . And now it would probably be too late, and Chris beyond recovery: self-respect would be gone, and there was nothing else.

Again he questioned himself as to Chris's attitude towards Annie. Only two things were possible, either he was in love with her still, or he thought that he ought to be, and, as had been said yesterday, the two came to pretty much the same thing. The only difference, pondered Dick, astonished at his own acuteness, was that in the first case Chris would do something desperate, and in the second that he would probably only pretend to. But either must be prevented, and this was only possible by getting him away from Foxhurst. . . .

There was a movement in the carriage as the train whisked over the junction lines a mile from home, and his father put aside the absurd newspaper and came across to the opposite corner.

"We drive home then first, Dick, and lunch. Then we have the carriage again at half-past two."

The priest nodded.

"We'll have the blue room got ready — it's near yours — in case we get him away."

"We must get him away," said Dick brusquely.

"Yes, well —" and his father looked at him doubtfully.

"We must. Why, you said so yourself."

"My dear boy, we will do our best."

Dick looked at him, and said no more.

Amplefield seemed somewhat unreal to the son of the house as he passed through the hall and sat at lunch with his father. It was as when someone comes to a house after a death there. Things were so familiar and so powerless to help, and yet it appeared that all that was needed was a violent effort of the will, and all would be as it had been before. If he only could wrench time backwards or forwards, and set Chris there as he had been two years before, or as he might be a year hence, elaborate still, it might be, full of affectations and poses, and yet with an unbroken heart! The very poses were better than this naked reality.

Dick looked up vaguely at his father.

"Have you told them we shall be there tonight?" he said.

"Not yet."

"And the room?" pursued Dick determinedly.

"Not yet. My dear boy, you must not be so positive. Perhaps he won't come."

"He must come."

"Or Rolls may forbid us to see him."

"I shall see him."

"Dick, you mustn't be violent."

"I shall see him," repeated the priest.

There was no more to be said. Mr. Yolland registered a resolution to keep close to Dick whatever happened. There must not be a scene.

It was a curious drive through the russet autumn country. The day was a little overcast, and it appeared that what light there was radiated from the golden woods rather than from the gray sky. The grandchildren of the pheasants who had crowed two years ago at the coming of the gentleman in the fawn-colored coat, crowed again now as exultantly as their ancestors; the world was what it had been; it was men's lives that had changed.

As the phaeton whisked up Foxton Street, Dick kept his eyes steadily in front of him, looking out for the red towers on the left; he was only aware out of the corners of his eyes of the little bow window of the "King's Arms" and the graveled space before the steps. Then the carriage slowed, wheeled sharply, passed through the gate-posts and turned up the lime avenue.

Dick scarcely noticed the processes of stopping, climbing out, and following the butler through the corridor. It all appeared so inevitable, as if he acted in a play of which each word was arranged; yet, though he knew his part in substance, he had not learned it in detail; he was far from word perfect. But he did not doubt that he would take up his cues.

Then the door opened, and the tall man whose figure had been so constantly before his eyes for the last twenty hours turned in the window seat with a book in his hands and stood up.

Dick heard his father's voice.

"I have had news, John — the news you asked me for. I thought I had better bring Dick, too."

"Ah!"

Then a courtly hand waved to a couple of chairs, and Dick found himself stiffly sitting, staring at the hard face seen in shadow against the high window.

"About Miss Annie, then?"

"Yes, she is to marry Brasted."

"When did you hear this?"

"Stirling told me yesterday."

"You did not write?"

"No. I thought it better to get Dick down. He has known Mr. Dell longer than either of us."

"I see. But I thought it was understood that I was to have the charge of Mr. Dell for the present."

There was an oddly hard tone in the voice. He spoke as one aloof at a distance.

Dick's resolution rose to meet it. He was aware that there would have to be a struggle, and his own sense of fury told him of the weight of this other personality that called it up.

"I am not satisfied, Mr. Rolls. Chris is an old friend of mine; I know him very well."

"Yes, Father Yolland?"

"I do not think this treatment is the best for him."

"Indeed. Has he written to you then?"

"No. But I am quite certain. I have thought it wrong from the beginning."

"And why are you now interfering?"

Dick's anger blazed a little. He could hardly keep himself from crying out.

"You forget, sir, that this man is my friend. I have a perfect right to do as I like."

"Dick, Dick," murmured his father.

"I have heard about what happened at the 'King's Arms.' I think it was perfectly brutal. Do you deny it, sir?"

Mr. Rolls' stiff figure was like an image.

"It depends on what you have heard, Father Yolland —"

"That you exposed him before them all — that you told them all that I had told you."

"I beg your pardon, but Mr. Dell told me also."

"All the worse then," snapped the priest. "You broke his confidence as well."

"Well, Father Yolland?"

"Well, sir, well! Well, I have come down to take him away. My father agrees with me."

The other broke in.

"John, you know, I must say I think I do agree with Dick. You see —"

Mr. Rolls lifted a hand.

"Mr. Dell is a free agent. He is not in prison. If he wishes to go, he can go."

Dick rose.

"Well, then —"

"Sit down a moment, Father, please.... But I am astonished that you should come here and speak like this ... It is for Mr. Dell to reprove me if I have done wrong."

"Chris reprove you? Why, the man is like wax —"

"Exactly, Father Yolland. Or rather he is beginning to be. And you do not trust me to mold him. There is no more to be said."

Dick hesitated an instant. He had not expected him to take this line. Then his resolution triumphed.

"I did not mean to insult you, Mr. Rolls....I — I beg your pardon — I was angry. But I still think that you do not understand him."

The other waved his hand gently.

"There is no more to be said, Father Yolland. Then I suppose you wish to see Mr. Dell. I will send for him."

"I must see him alone, sir."

"Forgive me, Father Yolland, but you shall do nothing of the kind. At this moment he is my servant, and you are in my house."

"I will not see him in your presence, sir."

The other got up, went tranquilly across to the bell and rang it. Then he turned his melancholy eyes on to the priest.

"You need not, Father Yolland, if you do not wish it."

"Dick, Dick, be reasonable," broke in his father's voice.

"But I shall send for Mr. Dell now," went on the other, "and tell him the news you have brought. He must not hear it elsewhere. I hold myself responsible —"

The priest sprang up.

"How dare you, sir —?"

"I hold myself responsible so long as he is in my charge. You may remain here; you may tell him yourself, if you wish. And if he chooses to go with you, he shall."

Dick stood trembling a moment. Then he sat down again. It was impossible to find fault; all was apparently entirely above-board. And after all, the actual telling did not matter; it was on the treatment afterwards that all depended, and he would have Chris to himself this evening. The door opened.

"Simmons, kindly send someone out to find the under-gardener. Tell him I wish to speak to him."

The door closed. Rolls went back and sat down with his back to the window.

"Now, Father Yolland, will you tell me what you wish? Are you to tell him, or shall I?"

"I will tell him."

Then the minutes began to pass in silence in the curious old-world room. The western sun broke through its clouds presently, and the glare behind the stiff figure in the chair grew intolerable in its brightness. The whole chamber was flooded with mellow light that fell on the paneled walls, the old carved press and the portraits, and even the dark corners became saturated with reflected splendor.

Dick sat in a daze of bewilderment and suspense. How smoothly and easily all had gone — with the smoothness of inexorable wheels whose motive power is hidden. His own was the only passion that had broken the peace, and as that ebbed from him, it left behind a dull resentment against the man who had caused it, the resentment of a weak nature against a strong one. Though there had been no bullying or storming, yet the weight of the personality had been overpowering.

There he sat then, that monstrous incarnation of a force whose roots the priest felt now more than ever before, sprang from something lying far behind that by which most men lived. Others were swayed by pity or passion, but this man, surely, by that which is to human emotions what substance is to accidents, an element to its energy. And through all swelled and swelled his anxiety, distracting and absorbing the point of his attention — as a man in the presence of mysteries of birth or death counts the ticks of a clock or sees irrelevant faces and houses in the red coals of a fire.... How would Chris look and behave? What would he say when he heard? Above all what words were to be used to tell him? He had better tell him first that he had come to take him away — that he would be provided for, and then break it to him quietly.... Perhaps he was exaggerating what would be the effect of the news; it was very possible that Chris had altogether outgrown his love for that wretched girl; at least he must have become accustomed long ago to the knowledge that he had lost her — to the knowledge that some day she would belong to somebody else. Oh! it would surely all go quietly enough; this brutal presence in the room, this detestably tranquil man as silent and inexorable as God — surely he could not make any difference. The three would drive back presently, and dine at Amplefield that night. ...

There were steps in the flagged passage; the heavy steps of a working man in his boots.

Then the door opened, and a man in corduroys came forward and stopped.

(3)

Dick rose to his feet in an instant.

"Chris!" he said, and stopped, forgetting even to put out his hand.

The sight was so astonishing. There stood the man whom he had last seen three months before in a trim well-cut suit, well-

groomed and tidy; now in heavy gardening clothes, stained about
the knees, with great earth-colored boots, a weather-beaten buttoned corduroy jacket showing a leather belt below, a red handker-
chief round his throat, ill-shaven, closely-cropped, and with an old
cap in his hands. He bore himself as upright as ever, but there was
an odd fallen look about his tanned face; his lips were drawn down
at the corners, and his eyes looked out narrow and furtive, turning
now to the priest, then with a quick glance to right and left where
the other two men sat, then back again to his friend.

"Chris!" said the priest again, taking a step forward and holding
out his hand. "We have come to take you away."

The other made no movement; he glanced swiftly towards the
window where his master sat, and then down to the floor. But he
drew himself up a little as he spoke.

"You sent for me, sir?"

His voice was almost emotionless, and Dick sickened at the sound
of it.

"Chris! For God's sake."

The man in the window cleared his throat. He had not stirred at
the entrance or the words.

"These gentlemen are come to bring you some news," he said.

"Chris! Take my chair," cried Dick, indignant at the performance.

"I beg your pardon, Father Yolland," came the steady voice from
the window. "It is not customary for my servants to sit down in my
presence."

"Ah!" cried the priest, seeing how he had been trapped. He perceived in an instant that the whole occasion was being made to
serve for a further humiliation of this poor broken brute.

"Dick, Dick!" came from his father.

"I can't stand it, it's devilish," raged Dick.

"I am sorry to be obliged to ask you to behave yourself, Father
Yolland," came the passionless voice again.

Dick drew a long trembling breath; he was powerless and he
knew it. Meanwhile he could not leave this miserable figure to bear
itself with such pathetic dignity.

"Then I will stand too," he said sharply "Chris, we have come to take you away from this place — tonight — we have the carriage here."

There was a dead silence, only the man's eyes looked furtively towards the window.

"Chris, Chris, do you understand? You need not stop here; not another moment. Get your things together. . . . I — I will tell you the rest when we get home."

"I beg your pardon, Father Yolland; you will tell him now. Or I will, if you prefer."

"No, no! Not you. For God's sake, Mr. Rolls, let me tell him alone."

"Look at him, Father Yolland. Do you think it kind to keep him waiting?"

It was intolerable to hear this cold comment on a present agony, but Dick stared again at Chris, and there was a miserable entreaty in his eyes that cut the priest's heart like a physical stab. Those down turned lips too were moving as if he beseeched for pity; he was fumbling his hat in his hands.

"Oh! Chris," he cried, with a great sob. "Don't look like that. It's not so bad. You won't mind so much as that. . . Chris! I can't bear it!"

"Shall I tell him, Father Yolland?"

"No, no, no! I'm his friend. He knows that, don't you, don't you, old man?" sobbed the priest. "You'll take it from me — not — not — not from him. Oh! don't look like that. . . . Yes. . . . I'll tell you at once. It's — it's about Annie."

There was again a dead silence. The two elder men sat like images, and the two younger stared for the first time straight in one another's eyes. Dick's were blind with tears of pity and anger at the hateful brutality of it all. He could see no more than a pale tanned face with burning eyes swimming before him. It was the first time he had spoken her name to this man for nearly two years.

Then he thought he understood, choked back his tears, and made a great effort to control his voice.

"No, no, she's not dead; she's not ill. She's perfectly well. She's going to — to be married. . . . There! There! You don't mind so much, do you? You guessed it, didn't you?"

Some sound broke from those down-turned lips that had seemed

set like a trap just now, and again the priest thought he understood.

"Oh! Oh! There's nothing against him. He's a good man, I suppose. It's — it's Brasted."

The corduroy figure began to sway ever so slightly, and Dick
flung his arm round it in a passion of pity, laying his other hand on
the rough shoulder, and looking up entreatingly into those agonized eyes.

"Chris! Chris! Don't look like that. There's nothing against him,
you know, except what he did to you. It must have happened some
day. You knew that. . . . And . . . and you've got accustomed to it by
now. . . . And now you'll come away quietly with us; it'll be all right;
it'll be all perfectly right. Father, tell him it'll be all right. We'll look
after you. You shall do what you like. You shan't be here another
hour. And — and you'll just get your things together. I'll come with
you. And you shall go right away, if you like — to Italy — anywhere. It'll be all right. . . . Chris! Say it'll be all right."

He felt hands seeking his own as if to disengage them, and he
gripped more tightly, but there was no mistaking the movement,
and in bewilderment he stepped back and stood staring at the figure that remained upright and steady now.

Then he heard Chris's voice again, very low and broken; and it
was not speaking to him.

"Is that all, sir?"

"Chris!" he cried again passionately.

"I beg your pardon, Father Yolland, my servant is speaking to
me. Yes, that is all, Dell, unless you wish to say anything."

"No, sir," came the low voice once more.

"Very well then; you take it like a man. Do you hear, Father
Yolland?"

"No, no! it can't be," cried the priest. "Chris! You don't mean
you are not coming?"

"Do you wish to go with Father Yolland, Dell?"

There was a pause in which Dick heard nothing but the hammering of the blood in his own ears. Then came the answer.

"No, sir;" and then after another pause, still more low, "it is not worth while."

"You hear, Father Yolland?"

Dick sprang forward and seized his friend by the arm.

"Chris! You don't mean it, you don't mean it! Say you will come! This man is killing you."

The arm remained passive, and the downcast eyes did not even look at him.

The man in the window spoke again.

"You have had your answer, Father Yolland. Kindly let my servant go to his work."

"Chris! You don't mean it! You shall have anything you like."

Then he felt a hand put on his shoulder, and turned to see a lean face and strong melancholy eyes looking at him.

"I mean what I say, Father Yolland. Have the goodness to stand back."

Dick relinquished the arm and stood staring.

"You can go, Dell."

As in a dream the priest saw his friend turn to the door and lay hold of the handle. He could not bear it.

"Let me go, sir. . . . Father, stop him, stop him! . . For God's sake! . . ."

He saw Chris shake his head as if to himself; then the door opened and closed again gently, and there was a sound of heavy boots on the flags.

Then a change came, swift and unexpected.

"Mr. Yolland, forgive me, but I must go after him. He means something this time. Kindly order your own carriage. I will send for you both if there is any need."

Then the door opened once more noiselessly, and the fierce presence was gone.

Dick stood dazed.

"What does it all mean? What's it about? Father, I don't understand."

CHAPTER VII

The Operating Table

(I)

The father and son dined in silence that night at Amplefield. They had hardly exchanged a dozen words since Rolls had left them and gone out. There had been no more to say. They had followed him a minute later, entered their own carriage, and driven off, and had caught sight of him going up the path to a little yellow-brick house that stood back from the main street of the village.

Dick abruptly told the groom to stop when they got a hundred yards further on, and leaned out towards a laborer who was passing the carriage.

"Can you tell me where Mr. Dell, the under-gardener at Foxhurst, lives?"

The man told them they had passed the house. Dick twitched with impatience and repeated his question. It was the yellow brick cottage, he was told, at the end of the village. The chaplain lived there too, it seemed; the house was Mr. Whalley's. Then they had driven on without a word.

The evening had passed in silence. Mr. Yolland sat in his room before the fire; Dick was upstairs. Then they had dined.

When the men were gone Dick turned to his father. "It's no good," he said, "I must go back."

Mr. Yolland lit his cigar carefully.

"There's no good your staying," he said. "I can see that. I'll promise to go over again in the morning and let you know."

Dick jerked in his chair.

"No, no. I don't mean that. I mean Foxhurst. I must go there again. . . . Yes, tonight."

"My dear boy!"

The priest sprang up.

"It's not the least use. I heard what he said."

"Who? What?"

"Rolls. He said that Chris meant something."

"Yes, I heard that."

"Well, you must see. He meant — he meant —"

"Dick, sit down again. Look here, we must trust him. He knows more than we do. Besides, it's no good interfering. We did more harm than good."

"I can't — I can't. I could never forgive myself Oh! Poor brute!"

"Dick, we must leave it. You must see that. It's gone too far."

"It hasn't. I must see Rolls again; he doesn't understand a bit. May I order the dogcart?"

Dick was at the bell, waiting with his hand on the handle.

"Wait a moment. What are you going to say to him?"

"I'll — I'll go down on my knees if he wants me to. He must let Chris go."

He looked at his father again an instant, and rang the bell.

"Dick! You're wrong. You'll be sorry. What explanation can you give?"

"I'll tell him the truth — that I can't bear it; that I couldn't sleep without coming again. He'll understand."

Yes, he certainly would understand, thought Mr. Yolland; it would be hardly possible to mistake Dick's face; it was no longer furious; it was just utterly miserable and worn; his meditation upstairs had apparently done him good.

He went out into the hall to see Dick off, and met him coming down from his room where he had gone to change his cassock, with a bag in his hand.

"I had to," said Dick briefly. "If he'll put me up, I'll stop."

"What time shall we lock up?"

"It's nearly ten now. If I'm not back by twelve you'll understand."

Mr. Yolland went out on to the steps into the night air all aglow with the blazing lamps and the breath of the horse, and saw his son climb up. Then he nodded goodnight, with his hands in his pockets, and watched the patch of light down the drive as far as the turn. Then he sighed, and went back into the house.

Dick was indeed cooled by his meditation, and the process had been partly intellectual, partly emotional. First of all, he had gained nothing whatever by his intemperate anger, and he had been insulting and ungrateful into the bargain. Next, he had made the case more difficult all round. Presumably he had forfeited what tiny responsibility had been his in the matter, and, worse than that, he had appealed to Chris and been refused; it would be extremely difficult to claim either right or courtesy in the further stages. Lastly, he reflected that Rolls could not possibly be an incarnate devil, and if he was not that, he might just possibly be — something else. Anyhow he had to go and see what was happening.

As the dogcart spun along the soft dark roads, he began to consider what on earth he should say. He saw that that depended entirely on the situation he found when he got there. He would be there soon after half-past ten; Rolls would probably be in his own room, and he determined to begin with an apology. He would say he was sorry for his attitude this afternoon, but that he was almost mad with anxiety. Then he would say that he was still very much upset, that he had come over to see what news there was — oh, that would explain itself. Then he would somehow get to see Chris the first thing in the morning, and he would put it all to him again, reasonably and persuasively. He would explain that he had changed his mind, that Foxhurst was not suitable, that he begged him to consider whether a year in Italy would not be better all round. Oh! he must prevail; it was such a sane, straightforward plan.

But he would not allow himself to contemplate any other situation than the one he proposed to find. Rolls in his study; Chris gone to bed, brokenhearted no doubt, but in a reasonable frame of mind — not with that deathly impassivity he had seen in him this afternoon. Possibly even Rolls would allow him to go across to the yellow-brick house and see if all were well. The chaplain at any rate would not be gone to bed.

So he sat and spun plans, looking out at the tiny world which he could see — the horse's back and head and ears, the harness on his flanks and shoulders, the black, slender shafts, the black leather railing in front, the traveling yellow light moving like a pale sheet on the grass by the wayside and the October hedges to right and left; out too at the vast world that he could not see, of black shadowland, an invisible sky, and now and again monstrous outlines of trees and woods.

Then a light showed far ahead, a bedroom window in the timber-and-plaster cottage at the turning to Newton; the light vanished and reappeared and vanished again, but the house was dark as the cart span past it and the horse's hoofs rang sharp and distinct from the cobbles.

Another light or two, a gas lamp, and now there was a pavement on the right, and that was Foxton steeple against the heavy sky. They would not be long now.

The night was very still, for the village was gone to bed, and lights were fewer and fewer as they went up the winding street. Then the "King's Arms" showed a swinging door and brightness beyond, and a gust of talk flowed out for a moment. Dick set his teeth — were they still talking of that miserable affair, he wondered. Then the last houses, and a blank wall.

Dick touched the groom suddenly on the arm.

"Here," he said. "Wait for me. . . No; drive on to the lodge, as soon as I'm out."

The man checked the horse and drew up opposite the cottage path.

Dick had not intended it, until he saw the actual lights of the cottage in the front ground floor windows. and then he was entirely unable to do anything else.

He could not wait to hear from Rolls. He would just ask for Father Baynton and have a word with him, and then go on up to the Hall.

As he went up the path, after latching the gate noiselessly behind him, he saw the light disappear, and then immediately reappear over the front door; then that too faded, and by the time that he reached the door, a glimmer shone from overhead. He was just in time then. That would be the priest going to bed.

He hesitated no longer, and tapped gently with his knuckles.

The door opened instantly, and Rolls stood there, a lean figure that seemed gigantic against the dimly lit staircase wall, with his finger on his lip.

(2)

The priest looked up at the dim face above him with a keen sense of guilt.

"I — I am very sorry —" he began to stammer; but an arm shot out and touched him for silence. So the two stood a moment.

Then the elder man took him by the arm.

"Tiptoe," he whispered.

Dick went in silently in an agony of doubt, and waited in the dark entry until the door closed noiselessly; then, still on tiptoe he followed the other into the parlor. He noticed that the door was left ajar.

"Kindly explain," said the steady whisper from the darkness lit only by the faint red glow of the dying fire.

"I — I could not help it. I was mad with anxiety. . . . I — I beg your pardon, sir, for what I said this afternoon."

There was no answer, and he could wait no longer.

"For God's sake —"

"Hush. Yes. Since you are here you must stop. I heard your wheels. Will you promise to obey?"

"I will."

"Before God?"

"I will."

"Well. He is getting ready to do something. . . . Now, be steady, you have promised. . . . He is waiting till Father Baynton is in bed."

"Ah!"

"Father Baynton is listening. He will put out his light presently. . . . Then I shall go up. . . . You must wait here."

"Oh! For God's sake —"

"Be quiet, Father," hissed the sharp whisper. "You do not understand. . . . He shall not hurt himself. . . . We have seen to that. . . ."

"Tell me, tell me. . . ."

"Whalley has his razors and knife. Besides, he does not mean that. He asked for a rope tonight. He said it was for his box."

A little moan broke from the priest. Then he felt himself caught fiercely by two strong hands on his arms.

"I am ashamed of you, Father. . . Sit down, or you shall not hear a word."

Dick felt himself guided to a chair. He bit his lips furiously to keep back the quick breaths that shook him like a storm, and it was a full minute before he could trust himself to whisper.

"Tell me. . . . I am quiet. . . . I swear I will not speak."

"Now kneel down."

Dick rose shaking, groped for the chair and knelt obediently before it.

"Make the sign of the cross . . . remember the Presence of God Almighty. . . . Now listen. . . .

"He has been writing tonight . . . then he was praying a while. . . . He has fastened a hook over his window. . . ."

"Stop him," whispered the priest, but his voice cracked softly with misery.

There was a hand again on his shoulder instantly.

"I shall stop him, at the last moment. . . . He does not know I am here. . . . I must take him in the act. . . . We may have to wait an hour or two. . . Do you understand?"

Overhead there sounded the crack of boards and a footstep. Dick drew his breath sharply, and the grip tightened on his shoulder.

"Baynton," whispered the voice. "Now pray. Have you your beads?"

Dick fumbled feverishly a moment.

"Yes."

"Then pray. . . . I am going to the stairs."

The grip loosened; there came a tiny pat on his shoulder, and then a faint noiseless vibration, and as he turned his head, he saw the thin figure pass out like a ghost. Then silence settled down again.

For a moment the priest hesitated, with parted lips and eyes wide and staring.

Then he gripped his beads. This was the only way.

It must be the Sorrowful Mysteries — what else could it be? Christ in the garden, Christ scourged, crowned, bearing His cross, and crucified.

There began an extraordinary process in the priest's brain. It was as if three realms lay beneath him, and he contemplated each; saw, heard and thought on three planes. He saw the Garden, as he had seen it a thousand times, moonlit and black, and a Figure striped with shifting shadows, flat upon the ground; tense in every muscle, and from it arose an exhalation of agony that broke upwards into moaning and downwards into undreamed of pits of despair. And meanwhile the prayers began to patter to the Father who was in heaven, to the Mother who stood apart as silent as her Son.

He heard the deathly stillness of the house; once a mouse that scratched behind boards, once the creak of a stair, once the rattle of a mattress as someone climbed into bed, once footsteps on the road outside twenty yards away.

And his brain snatched at fragments that sped past — wonder at the compliance of the priest upstairs, amazement at the fierce intensity of the quiet figure that had been with him a minute before, and whose presence still seemed to burn upon the dark; and above all, and again and again, Chris, Chris, Chris. It appeared to him that it could not be Chris waiting upstairs in the little back room till the house was asleep, any more than it could truly be Chris whom he had seen in corduroy this afternoon. Chris must be somewhere else. . . There were irrelevant fragments too, of thought and imagination that fled past him on a stream; speculation as to when he should get back to town; a vision of the dinner table of two hours before, its white linen and silver, and his father's face with the red light upon it from the candle shades; a little wayside station he had seen sometime — he wondered when it was — till he remembered that it was this morning; he had seen a porter and a retriever-dog and a truck of luggage; a sight of his own room in Soho — the plaster images on the mantelpiece, the rug awry, his large Mechlin breviary open upon his desk.

Then again the present whirled into view; he saw the back of the chair at which he was kneeling and a glimmer of red from the fire on some angle of wood.

The mouse scratched again, and in a moment his whole being was in his sense of hearing; and the silence became audible in a kind of vast hiss as of a monstrous kettle, and in an instant vanished in another creak from somewhere, above, outside or within, he did not know.

Once his hands touched and sprang apart, each shocked by the wet chill of the other; and his mind fled back to the beads; he must have said a hundred by now, and all in the presence of the moonlit garden and the figure that writhed there. — O! Jesus Christ, remember and have mercy!

Then he was standing up, without conscious volition; he only knew that he could not remain there; he was aware of a carpet under his feet as he moved to the door, and an ache that rose from his heart and seemed to pervade his entire body.

There was a vibration from somewhere; the whole house seemed to shake with it, and he knew that a sound had broken from his open throat. He did not know whether it was a whisper or a cry. Then he understood that someone had moved upstairs, and again his whole being was in his ears.

Then a handle turned somewhere, and a gleam of reflected light showed the marbled paper on the wall above the stairs.

For him that sight and sound was as a plunge from beneath water to upper air. Images, arguments, and the touch of beads, even the physical pain at his heart vanished in an instant into one great mental picture of an open door on a landing, and a man who stood there with lighted candle, his lower lip sucked in, his head sideways to listen more intently, his feet bare on the boards. . . He thought he saw him in silk pajamas. . .

The room behind this man, for the priest contained but one thing, a hook above a window, and a noosed rope hanging from it.

It seemed to him that he could hear breathing now, but he did not know whether it was his own. He only knew that Chris stood alone, not five yards away, staring and listening for the silence he desired. It was horrible to contemplate his unconsciousness; he thought himself alone, and there were at least three watching and listening too. The whole world appeared to stop and listen and watch.

Then again there was a movement, the light died again on the wall; there was the sound of a door closed softly, and the tiny, careful snap of a latch; and a second later another creak from the stairs.

It seemed then to the priest as if a hand or a breeze caressed his hair behind, as his skin prickled, and the cold swept from his shoulders down his back; but with it came a sense of steadiness; his heart leaped thrice in his throat, the pain began again, his muscles grew tense to resist it, and he took another noiseless step into the entrance passage.

There, he understood; and he observed each detail, in spite of an odd sensation as if he were rising from the floor and a murmur that rose louder and louder in his ears.

The stairs ran up before him, on the left of the door, and turned again to the left; there could not be more than a dozen all told; for barely above the height of his own head sprang the banisters that fenced the landing. These were visible against a faint light that shone from beneath a door on the right.

It was at that door then that Chris had stood just now, and it was in that black angle of the stairs that the watcher had stood.

Then suddenly he saw a figure lean and black emerge noiselessly from the wall and stand beyond the banisters, faintly outlined against the twilight of the landing; a pale line showed the back of his collar.

Then suddenly sounds began, shockingly loud in that stillness, breaking through the murmur that ran like a torrent in Dick's ears; there was a vibration or two, a faint clatter of chair legs, and then a very low voice talking in a soft incoherence.

The rest happened in an instant.

The black figure vanished; there was the crash of a suddenly opened door, loud footsteps, a gabbling voice or two that mingled with a mad screaming and waxed into a roar as if the heavens had split. Then he perceived a rush of air and knew that he was falling.

CHAPTER VIII

A Recovery

(I)

It was a very bright hot day at Amplefield. The winter had been followed by a slow, luxuriant spring, and the crescendo of life had swelled, like a well ordered movement of an orchestra into the sublime climax of midsummer day; each instrument, from may and hazel to ash, had added its tone; day had followed day, each pausing longer than its predecessor like the slow beats of a baton that adds a rallentando for greater effect; now the last chord of color and life had broken on the world, and the creation stood revealed.

To desert elaborate metaphor, it was one of those days when poets and even farmers feel that there is no more to be said, no suggestions to be made to Almighty God. The sky was one deep clear vault of blue, resting on humming woods; the park was a study of amazing greens, lit by yellow meadows, and culminating in the blaze of hot flowerbeds round the white comfortable house, whose external glare was pleasantly contrasted with the intimation of cool, dark fragrant rooms within, seen beneath striped awnings and through tall windows opening to the ground.

The place was obviously *en fête;* at either end of the long oblong lawn to the south stood a white marquee, with curtains looped back in front; groups of chairs, not yet sorted, stood about on the gravel, and busy men in shirtsleeves hurried to and fro in the brilliant light, carrying glasses and carpets, and large tin boxes. From the east end of the house where the kitchens stood came a murmur as of bees; and three or four vans stood on the gravel in the shelter of the north shrubbery.

There was a small company of ecclesiastics waiting in the smoking room, until the gong should announce that lunch was ready — Dick Yolland, Father Maples and Father Baynton, all alike in seemly

black, and Roman collars; Dick, however, was at present in an al-
paca jacket; there was no need to be stifled until convention demanded it.

He was wondering what on earth to say next, as he sat in his
armchair, with his back to the window; and he looked with a kind
of despair at his stout parish priest who sat opposite smiling to
himself. They had already said all that was possible about the
weather and the coming entertainment and the farmers' views of
the crop-prospect; they had also discussed a rubric or two, as is
proper among clerics, and had speculated on a rumored conversion, and there was really nothing more to be said. Dick had not
wanted Father Maples at all; he had only asked the monk to come
over to lunch before the garden party, because he particularly
wished to have some conversation with him, but the two priests
had appeared together half-an-hour before; and Dick could not
find it in his heart to tell the uninvited guest that he wanted to talk
in private to the other; Father Maples was always so certain that his
own presence was welcomed that to hint otherwise would be as
brutal as the breaking of a child's toy.

So here they sat, still waiting for the gong, or the coming of Mr.
Yolland who had been last seen half-an-hour before interviewing
the bandmaster in the kitchen yard.

Father Maples shook his head sadly.

"I suppose Lord Brasted and his good lady will not be here till
five o'clock? I had once hoped that Miss Annie would find the Faith.
We have been sadly remiss, you and I, Father Yolland. They only
got back on Tuesday, I hear."

"On Tuesday," said Dick, trying to be genial.

"I hope her ladyship bore the journey well."

"I believe so. They left the yacht at Southampton, and came
straight up."

They had said all this at least once before; but Father Maples
basked in the prospect of seeing the titled lovers and talking with
them before the crowd, and tasted the anticipation like a gour-
mand.

"Mrs. Hamilton will live with them, I understand."

"Well, the house is hers, you see. I suppose they will live chiefly at their own place."

"And Master Jack?"

"Jack will be here, as before, I suppose. But I haven't seen any of them lately."

It was an infinite effort to Dick to go on talking. He had only got down from town last night, and he wanted news as much as anyone; but it was not news about the Brasteds; that was all settled in a perfectly suitable manner; they had been married after Easter; they had been in the Mediterranean ever since; they had come to Hinton for a week before settling down at Esher; they were coming to the garden party at Amplefield to be inspected by the county. There was not one convention that was not being observed. There was really nothing more to be said.

But Father Maples' mind was one of those that hung about conventions as a bee about honey flowers; he was an excellent representative of those persons who have succeeded in establishing the doctrine that the average is the most excellent, that the House of Lords is the elite of the nation, and that the *Times* newspaper is the Voice of God in all but Faith and morals.

"And Mr. Rolls is coming?" pursued the clergyman, still intent upon the County.

"I believe so," said Dick. "Isn't that so, Father Baynton?"

"He is coming, yes," answered the chaplain. "He said about five o'clock."

The gong sounded; Mr. Yolland appeared simultaneously, and the four went in to lunch.

Dick was extraordinarily anxious to get at facts, but he could not put his questions in the presence of Father Maples. He wanted to know a great deal, and his father had not been able to tell him much.

Dick had not seen Chris since that ghastly night in the previous winter, when he had seen his face for an instant with the candle-light on it, as he came out of his swoon on the stairs. The priest had stayed the night at Foxton, and had been sent home next morning after a very short interview with Mr Rolls, and two days later had returned to town, very quiet and subdued. Since then he had received two letters from the curious old man of whom he had become so desperately frightened, telling him that Chris was going on well, that there was no need for anxiety, and that there would be better news presently; but he had been given no details, and had been reminded of his promise not to interfere. His father too had confessed to complete ignorance of what was happening at Foxton; he had only assured Dick that he was satisfied that Rolls knew better than any of them. But then last night there had been a little more news, it seemed that Chris was no longer working in the gardens; he was back again at the house as Mr. Rolls' guest, and that was absolutely all that the priest knew.

Lunch ended at last, and Dick threw an imploring glance at his father, who understood.

"Come with me, Father Maples," he said, "I have a book to show you."

Dick turned to the monk.

"Now, Father, shall we go to the smoking room?"

When the door was shut, Dick went across to the fireplace, and then faced round as the other priest sat down.

"Now, Father Baynton, you know what I want to ask."

The monk looked up mildly.

"Of course, my dear Father. I think you may be quite happy. Mr. Rolls is satisfied."

"And Chris —?"

"You will find Mr. Dell very happy, I think," said the priest slowly. "He is back again at the house, you know."

Dick turned and began to finger an ashtray; he had forgotten to take a cigarette.

"It is all most extraordinary," he said. "I don't understand it in the least. He is really happy?"

"It is all successful, I think," said the priest as serenely as ever.

Dick felt a spasm of impatience at this tranquil little man who took miracles as a matter of course.

"And his faith? Do you mean to say —"

"He is a perfectly convinced Catholic, Father Yolland, — if you mean that."

"And all the time it was going on —" began Dick again.

"My dear Father, Mr. Rolls is unlike anybody else. It was not my business to interfere. I did express a doubt once or twice, but he was doing nothing immoral."

"But that night —"

"It was not my business. I only watched lest Mr. Dell should do himself an injury."

"Why did Rolls wait so long?"

"I thought it rash, Father, but if you had lived with Mr. Rolls, you would have learned that he does not make mistakes."

Dick faced about once more with his hands behind him.

"I suppose he waited in order to catch him at it, to show him what he was doing. Do you know what he said to him?"

The little brown face grew grave.

"Yes, I heard it, Father. It was very terrible, but it was perfectly true. Mr. Rolls would have been an orator, I think, if he had cared to be one."

"When did he say it? What did Chris do?"

"He said something as soon as he found him, and then you fainted, you remember, and we came out.

Then, when you were gone to the house, he talked to Mr. Dell in my presence, and he stopped with him all that night."

"But — but —"

Father Baynton looked at him solemnly, as he threw himself into a chair.

"The building up, Father! I understand the breaking, but how did he build him up?" cried Dick.

"Mr. Rolls thought Mr. Dell had plenty of vitality," said the chaplain; "and so it proved to be."

"But what did he do?"

The other pursed his lips a little.

"So far as I could understand, Father, he allowed Mr. Dell to ask him questions. They were together a good deal. Once —"

"Yes?"

"Mr. Rolls talked to me one evening. That was about two months ago. Mr. Dell was coming to confession — and I was very grateful for what Mr. Rolls told me."

Dick looked at him narrowly and intently.

"Well, Father?" he said breathlessly.

"Well, he told me that Mr. Dell was in a receptive state. He asked me to talk to him at length. He said that he — Mr. Rolls — had been keeping him at arm's length, to — to provoke him, I understand."

Dick fidgeted a moment, and stood up again.

"I don't understand in the least. What do you mean by 'provoke'?"

The chaplain drew a breath as if for an effort.

"It seemed that Mr. Dell was really interested — interested and humble. He had been asking Mr. Rolls a number of questions about himself and Almighty God."

"Yes?"

"And Mr. Rolls had been rather cool to him," said the monk.

Some sort of faint mental image did begin to form itself now before Dick. He perceived Chris, melting, humble and receptive — like a man's body after typhoid — with the hardened elements of character broken and re-sorted. In this mood, of course, he would be intensely appreciative and appetent; his very warm heart would assert itself, reaching acquisitive hands through the débris of tumbled unreality — his desire would be further stimulated by his master's deliberate aloofness. . . .

"Yes?" he said.

"After that confession Mr. Rolls saw a great deal more of him," said the chaplain; "they were together a great deal; and a week or two later Mr. Dell came back to the house as a guest."

Father Baynton looked primly down his nose, and Dick saw it was useless to expect descriptiveness from him. There was a kind of natural dullness about this priest, an astonishing simplicity, that was at once disappointing and reassuring. But things seemed a trifle clearer. It was as when outlines begin to show through dispersing mist. Yet the mist was not yet gone.

"And when shall I be allowed to see Chris?" he asked.

"Mr. Rolls commissioned me to tell you, Father, that he would bring Mr. Dell over here this afternoon."

The tongs fell with a crash, as Dick sprang upright.

"Good Lord!" he said. "But he can't! Not this afternoon. The Brasteds —"

"I think that is his reason, Father Yolland. You understand —"

"It's madness," cried Dick, "there'll be a scene. You don't know Chris —"

The priest shook his head gently.

"There will be no scene, Father Yolland. Mr. Rolls thinks it necessary. I fancy it is a kind of test. You may trust him entirely."

Dick stood motionless, trying to understand. He might have expected something startling, but he had never dreamed of this; it was surely too fantastic to be true. And even if Chris behaved himself with decorum, what of the others — Annie and her husband, and her mother?

"Does he know?" he asked suddenly.

"He did not know when I left this morning," said the other quietly. "And Mr. Rolls gave me a message for you."

"Well?"

"He begs you to avoid both Mr. Dell and himself till the interview is over. They will arrive a few minutes after five o'clock."

Dick stood staring and wondering.

Then he put out his hand mechanically and took a cigarette.

(2)

The lawn was well filled by half-past four, but the lions had not come. They could not be expected to appear before five, and they could hardly be much later, as the cards that had been sent out had informed the guests that Mr. Yolland would only be at home until six o'clock, and presumably the Hungarian band would also cease to play at that hour.

Therefore five o'clock was obviously the moment for the entry, and we all wished to make quite certain of assisting at it.

It was all so extremely suitable, we told one another, and the whole story was so very touching and beautiful. Poor Miss Annie had made a sad mistake once with that Mr. Dell, who, it was understood, had gone to the dogs, and had been so very kindly taken on as gardener at Foxton. — Yes, the Brasteds intended to be at Hinton at least two months in every year. He was an old friend, and how touching it was that the poor girl had found that old friends were best. — Otherwise they would live at Esher. — No, Lord Brasted had withdrawn from the race from Paris to Berlin; he was quite giving up motoring. — Yes, Father Yolland was here, and two or three other Popish priests; they had not succeeded in bagging Lady Brasted after all. — They had not tried? Nonsense; we know much better. All Popish priests . . . . Yes, Mr. Yolland was looking very well, but how stout he was getting. — These ices were quite excellent; and what about another cup of tea? — We thought it was a little hot out here, but how much better than a gray day like last Wednesday when poor Mrs. Ffoulkes had had her garden party. —

And so on, and so on; and the sun began to lose its virulence, and the band crashed from below the terrace, and wheels came and went on the gravel beyond the house, and two toy terriers had a hysterical turn-up in a geranium bed, and cups clashed, and we all quacked together, and beautiful young men in Panama hats carried ices to beautiful young women, and stout old ladies looked severely at one another from green garden chairs, and red-faced old men bawled golfing shop, and the grass began to turn damp and dark green from the treading of many feet, and at last the stable-clock struck five.

Dick had been perfectly miserable all the afternoon, and had gone about here and there in his long hot coat and hat, and said the proper things, and sat down by the dullest people, and wished to goodness that he had never come down from town. It was hateful that Chris should be brought here. There was bound to be a scene of some kind. Everybody knew about him now; it was all shocking bad form.

And what would happen if he was publicly snubbed by the Brasteds? Was it possible, in fact, that Brasted himself could do anything but snub him? And what on earth would happen then?

And what would Mrs. Hamilton say, and Annie? And it was all an abominable piece of bravado on Rolls' part. What earthly good would it do to anybody?

When it struck five he jumped up, to the fury of poor Mrs. Ffoulkes herself, with whom he happened to be talking, and moved nervously off without another word, eyeing the steps down which the actors must come; and even as he looked he saw a group appear from the house behind. The lions were punctual to expectation.

He was scarcely aware of the lull on the lawn, when the group began to descend the steps, with his father walking with Mrs. Hamilton in front, but he moved quickly aside, wheeled a little behind, and stood watching from thirty yards away.

First came that dignified lady in purple, looking quite magnificent with her gray hair and clean, handsome face; and on the near side of her mother came a radiant figure of a girl in pink-and-white, with a heavily fringed parasol in her hand.

She looked better than Dick had ever seen her, walking very upright and sedately, looking out with a pale innocent face at the crowds that began to gather; her splendid black hair showed regally under her white hat, and her eyes were shining.

Then came two men Jack on this side, looking delightfully young and proper in his gray suit and brown boots, carrying his head rather high over his white collar, and a large red-haired man beyond him, with an ample white waistcoat, and a Panama hat.

It was all as dramatic as a play. The band crashed and boomed, the sun shone, the flags drooped, the butterflies danced, the crowds stared and murmured, and the triumphal party went forward in the midst to the center of the terrace-walk where half-a-dozen chairs and a couple of carpets were ready to receive them. It was an apotheosis of Suitability.

Then Dick turned once more towards the house.

The upper terrace was almost empty now; a couple of footmen only passed along it and disappeared through the tall door into the darkness of the hall, and Father Maples, who had found himself stranded there with a friend, hurried down the steps to join the gathering across the lawn. Then for a minute or two the walk was empty.

Dick knew perfectly well that he ought to be with his father, but he also knew that he was simply incapable of fulfilling that duty. It was five minutes past the hour now, and the others might be here at any moment. He was torn two ways at once. On the one side he had conceived the plan of intercepting Rolls and Chris, and entreating them to go away again; on the other, he knew that it was entirely useless. Yet he could not go and mix with the other side, as if he were of their party; nor did he dare to contemplate joining himself to the two men in the horrible experiment. He must observe, he told himself.

So he stood sheltered by the dial, where Chris had sobbed two years before, and eyed the blank door in the white house.

At the cessation of the band he turned again for an instant to the crowd that seethed like meat flies on the lower terrace, and when he looked again two men were standing at the top of the steps.

Dick drew a long breath, sucked in his lower lip, and stood staring.

There was the old man, upright and thin as a lath in his long frock-coat and silk hat, with his face thrust out, looking across at the crowd, and there by his side was Chris in a light holland suit and Panama, with his hands clasping his stick behind his back.

They both looked completely at their ease, but hesitated, as if not knowing what to do. They must have come through the hall when the men were absent for a moment. Then a footman hurried out and appeared to apologize.

Dick saw Chris turn and speak to the other a moment; and even in that moment he perceived that odd indescribable air of intimacy between the two — that air which can neither be mistaken nor defined. Then the two, with the servant in front, came leisurely down the steps.

(3)

We were all, as I said just now, gathered about the chairs in the center of the terrace. I do not quite know why we were so much excited, nor why we forgot our manners and pushed so much; partly,

I suppose, it was because of the solidity of the bridegroom, who was fifty if he was a day, coupled with the extreme innocence and simplicity of the bride; singly, too, they were wealthy; together they were extremely rich; and these facts, together with a title, and a prospect of their future residence at Hinton, and the memory of their recent return from the honeymoon, and the tale about Mr. Dell, over whom we had shaken our heads many a time, and the Papistry of this house which was so seldom thrown open to the county — all these things made us first hurry to Amplefield, and, when we got there, push and crowd about the romantic couple.

At any rate, there we all were.

Mr. Stirling had got a place next to Jack, and was enjoying himself immensely, with a priestly face. I think he had an idea that all this fuss redounded to the glory of the Church of which he was so unworthy a minister; his wife was somewhere on the outskirts of the crowd. Father Maples' hot face turned and twisted through a vista of shoulders; Mrs. Ffoulkes, with her head on one side, was smiling languidly in the front rank. Mr. Yolland was talking to Lord Brasted in the middle, and Mrs. Hamilton was nodding and smiling to somebody else.

Annie, for a moment, stood hesitating when she reached her place; and then, very simply, she sat down.

It was beautifully done, and I craned my head to look at her, to see if she knew how beautifully; it was her first attempt, I should suppose, at taking her proper place among her neighbors, and was most creditably achieved. She was the only person sitting down, and yet she did not look at all arrogant; it was as if she had been born to it. There she sat, letting down her parasol, looking about sixteen, rather shy, extremely innocent and pretty, and yet sufficiently at her ease. I found myself smiling like a fox terrier, with enjoyment.

Then I was suddenly jogged fiercely, and turned round with some asperity; but it was only Dick Yolland, rather pale under his freckles, with his mouth open, and his hat tilted back a little.

"Let me through," he said.

I did not understand in the least, but I obeyed, and he got in front of me; yet not so that I could not see what happened next.

Immediately in front of Annie the crowd was less dense; it was more like a loose scrimmage at Rugby football, and a moment after Dick had pushed before me I observed Mr. Rolls' melancholy face make its appearance. I looked at him with a good deal of interest, and I noticed that other people did so too, for it was not very often that he appeared at public gatherings, and his impressive bearing was further haloed by the rumors that hung round him. He looked very distinguished, very melancholy, and his head was a good eight inches above those of his neighbors.

Then Mr. Yolland stepped forward.

"Ah! John!" he said, and the two shook hands right in front of Annie, whose profile was all that I could see now.

As Mr. Rolls moved out I caught sight of another man following him; and I too, like Dick a few moments before, perceived in that unconscious naturalness and ease of the two the indication of a singularly close relationship. I had never seen him before to my knowledge, nor did I recognize him now, though I had gossiped of him a hundred times.

He had rather a long face, smooth-shaven, with projecting chin and a full mouth with down-turned corners; he had black hair, a little grizzled over the ears, as I could see under his Panama hat, and black eyes. I was not particularly aware of his clothes, and so I gather that he was extremely well-dressed.

He stood there waiting until the two men had spoken a word or two, and then he stepped forward, smiling. I noticed then how very pleasantly his face lighted up, and how very white his teeth were. He looked like an actor, and yet he was not at all theatrical in his bearing.

At this moment Dick trod violently back upon my toes, and my anguished expostulation did not even make him turn his head. When I recovered sufficiently to look again, a curious change had taken place before me.

Lady Brasted was standing up, rather stiffly, I thought; her lips were parted, and she was staring. A great rosy flush swept over the cheek that I could see, and ebbed again, leaving pallor behind. There was a change too in the position of the other group. That pleasant boy Jack, beyond his cousin's chair, had stepped forward and was staring too; Brasted himself seemed petrified by something, and stood absolutely motionless beside his mother-in-law, who also resembled a statue of astonished indignation. A subtle change had come over the crowd; the hum of talk had died, and except for the cooing of a pigeon half-a-mile away in the park, there reigned a complete silence.

It was obviously a Moment, though I did not in the least understand why.

Then the man, who was of course Mr. Christopher Dell, bowed quite naturally to Lady Brasted.

"May I congratulate you?" he said in a very pleasant, easy voice, "and — er — and Lord Brasted?" and he bowed almost imperceptibly to that nobleman.

It was done, and I thought very nicely done. There was nothing else remarkable about it. Then he put out his hand, but there was no movement from the girl.

The silence became simply electric, and broke immediately afterwards in a rustling storm of whispers as Mr. Dell, still smiling pleasantly, withdrew his hand, and bowed again. It is very difficult to describe all this without giving an impression of theatricality; but there was absolutely nothing of that vicious charm about his manner. However, the situation was dramatic enough, though, as I have said, I did not in the least understand why; but even that was saved by the stepping forward of Mr. Rolls from where he stood with his host, watching.

"Come, Chris," he said, and took his friend by the arm.

Then once more, as the truth began to dawn on me, Dick first trod violently on my toes as before, and then dashed forward to where the two men were turning away.

I suppose it would be an hour later that Dick found me walking below the lower terrace, quite alone.

I had employed my time well, in hearing half-a-dozen versions of the whole story. Mr. Stirling, for whom no one has a greater respect than myself, had expatiated on the brazen hardihood of an abandoned Papist, and the very proper punishment that had been meted out; Father Maples, whom also I reverence very deeply, had gasped and spluttered at me like an eager codfish, taking me by a button, and telling me how he had known the whole thing all along, and how he had always prophesied that Miss Hamilton would marry her present husband. Mrs. Ffoulkes had hinted at the frightful career that had blighted Mr. Dell's claim to respectability, and had begged me to come and see her next week when all the details should be revealed, so far as it was proper for her to do so.

And the Vicar of Foxton had informed me that Mr. Dell was no longer gardener at the Hall, but was supposed to have gained an extraordinary and sinister influence over his remarkable host.

I got away at last, and rushed round the shrubbery and out below the terrace, where I could not be observed from the lawn, in order to smoke a cigarette and meditate on what I had heard; and it was here, as I walked on the trampled grass whence the band had just taken their departure, that Dick, as I suppose, viewed me from an upper window, and came down to tell me his news.

I had known Dick a long time; in fact I remembered him in Eton jackets; but I had never seen him so much excited as he was now. He came down the center steps, hatless, with his tails flying behind him, and caught me by the arm.

"My dearest man," he said, "God bless me! It's all perfectly right, and the brutes have all gone away at last, and Chris and Rolls are stopping to dinner, and I'm going back with them afterwards. You must stop too."

"I don't in the least know what you're talking about," I said. "And I certainly can't stop to dinner."

He paid no attention at all.

"And Chris is all right. Old Rolls is going to settle something on him — oh! I oughtn't to have told you that. But he is! And he's going off to Italy in a week, and I shall join him there in September. Good Lord! How pleased I am!"

"Kindly tell me what on earth you mean. I have never even seen the man before today."

"What! Don't you know Chris? Come in instantly and make his acquaintance."

"Dick! I won't. You must tell me first."

So Dick told me.

I don't know how he succeeded in keeping away from his dear Chris for half-an-hour, but it was nearly seven before we turned at last up the steps, and came on to the lawn, all glorious with evening sunshine and geranium beds and long shadows from wall and dial and trees.

There was a man in a brown holland suit standing at the house door, as if he looked out for someone; and when he saw us he came down the steps from the terrace, smiling.

The End.